KRALLIS

LLOYD INGLE

Ordering Information:

Prime Seven Media
518 Landmann St.
Tomah City, WI 54660

Printed in the United States of America

1

Aware that normality would not be achieved easily after the mayhem that he, and kinsman Reuben Scamp had wreaked in Australia. Andreas *was* however highly incensed, when a mere ten days after the return from Melbourne, Viv Bailey, his fellow solicitor and business colleague, rang to inform him that the partners at Mowll and Mowll solicitors, required a full and detailed report on the Melbourne trip, *as soon as possible*. Andreas's initial knee-jerk reaction, was to tell him to take a running jump, but knowing that such an action would merely delay matters, he said nothing, a trait acquired in his youth, *whenever* seemingly insurmountable difficulties arose. At odds with the turmoil in his mind, he *gently* put down the phone, and with eyes cast upward to the ceiling seeking divine intervention, he railed, "Why the *hell* couldn't I have been given a bit more time than *this* to get over this affair!"

The *affair,* concerned investigating discrepancies, discovered in the returns, of the previous three annual financial statements from Melbourne, with the *whole* problem, being unceremoniously dumped in his lap by Viv. Having experienced Viv's *little* problems before, he pushed for his sparring partner Reuben to accompany him, with Viv's all too ready acceptance, almost guaranteeing that the problem would *not* be straightforward, or indeed little. Initial feelings of excitement, were soon supplanted by doubt, due almost entirely to his innate Romany, suspicion of everything. Logic too, screamed at him, that having *three* separate discrepancies, in consecutive years, would not make the task an easy nut to crack, and if money *had* been embezzled, the perpetrators would by now, have been able to cover their tracks, unless their continued success, had made them complacent. Having conveyed his thoughts to Viv, it was a push-over, getting a sanction for a crash courses in unarmed combat, stressing that it was just as a precaution, omitting however, to mention that it would run parallel with a course in weaponry, that he had in mind. Those safeguards, had actually proved pivotal in their fight for survival, as almost from the outset, their worst suspicions had proved to be unerringly correct, with a triad-organised consortium having embezzled clients' money to fund a drugs cartel. Despite the overwhelming numerical superiority of the organisation they faced, he and Reuben had managed to smash the entire operation, but not without shedding blood. Using the skills that they had been taught in Bristol, and honing them along the way, they evolved into a formidable, and ruthless, dual killing machine, enabling them to survive, and finally achieve a successful result. In Lou's warm and loving embrace, he had succeeded thus far, in suppressing the trauma, but the horror of it all had just been dredged up by Viv's two minute phone call. Knowing however, that a report *would* have to be made at some stage, he sighed philosophically and resolved to submit a report later in the morning. Then smiling contemptuously, a sudden idea came into his mind, *I'll give them a bloody report all right!*

Having promised to take Lu and the kids to Bristol on a shopping trip the previous evening, he informed Lu of his intention to pop in to the office with the report, saying with a grin, "I'll pop in the house, and write it now, but don't worry love, it won't take long!" Returning to the car in two minutes flat with a folder containing his submission, he declared that he was now ready for the trip. She said, "Christ that *didn't* take long!" Andreas smiled and told her that he did not want Viv wasting too much of his valuable time, reading a load of old tosh. Depositing his young daughter into the rear car-seat, he glanced in the rear mirror, and smiled as his lovely wife, on reading the single sheet of paper, clapped her hand to her mouth, stifling a surprised gasp. Grim-faced for the duration of the journey, Andreas painstakingly parked the car, and opening the car door he declared, "No need to disturb the kids, I won't be *that* long!" Kissing her cheek, he strolled confidently through the majestic portals of Mowll and Mowll, and was instantly afforded a hero's welcome by the office girls. Accepting the accolades with good grace, he wondered if they would be quite so appreciative, if they knew just what they did, to attain the desired result. "Is *he* in?" He asked sarcastically. Sally, Viv's personal assistant, answered politely, "No, he's got a meeting in town this afternoon, but he'll be having a spot of lunch in the Green Lady, if you want to see him!" "I think I'll forego that pleasure! He answered with a smirk, "I'm taking Lu and the kids to Bristol, on a shopping trip, but could you give him this report, if and when, he deigns to honour this establishment, with his presence!" Handing over the envelope, he returned to the car remarking, "I've got to fill up with petrol, so we can get eats at the garage as well, *and* it'll give the kids the opportunity to see their uncle Gunnar!" Lu grimaced and issued a warning, "Okay, but do *not* drive through the car-wash, *or* allow the boys to get oil all over their clean clothes!" "As if I would!" He retorted, wearing an entirely false facade of having been mortally slighted. Pulling in at the garage, they saw that Gunnar was chatting to a pretty young, twenty-something, sitting at the wheel of a shocking pink mini Cooper S, and finally tearing himself away from the coral vision, he ambled across to the car, where Andreas sat drumming his fingers impatiently on the window rim. Gunnar scowled, "Whatever you want, there will be no discount, not now not ever!" Andreas answered with a grin, "I haven't asked for anything yet, so you can stop whingeing!" Gunnar averred starchily, "I know what you're like, always after something for nothing!" Then grinning Gunnar asked, "By the way, I hope you remembered the koala that you were supposed to be bringing back for Pa?" Andreas laughed, "I don't think he knows what a koala is. I'll tell Ma, that it was impounded at the airport!" Reuben asked, "How did the the trip go?" Replying, Andreas remarked, "We actually *managed* to sort out Viv's not so little problem!" Gunnar grinned, "Yes and if I know you and Reuben, you'll have caused more problems than you solved!" Andreas retorted, "Stop bloody moaning, and fill my tank up. I'm taking my wife and kids to Bristol for the day, so make it snappy!" Gunnar remarked, "I have the thought that your family, are the only ones *capable* of parting you from money!" Lu interrupted, "Are you two going to stop slagging each other long enough for us to make a start, or will I have to get out of this car and sort both of you out?" "That's good enough for me!" Andreas replied, and reaching for the hose, he quenched the thirst of his trusty steed, then headed for the shop, to purchase the necessary journey accompaniments of crisps, chocolate. Walking across to Gunnar, he gave his oldest friend a hug, and smiling he got into the car, setting off once more for Bristol, but having driven only a few yards, he noticed Gunnar in the right wing mirror, running across the forecourt shouting, "Hey you bastard, you haven't paid me for the petrol!" Making a hasty gear change, Andreas pulled away, and glancing in the side-mirror, he laughed loudly, seeing Gunnar throw his cap down into the dust with disgust. Lu remarked, "You bastard, why do you always wind him up!" Andreas laughed and continued driving, until nearing Bristol, he turned to Lu, "Bloody good job we didn't mention this trip to Pa, he'd have wanted to come with us, and we'd have had to put up with him snoring all the way there. Getting drunk as a lord, on arrival, then being out like a light all the way home, farting and burping!" The boys screeched with laughter, and Lu retorted with an artificial scowl, "*Hey* you lot, that's my father you're laughing at!"

Parking the car haphazardly in the usual car park, they disembarked, stretched their limbs, then picking up the carry-cot containing the still sleeping Rosie, Andreas walked to the edge of the park and sat on a bench. "Rosie has to wake up Lu!" He called to his ever loving, "I'm buggered if I'm gonna spend the whole day, carrying her round sodding shops!" "You bloody numbskull!" She retorted, "Her buggy's in the boot!" Despite the barb, hurled by his long suffering wife, that bruised his alpha-male ego, he did not respond, being still hung over with guilt from his dalliance with Angela, his newly promoted second-in-command in Melbourne, he deemed it providential to keep his mouth tightly shut. Managing to visit a host of shops in a very short time, with very few actually being negotiated without purchasing anything, provided a querulous Andreas, who had long since given up the ghost of trying to keep a tally of all that had been spent, with a momentary ray of sunshine, in an otherwise long dark tunnel. Despite the added bonus of a sleeping baby, despite all the hustle and bustle, Andreas became more irritable as the day wore on. Noting his agitated state Lu, fearing the worst scenario of him losing his temper with someone, suggested dining in one of the many restaurants, that appeared to line every street. Opting for one that would have been new, several hundred years ago, Andreas believed hopefully, though erroneously as it turned out, that it might turn out to be a few bob cheaper than the others, and when the bill had been presented, he carefully inspected the sheet of paper, to see if a mistake had been made, and when the tally proved to be correct, a scowling Andreas had to hand over a fair wedge of his hard-earned, with Lu grinning at his discomfort. Fortunately Rosie slept through that too, as she could be a little sod, when she was wakened before having a full sleep, and being thankful for small mercies, Andreas mused, *I wonder where she gets that temper from. Her mother is extremely sweet tempered and it goes without saying that she cannot possibly have inherited it from me. Mind you, Uncle Riley can be a bit wicked with his tongue at times!* Feeling distinctly self-satisfied with his take on genealogy, he smiled and pushed the buggy carefully along the road, until nearing the car park, he told Victor to push for a spell, while he put the packages in the boot of the car. Taking the bags from Lu's hands, along with those occupying the buggy's under-carriage, he walked to the car-park, and depositing everything in the boot tidily, fearing the worst *if* they just *happened* to spend enough of his hard-earned to *over-fill* the boot. Sneaking a glance, while locking the boot, he noticed that he almost out of sight from Lu's panoramic vigilance. Heading for the nearest boozer for a *swiftie,* he threw back the cognac hastily, then strode from the tavern, and caught up to the family, with all being achieved in less than five minutes. Lu scowled at him the instant she got a whiff of the ambrosia, but in mitigation, Andreas whinged, "It was only a small one!" One hour later however, his misery was at last alleviated, with everybody finally tiring of spending his money, they decided that they wanted to return home. Squashing the remaining bags *and* the buggy into the already overladen boot, he decided to have a couple of minutes rest before setting off for home. An act that immediately became another rod with which to flay his already well lacerated back, but finally bowing to *petticoat power,* he set off for home, noticing immediately that Rosie had dropped off once more. He thought, *just like her bloody Grandfather,* and *it's a pound to a penny, she'll fill her bloody nappy.* Ordinarily he would not have minded the little one sleeping, but knowing that it would almost certainly mean her not being able to sleep later, wrecking the nefariously carnal scheme he had in mind for her mother, which did *not* include sleeping. A cunning plan sprung to mind, *Maybe I could slip a little brandy into her night bottle,* and conceding with a lascivious grin that where sex was concerned, he could be as devious as all hell, he grinned. "What are you so bloody happy about?" The lady of the car demanded, and with an even broader grin, he replied facetiously, "Nothing love, just thinking of how nice the day has been!"

Arriving home, Rosie promptly wakened and while everyone else was out on their feet, *she* was running round like a hyper-active dervish, Andreas thought, *I bloody knew this would happen. Now where did I put that sodding brandy?* Before his nefarious plan could be put into practice however, Ma and Pa arrived, being followed closely by Vee, Michael and Lily-Ann. With the desired tranquillity, further discombobulated by the arrival of Guaril and Barbara Johnson later, Andreas took out a second flagon of cider and sighed philosophically, *there goes my plans for the night. Oh well, you can't win them all.* The evening passed pleasantly enough even if had ruined his plans for a night of carnality but he *did* manage at one stage to sneak into the kitchen to secrete a wee drop of brandy into Rosie's bottle, *just in case.* Reflecting that the day had certainly not been his most enjoyable, and considering that it was fortunately not yet over he thought, *always look on the bright side of life.* Lu told them all about the report that he'd handed in at the office, remarking laughingly, "He gave them a sheet of paper with one word written on it, SORTED in capital letters!" Andreas's caustic wit as ever, was a source of much humour, but the truth behind the ironic missive, was that he was actually still so hung up about what had been necessary to ensure their survival in Australia, he was disinclined to write a report on all that had happened or even be reminded of it. Needless to say that by the time everyone had left, Andreas and Lu were so exhausted from the shopping, and the impromptu party, that both fell asleep immediately, however, the evening had not been a complete disaster. Rosie slept all night.

2

Despite the alcohol excesses of the previous evening, Andreas duly made up for the forfeiture of libidinous delights that he had promised himself, and true to form, his beautiful wife went straight back to sleep on completion of the act, and failing to rouse her for more of the same, he had a long, cold shower. While towelling himself dry, he made a mental note to organise the purchase of a power-shower, *just wait til that bloody jet hits her*, he thought, *this is pay-back time for denying me my conjugal rights*. Entering the kitchen, wearing his once white bathrobe, he put the kettle on for coffee and began preparing Rosie's breakfast, before she wakened from her brandy-induced sleep. Finishing his first coffee of the day, he heard her plaintive demands for Lu's attention, and dashing upstairs, he succeeded in halting the caterwauling before she wakened the entire house-hold. Returning to the kitchen with his daughter, he relieved her of the weighty nappy hanging down almost to her knees, and still experiencing coital cancellation symptoms, he grumbled, "That bitch upstairs knows when to have a lie-in!" After powdering Rosie and expertly positioning a clean nappy to her nether regions, he conveyed her to the high-chair and putting a milk sodden rusk in front of her on a plate, he took a backward step to watch his little girl, now eating her meal unaided, albeit making an unholy mess, realizing sadly that she would not be a baby for too much longer. The rapid advances in her progression into childhood, reminded him so much of her canny cousin Lily-Ann, and of course Lala, Andreas's sister, who's tragic demise just a few years ago, had denied the opportunity for realising her full potential. Lala, he was sure, would have loved her nephews and nieces, while their aunt would have adored *them*. Walking from the kitchen he had to pass the nappy that he had consigned carelessly to the floor, and gagging on the overpoweringly strong chlorine smell, he deposited the malodorous package into the wash basket, before *she-who-must-be-obeyed* arose. Musing with an arch grin, *she can bloody-well sort that out later,* and *she* rose shortly after, carrying an untouched cold cup of coffee. Visiting was the day's mission, and Andreas told her to get a move on, not having seen his younger brothers or Reuben since the return from Australia. "You'll be going on your own then!" She moaned, pointing to the wash basket, "I have *this* pile to do. Perhaps you could take the boys with you, to get them out of my hair for an hour or two!" She said caustically, "And under no circumstances whatsoever, are they to be taken to the garage. They get in such a mess, and it's the devil, getting all that oil and grease out of their clothes. I wish you'd get me one of those washing-machine things, it would make my life so much easier!" Being heedful of her words, he realized that laundering Rosie's nappies *and* the family's clothes, would be no easy task, and perceiving instantly that another trip to Bristol would be required before Christmas, he would purchase a washing-machine, as well as a power shower. Shaking his head, he wondered how he would ever find the time, and *still* not having vetoed Michael's apparently successful stream diversion, he realized that plans for the commercialisation of the stream could *not* go ahead until he had.

As soon as Lu had readied the boys, he set off for his first visit of the day, and being invited into the house of the Scamp domicile, Andreas thought, *changed days indeed*! Explaining that Reuben was out somewhere in his new car Bill growled, "I'm glad of an opportunity to talk to you anyway!" Mrs Scamp busied herself spoiling the boys, allowing the two men the opportunity to talk in peace. Bill made a brew and sitting two coffees on the table, he added a large helping of rum to his own, "You are carrying a precious cargo, so there will be none of this for you!" Andreas remarked with a smile, "One of these days, I'll walk over here and help you get rid of some of that rum you've got stashed away in that dresser!" Bill smiled and answered sarcastically, combining the two liquids with a straw, "Now wouldn't *that* be something to look forward to!" Slurping the amalgam rapturously, Bill remarked, "Reuben told me that you wanna trace your real father but if you want my advice, you'd be better letting sleeping dogs lie, you *could* be stirring up a hornet's nest!" Andreas commented, "I've got too much on my plate at the moment, but it *is* something that I *will* be looking into and I'd be obliged for any assistance *you* could give me, when I do finally get around to it!" Changing the subject Andreas asked, "How *is* Reuben, has he had time to relax since our return?" "He's certainly different!" Bill replied, "Your trip certainly appears to have made a man of him, and guessing that whatever you were about may not have been strictly legal, the pair of you must have made a pretty good team to clear up that spot of bother, *and* get back in one piece!"

Making no comment on Bill's observations, Andreas asserted, "I have to go now, I've got Guaril and Walthaar to see, and your missus will have those boys ruined if we stay any longer. I've enjoyed our chat, and I'll come again soon!" Bill said, "Aye and make sure to bring the boys with you, my missus loves the bones of 'em!" Andreas replied with a grin, "I'll do that and *next* time I'll walk here, so you'll have no excuse for hanging onto that rum!" Driving to town, Andreas reflected on the strange new relationship that *now* existed between Bill Scamp and himself, deciding that mutual respect was not such a bad thing after all.

Arriving at the flat that he rented out to Walthaar, even though Andreas had yet to actually receive a penny in rent, he found Walthaar entertaining a female, and judging by their flushed faces, he had been doing more than just entertaining. Managing however to compose himself sufficiently enough to welcome them, Walthaar introduce his family to his latest conquest, a pretty little thing who made as much of a fuss of the boys as Mrs Scamp had done, but getting the impression that his brother and the young lady had unfinished business to attend to, Andreas swiftly downed the coffee and inviting them over for a meal, left for Barbara Johnson's house. The semi-detached was still very much as he remembered, the only difference being Guaril's untidy presence, with Barbara not able, or perhaps reluctant to alter the endearing trait. Bringing out his guitar, Guaril played a song that he had been working on, which Andreas thought showed a great deal of promise, wondering however, how much of an input Barbara's expertise had been in the matter. Listening intently to the recital, the boys showed signs of restlessness at it's completion, and realizing that the time for leaving had come, Andreas gathered the boys together, and left for home after extending an invitation to the love-birds to dine at some time in the near future. Realizing that both Viv *and* the diverted stream would have to wait another day, he remarked to the boys as they set off, "I hope your mum's got something really delicious for us when we get home!" In that department as in every other, Lu had never disappointed him, and he for *his* part, had never failed to show his appreciation for her sterling efforts on his behalf. An absolute feast awaited their delectation and being cynical, Andreas wondered if all of this might possibly have something to do with a washing-machine, and if that *was* the rationale, it had certainly borne fruit. Resolving to visit Bristol the next day, he vowed that if such things could be had, he would purchase a washing machine *and* arrange installation. *If* it was half as efficient as Lu had led him to believe, then perhaps it would remove the stains from his bathrobe, and maybe, just maybe, it would mean that he got to spend more time in bed with his wonderful wife, *ha and she thought she was devious,* he mused with a sly grin. Glancing over at her husband, Lu was never quite sure of what was going on in that mind of his, when he smiled or grinned for apparently no reason, *it could be wind,* she thought, and smiled herself at the very idea. As she walked past his chair, he burped, and slapped her arse, and *she* laughed out loud at confirmation of her notion.

3

"No boys, you are definitely not coming to Bristol!" Andreas asserted, "I have to buy a washing-machine for your mother, and if I take the pair of you, I'd end up coming back with something entirely different, and no bloody machine. I promise that the three of us can go Christmas shopping next week!" Having placated them somewhat, Andreas set off before further entreaties would lead to capitulation, and pulling out quickly onto the road, he immediately spotted a figure that he knew only too well, and slowing the car, he pulled up a few yards in front of Maria, "I'm off to Bristol to buy a washing machine for Lu. Hop in if you want to come along for the ride?" "You can drop me in town if you like, but I'm not really in the mood for shopping!" "Okay!" He responded, disappointed at the response, "Town it is then!" And dropping her outside the same church where he had waited for her on his very first ever date with anyone, *a century* ago or so it seemed. Watching her walk away from the car, hips swinging, and arse jiggling, he was reminded of *wild* nights of passion, that were actually not so far in the past Sighing, he shrugged his shoulders, and continued his journey to Bristol, beeping the horn as he passed her by.

With Bristol being a little busier than it had been the previous week, Andreas was grateful for the fact that Maria *had* declined his offer, and feeling strangely elated, yet conversely isolated too, in the vast expanses of the city, he began the search for a suitable shop. Fortunately discovering *Goldwyn's*, soon after his arrival, he peered through the window of the vast emporium, and perceiving a plethora of washing machines, towards the rear of the shop. Striding confidently into the showroom, his inherent bubble of self-assurance was suddenly punctured, as he perused the vast array. Discovering that all were different sizes, with each possessing diverse functions, he was confused, and not really knowing what he was looking for anyway, he turned around, ready to call off the whole idea of spending good money, in purchasing something that he would probably never use himself. But fortuitously, a saucy young piece, with a plunging neckline, walked his way, asking if she could help him with anything, and passing up the opportunity to give a pert response, he replied soberly, "I'd like to ask your advice on purchasing a washing machine, and I'm confused by all the different functions. What I would really like, is one that has *all* the functions, and suitable for a family of five, er better make that six!" The saucy young piece smiled, "Follow me sir, I have just what you're looking for!" Rolling his eyes heavenwards at the suggestion, and following three paces behind, deeply preoccupied by the movement of her derriere, he thought, *You most certainly do young lady*. While being unable to avert his gaze from the amount of flesh on view, he readily agreed immediately to her selection, and while settling the bill, still finding it difficult to wrench his eyes from her decolletage, he asked about the possibility of also purchasing a power-shower. Yvonne, for that was the name emblazoned on the badge, pinned to the strap of her flimsy top, which in truth was actually the only available space, announced that they had just taken delivery of shower-units from Peterborough, and a power-shower, could very well be among them. Disappearing through a door at the rear of the shop, she re-entered a few minutes later carrying a box. "Bingo!" She declared, "But I'm afraid it's the only one!" With his mind apparently made up for him, and discovering that she was the manageress, he negotiated a deal, whereby he was able to purchase the two items as a job lot for cash. Informing him of the delivery, and installation date, the details of which did not register in his brain, as it was nigh on impossible, for him to tear his gaze from her ample bosom, long enough to concentrate, he did however, remember insisting on an early morning delivery. Walking to the door, still on a euphoric high, he paused to mop the sweat from his brow, omnipresent in spite of it being a chilly December morning. Looking toward the cash desk, he observed her, watching his exit, whereupon she smiled, and blew him a kiss. Returning the gesture, he thought philosophically as he walked away, *Yes you little mare, you knew exactly what you were doing. Just like a bloody woman. But hey, he had achieved his goal.* Having nothing important left to do, he indulged himself in retail therapy, then realizing how much he had spent on himself, he bought guilt-trip jumpers for Lu and the boys, then satisfied with his days work, he drove home.

Walking through the gate, he was almost bowled over by George, who had run out to greet him, and allowing him to carry two of the lighter bags, he followed his youngest son into the living room. Aiming the bag containing Lu's jumper at her head, he saw her sway to the right, and throwing out her left hand, she plucked the missile out of the air. For her dexterity she received applause from her sons, and a kiss from her husband. Telling her of the washing machine to be delivered soon, he confessed, "I'm sorry love, but a lorry went past the door, just as *he* was telling me the delivery date, then the bastard, buggered off for *his* tea-break, before I could ask him to repeat it!" Neglecting to warn her of the shower that he had purchased, and pretending that the assistant *wasn't* a voluptuous strumpet, sent to haunt a man's wildest sleeping moments, was devious to say the least, but the smile he received for taking time-out to buy his wife something to lighten her load, far outweighed any guilt that he ought, or perhaps ought not feel, and *could* portend a night of carnal delights, *if* he played his cards right and *if* Rosie allowed it. The new stratagem he had conceived in handling that particular last proviso, *should* provide the opportunity, appreciating that the *correct* dosage of brandy, would have to be administered to her night-time bottle. Unwrapping the jumpers, which proved a matter of pure luck or divine intervention, in *actually* purchasing the correct sizes, surely would have earned him more *brownie* points, which he fully intended to cash in on later that night. After having eaten the meal, lovingly prepared, and served by his beautiful wife, he played *hangman* with the boys, proving to be a source of much fascination to Rosie, and allowing her to help him, was instrumental in enabling the boys to win the games, which put *them* in a good mood too. The pursuit came to an abrupt end, when Lou began to yawn, and more loudly than was the norm. Taking it to be a sign of things to come, Andreas rose from the settee, "I'll see to Rosie's bottle babe, you sit where you are!" She responded coquettishly, "You are *such* a good husband!"

Shouting from the kitchen, while removing the brandy from it's hidey hole, he oiled the wheels of life and love, "It's called appreciation babe!" With the boys climbing the wooden hill early, and Rosie duly falling asleep, even before the mixture had been half-finished, the amorous couple retired for the night. The signs were now definitely favourable, and wasting little time in initiating proceedings, he began gently stroking her hair, a ploy that he used on the odd occasion, to secure his wicked way, and snuggling into his chest in supplication, strands of Lou's hair tickled his face. Tenderly edging her head from his shoulder, he kissed her passionately, and reading the unspoken signs that exist between lovers, he took her roughly, finding unsurprisingly that playing the role of a brute came all too easily for him.

Over breakfast the following morning, the man of the house asked, "Lu are you pregnant?" She retorted, "It'll be a bloody miracle if I'm not, the way you've been at me since you came home. What makes you ask?" Andreas replied, "It's just a peculiarity that you had in our love-making, when you were pregnant with Rosie, and it raised it's head again last night!" She suggested, "I'll consult Ma later, she will know!" Andreas made a mental note to begin looking for another house, *just in case*. He imparted his plans for the day, "I'm going to see Michael this morning, and after that I'll have to pop into the office to see Viv. I wanna run this idea of the farm making cider on a commercial basis, past the pair of them!" Lu was asked for *her* opinion on the scheme, and after deliberating for all of sixty seconds, she declared, "It sounds like a good idea, but with so many irons in your fire already, you could be in danger of over-reaching yourself!" He replied, "I take your point, but it makes sense to diversify, not only for the farm, but for business interests too, and putting all your eggs into one basket, could just as easily be folly too. You just never know what the future holds!" Leaving for the farm as soon as he had eaten, he decided to take Victor with him, having the thought that because his son had it easy for far too long, he was resolved to speak to Michael about Victor doing some kind of work on the farm. Driving leisurely to the farm, Victor asked his father, why the farm had been sectioned off, with Andreas explaining about the need to protect the farm from outside sources of disease. Andreas was pleased at Victor's interest, until parrying further questions as best he could, made it difficult to concentrate on driving, and he breathed a sense of relief when they finally arrived at the farm. Michael put aside the brush, with which he was clearing dried dung from the yard, and greeted them warmly, then ushering them inside the farmhouse for coffee, and a chat, he told them, "Vee is in the shop, and she is bound to have seen you arrive, so don't forget to go and see her before you leave!" Andreas and Victor followed Michael into the parlour, carrying their coffees, "Ted has done wonders diverting the stream, and I'll show you everything later, but Lu rang to say that you wanted to talk to me about something?" "Well two things really!" He replied seriously, "Firstly I would like Victor to work at the farm in some capacity. It will do him good to learn how the farm is run as a business!" Michael agreed, "That's a great idea, and I can use another hand, now that business is on the up!" Andreas sat down, "The second matter, is for you and Viv to consider the possibility of brewing your home-made cider on a commercial basis. *If* you're both agreeable, we could install the necessary machinery here in next to no time, with no cost to you or the farm, being a straight investment by the firm. You would receive remuneration for your expertise, *and* initially for the use of your property, but obviously if it takes off, we would need to purchase alternative premises, *or* build a suitable plant right here. Viv believes that he can broker a deal with local breweries, so it all hangs on *your* acceptance and *his* contacts. Think everything over, but keep in mind that we *do* constantly have to keep an eye to the future. We do not want another foot-and-mouth epidemic, without having sustainable alternatives in place!" A shell-shocked Michael said, "*Well* you've certainly given me plenty to think about, on your ideas for the future, but I'd like to talk it over with Vee!" Andreas remarked with a smile, "We don't need an answer *immediately,* but we *would* like a decision as soon as possible, and if you could come over to our place for lunch, we could come to some arrangement about Victor!" "Great!" Michael smiled, "You can be sure that Vee will want to see you, so the two of you had better go and see her before you leave!" And as soon as they entered the shop, Vee threw her arms around both her brother and nephew, "I wondered if you intended coming to see me. I've got some scones in the oven for you!" then looking at her husband, she said, "If Michael watches the shop for five, I'll put them in a bag for you!" Michael cast his eyes to the ceiling, but assumed a place behind the counter anyway. Andreas and Victor ended up wiling away an hour or so with Vee and Lily-Ann, who had just finished picking cider apples, and finally glancing up at the clock, Andreas decided that it was time to leave, "I'll have to leave now Vee, I've got Viv to see!" Helping himself to a few flagons of cider, Andreas placed them into the empty boot, while Lily-Ann placed the cakes carefully, on the floor, in the rear of the car.

4

Viv assumed a feigned air of surprise at seeing his colleague, "You must be as fresh as a daisy, with not having worked for so long!" Not rising to the bait, Andreas ignored the remark "I've seen Michael, and he *is* interested in making cider commercially, *if* there is enough interest from the breweries, but producing cider at the farm would come at a cost. Since shouldering the responsibility of the stream diversion, he has really matured in business ventures, and with his expertise in the field being so vital, I believe that if he were offered some kind of a partnership, it would completely tie him to the firm!" Viv answered soberly "Before we start handing out any gratuitous partnerships, I've been in touch, with several breweries and almost all, *are* prepared to sell the produce from their hostelries, seeing it as having a *quirky* appeal!" He paused, "*However* the logistics are not good, for instance, how can it be kept fresh long enough to warrant producing it in large enough quantities, to be a viable prospect?" It was a problem that Andreas had not foreseen, but as always, being like a dog with a bone, if there was a sniff of money to be made, "I really had not anticipated that problem!" He said dolefully, adding more in hope than anything else, "But I'm sure it will *not* prove insoluble!" Viv shook his head, "Well when you *have* solved the problem, come back, and we'll get it off the ground. They were certainly interested, so if you *can* come up with an answer, we *could* be onto a winner!" Andreas changed the subject, "Have you had any further thoughts on commercialising that part of the stream I earmarked?" Viv became animated, "Ah yes, I've had a look at the site, and decided that it *would* be a worthwhile venture. With little financial outlay, you wouldn't lose too much money if it were to flop, which I think very unlikely anyway. With the whole nation now moving out of the doldrums, people are looking for new ways to spend their hard-earned cash on leisurely pursuits, and being one of those, your scheme *definitely* has potential! Now then, we have to address your report on Australia, or lack of it. The brothers were *certainly* not amused!" Andreas's face clouded, and he responded coldly, "To be fair neither you, nor the brothers were there, and the report wasn't intended to be humorous. *If* you are all so concerned about what went on, Reuben and I will come to a meeting and *explain* everything in graphic detail!" Rising from his chair, Andreas glared angrily at his friend, "I assure you that if you wish to have such a meeting, you would understand just why it was not put down in what you and the brothers would consider, something to read in an idle moment. The reality is that you sent a couple of kids, wet behind the ears into a hell-hole, and the fact that we managed to come out of it successfully, came at a high cost to our safety and sanity. We shed buckets of blood, almost losing our freedom, *and* our lives in the process, so I have no intention of putting anything further than I have already in that report. The fact that Reuben and I are both home, walking around, is in no way thanks to anything you lot did, so don't *ever* ask for that report again. I hope

I'm making myself clear!" Knowing that he had hit a sore nerve, Viv tried to change the subject, "How's the family?" Leaving the query unanswered, Andreas glared at him as he opened the door to leave, "By the way, I *will* be in to work on Monday, where I'm sure you will find another *little* problem for me to solve!" Slamming the door behind him, Andreas collected Victor from reception and headed home.

Sensing that something was awry when Andreas stomped into the room, Lu sat beside him on the settee, and putting a solicitous arm around his shoulder, she cradled his head against her breast. Although still smouldering inside, Lu's ministrations at least went *some* way toward soothing his troubled demeanour, and after a further few minutes, he admitted that to her, that it was all to do with Viv and the report, "He should learn to keep his bloody mouth shut!" Suggesting a visit to Ma and Pa's he stated, "I haven't seen much of them since I came back?" "That's a good idea!" Lu replied, "I'll get myself ready, while you see to the kids!" Walking to Ma and Pa's, Andreas was grateful for the fact that he had made sure that the kids were all wrapped up warm, as the weather was perishingly cold, and being not quite acclimatized since returning from Melbourne, he rued the fact that he had not taken the time to clad himself in a similar way. Typically Ma was not surprised to see them but Pa, who had obviously been at the bottle was almost on the verge of tears seeing them all there together. Smiling resignedly, Ma asked, "To what do we owe this honour?" Lu answered for him, grinning pertly, "Something Viv said upset him, so he had to come and see his Ma!" Ma asked, "Was it about the report?" Andreas looked at Ma and grumbled, "I thought he would be above the sort of remark that he made!" Ma remarked, "Whatever it was he said, you know that deep down, he would not have meant it. Katie is working today, so why don't you go over, and tell him *exactly* what happened over there, then shake hands, and draw a line under it. You've been friends for too long now, to let such a thing come between you, and I'm sure he will be feeling just as wretched as you do over this matter!" Andreas smiled and kissed Ma's forehead, "Thank you Ma, you are right as usual. I'll go and sort it out now!" She said impatiently, "Well off you go then, and there's no need to hurry back, me and Pa will look after your family!"

Knocking tentatively at the door, Andreas was timorously invited in, and Viv asked him to take a seat, while he fixed them both a drink. Viv disappeared into the kitchen, and Andreas called out, "I suppose it's beyond the realms of fantasy that you have Tolley's?" Viv returned with two empty glasses and a bottle of Southern Comfort looking puzzled, "What the hell is that!" Andreas replied "Don't worry, it's an Australian thing. I'll explain later!" Shame-faced Viv said, "Before we begin this drink session, I'd like to apologise, and I really meant no offence. It was just a stupid lack of judgement on my part, and I'm really glad you came over, so we can clear the air!" Andreas smiled, sipped his liquor slowly, "Nice drink, shame it's not Tolley's though!" "Tell me all abut this fabulous liquor!" And after being enlightened, Viv suggested, "Perhaps we should import it! I wouldn't mind trying it if it's that good!" Between glasses of the soothing ambrosial Southern Comfort, Andreas recounted everything that had occurred in Australia, omitting nothing, including his dalliance with Angela, the new second-in-command in Australia. "My God!" Viv remarked at the end of the saga, "I thought there might be a *possibility* of violence, but never in a million years, did I ever dream that it would be as perilous as that. No wonder you were so furious at my stupidity!" Andreas shook his head, "Let's just forget it, and I really don't want any of what I've just told you to be known. I *haven't* even told Lu!" Viv grinned and suggested, "Especially about Angela!" Viv began to eulogise about Andreas's part in the precarious adventure, and taking a large slug of his drink, he corrected Viv, "If it had not been for Ronaldo, *and* the old man who hired the boat to us, I would not be sitting here, and don't forget that it was Reuben who actually took out Hendy *and* the sniper!" Viv nodded, conceding that Andreas was indeed correct, "There must be some way that we can show appreciation for their bravery!" Andreas agreed, suggesting, "Reuben has already been paid, but if the firm *really* want to thank him, Jimmy Kelly is nearing retirement age, and Reuben would an ideal replacement. It would mean going on a business-study course, which the firm could subsidise. Ronaldo is happy as he is, but I *would* like the firm to sponsor the education of a bright young lad, who gave us information, that was both helpful, and valuable!" "That's the least that we can do!" Viv conceded, "I'll make the arrangements tomorrow. Now is there anything else?" Andreas declared with a smile, "Well yes there is one small matter. When we blew up the filling station, the wash destroyed the wharf from where we hired the boat, and I promised the old man, that I would have a new one built for them!" "That will also be arranged tomorrow, and now we've got that all sorted out, can we get down to some serious drinking?" A few hours later Andreas staggered rather than walked the distance to Ma's and as soon as he entered the room, Ma remarked, "Oh I see you've settled things then!" Andreas slurred with a silly grin, "Yeah, that's *sorted* too. Come on you lot, let's go home!"

Outlining his plans for Reuben's future over breakfast, Andreas informed Lu, that he would be popping over to see him, "If he agrees to putting his future plans in my hands, I will have the unpleasant task of informing Jimmy of my decision, and I'm certainly not looking forward to *that*. Jimmy and I have been friends for years now, but the future *has* to be addressed. He cannot go on forever, and I have to make contingency plans, but I'm not sure how he'll take it!" Believing that fresh air would waken him from the alcohol induced torpor from which he was suffering, and opted for a brisk walk to the Scamp's place, which *should* completely clear his mind of cobwebs. Arriving at the Scamp house with his faculties now three quarters repaired, he found Reuben still eating breakfast, and realising that business was almost certain to be on the agenda, his parents rose from the table. Stopping the exodus Andreas said, "Please don't leave, I'd like you all to hear what I have to say!" And cutting straight to the chase, he turned to Reuben, "I'd like to offer you the position of *manager* at the Gymnasium Club, subject of course to terms and conditions. It would necessitate attending a course at college, *and* you would still have to work under Jimmy, until such time that you have passed your course, and deemed ready to take over!" Finding three silent and open-mouthed members of the Scamp clamp facing him, he continued, "You already have a tidy sum of money, and the position on offer, is intended to set you up for life!" Reuben sat back in his chair dumb-founded, but his father suddenly discovered his tongue, "At least it will stop him gallivanting all over the place in that bloody car!" His mother kissed Andreas on the cheek and said, "Thank you Andreas, and he'd better sodding say yes, or I'll take my whip to his arse!" The accompanying smile as she trundled off to the kitchen to make coffee, displayed an array of gold fillings, leaving Andreas racking his brains, to ascertain when if ever, he had heard her utter a word *or* smile before.

He walked slowly homeward, feeling more *compus mentis* by the minute, and declining Lu's offer of breakfast, "I want to get this manager situation sorted out, and the sooner the better!" Having problems *en route* concentrating on his driving, he stopped for ten minutes, to clear his mind, and once equilibrium had been restored, he headed once more for the gym. Pulling up in front of the club, he noticed that even at that early hour, there was already a few cars in the car-park, *business is looking up,* he thought. Without a word, Jimmy rose from his chair, took two cups from the cupboard office, and while waiting for the kettle to boil, he said, "What ails you son. It's kinda early for you to come visiting?" Andreas took a sip of coffee, and with no preamble, he outlined the intended plans for the future. Jimmy's face gave no sign of reaction, prompting Andreas to ask, "Well, what do you think?" Jimmy put down his coffee, "How long will this course last, I'd like to know how long I've got!" Andreas asserted hastily, "Jimmy, it's not a short course, and he'll have to learn how to run this place from you, so it would be a while!" Sullenly, Jimmy shrugged his shoulders, and the moment that Andreas had been dreading had arrived, "I don't know for sure how long, it could be a year, maybe longer!" Sensing Jimmy's distress, and with his voice almost a whisper, he said, looking guiltily at the floor, "You will receive a lump-sum in recognition of your service, and a generous pension to supplement what you would receive from the government!" "All that is fine and dandy, but as generous as the terms are, what about *me?*" Jimmy asked, "This place has been such a huge part of my life for so long, that I don't think I would survive too long, if I weren't here!" Andreas thought for a minute, then smiled, "Look Jimmy you can have everything I've already offered, which starts as of now, *plus* you would still be in charge of training future champions, for as long as you wish. How does *that* sound?" Jimmy's demeanour changed immediately, "Andreas, that would be a dream come true for me, and would also give me the opportunity to look after my sick wife, a whole lot better than I do now!" Pausing, Jimmy observed, "Little did I realise that the little boy who came in one day looking for a place to train, would be such a large and wonderful part of my life. You have always done right by me, and I have to be fair, there could not be a better replacement for me than Reuben!" He thrust out his hand, and as Andreas took Jimmy's large misshapen mitt, he said warmly, "Jimmy, I promise you one thing. I will *always* look after you!" Driving away from the club, Andreas was very much lighter in heart, having successfully negotiated Jimmy's release *and* his replacement, all with the minimum of effort and fuss. Heading for home, he was *not* surprised to find on arrival, that a hot meal was already waiting for him, *just like her mother,* he thought. Lu remarked, "You're looking very smug, what have you been up to?" "You mean you don't know?" He suggested sarcastically. "I do not know *everything!*" She retorted, "Only bits of things, and I think sometimes, it is just as well!" She came up behind him while he was eating, put her arms around him, "I've got some news for you. Ma told me that I *am* pregnant!" He stopped eating and asked, "Why didn't you tell me last night?" "You were in no fit state to be told *anything* last night!" "Christ!" He remarked, "The way we're knocking them out, I'd better have my dick tied up and knotted!" "Don't you bloody dare!" She said, with a purely artificial pout. Reflecting later that it had been a strange and fulfilling morning one way and another, he wondered if the afternoon would be as productive, and with that in mind, he made ready to take the boys to see Viv, to legalise the morning's work, and address the small matter of a new house.

5

"What on earth do you want with another house?" Viv asked. Andreas replied, "It isn't that I *want* another house, It's just that all of a sudden I *need* a larger one!" The penny did not take long to drop, and grasping Andreas by both shoulders, he offered his congratulations, "Are we allowed a celebration?" "Not for a while!" Andreas replied, "I've got to get over last night first!" Then changing the subject, to one that had been at the back of his mind ever since Reuben suggested the matter, Andreas said, "I'd like to trace my lineage, but do not know how to go about it, and having no birth certificate complicates things somewhat!" Viv said, "It will certainly not help, but leave it with me. I'll look into it for you. Am I permitted to ask why this has arisen all of a sudden?" Andreas informed his colleague, "It all started, when the old man, from whom we rented the boat in Australia, made the remark that I had the look of a Roma, and with it having been suggested several times before in my life, it made me wonder about who I really am, and where I came from!" "Leave it to me!" "It sounds the kind of project, that I'd enjoy getting my teeth into!" Informing Viv of the morning's successful agreements that he had brokered, he received Viv's approbation for a job well done, but noticing that the boys, were wriggling restively in their seats, he called a halt to the discussion. "I'll have to leave, the boys are getting fidgety!" "Right then!" Viv suggested, "You'd better get them home, and *don't* worry, I'll sort out your ancestry somehow, but it *could* take a little time!" Adding with a smirk, "And, *if* you're a good boy you can come in next Monday, and start work!" Closing the door quietly behind him, Andreas reflected, *I'm glad I'm not sarcastic like that.*

Andreas was elated with all he had accomplished that day, with even the boys' seemingly endless squabbling in the rear of the car, not being able to dislodge the smug smile from his face. When they finally reached home, with his offsprings' contretemps still ensuing, he found that they had a surprise visitor. "Ho Gadjo, long time no see!" Came the voice from the living room. "*Here* for dinner again are you?" Andreas asked sarcastically, "Which would not surprise me in the least Gunnar, you're *always* on the bloody mooch for something!" "Well if it's on offer, and I haven't got to pay, who am I to refuse!" Andreas conjectured, "What *does* bring you here then?" But before there was time for Gunnar to respond, Andreas conjectured, "Hmm let me guess now, you've got a car that you can't get rid of, and you wanna dump it on me?" "I've got several nice little runners as it happens, all as clean as a whistle!" "Let me hazard another guess!" Andreas postulated, "You want my people-carrier?" Gunnar grinned archly, "Not as silly as you look are you? Come to the garage tomorrow, and see if there's anything you fancy. Mind you, it'll have to be a fairly large one, as I understand you will soon have another seat to fill!" And shaking Andreas's hand, he asked with a grin, "What else have you been up to, besides knocking up my sister?" Andreas explained about the successful scheme for the changeover in managership at the Gymnasium Club, and enlightened him of the meeting with Viv. "Why on earth would you want to know if you are a gypsy or not?" Andreas answered brusquely, "Well it would stop you calling me Gadjo for one thing, but it won't be easy without a birth certificate!" Gunnar's swift response, stunned Andreas, "You *do* actually have a birth certificate. I've seen it. Your mother's cousin gave it to Ma and Pa, when they handed over the money for your adoption!" Turning to Lu, Andreas asked, "Would you mind if I went over to Ma's, I really *can't* put this off until tomorrow!" Smiling sympathetically, she said, "You go babe, I know it's important to you!" Speeding to the house in less than five minutes, the two brothers noticed that Ma had already put out two plates of stew, "There you are boys, I know you haven't eaten!" "Thanks Ma!" Andreas said, "I suppose you know why we're here?" "Of course I do. Lulu phoned me just before you arrived. Give me a minute or two, the certificate is in the bedroom, with those insurance policies that you made us take out!" Two minutes later, she re-entered the room carrying a sheet of paper, that Andreas was convinced would open the window to his past. But when he looked at the document, there was no name in the father's column, so it was back to square one. Pa unusually ventured the thought, "Never mind son, maybe Viv can turn something up, he's a devious bastard at the best of times, but if you need help with this sort of thing, he's the man for the job!" Pa's words had a ring of logic about them, and leaving Gunnar to devour his stew, Andreas returned home, downcast but not *completely* disheartened, birth certificate in pocket.

Going to the office the following morning, he handed the certificate to Viv remarking, "Ma had it all the time, but it's not much use, the father section has nothing entered in it. Viv scrutinised the paper, then with a smile he declared, "It's not *entirely* worthless, it has the office of registration stamped on it, so at least we have a foothold!" Andreas felt stupid for not having spotted it himself, but despite that, Viv's observation had given him new heart. He smiled, "I knew I could depend on you!" Rising from his seat, Viv informed his colleague, "I'll be on the phone for most of the morning, so you may as well just leave it with me, and do whatever is next on your agenda!" Deciding to have a *shufti* at the car that Gunnar wanted him to take off his hands, Andreas drove to the garage, where he found Gunnar on the forecourt, head under the bonnet of a car. "Come on then where's this wreck of a car you want to dump on me?" Andreas demanded. Gunnar remarked, "Come on round the back. I have a car that could have been made, with you in mind!" Following his brother to the rear of the garage to see this wonder of modern engineering, Andreas was immediately forced to concede that the car was a stunner, but in no way could he let Gunnar know just *how* impressed he was. A gleaming silver Citroen DS break, obviously *fairly* new, with the added fillip of not too many miles on the clock, and with plenty of room for his expanding family, it *would* have been exactly the car he would have chosen, *if* he had been looking for a different car. Already being taken with the car, *without* Gunnar's spiel, he resolved to negotiate as good a deal as he could possibly get. With bargaining akin to a game between the two of them, Andreas propounded, "*If* I were looking for a new car, which I'm not, what would be the asking price, and how much for a trade-in?" "Who do you think you're kidding?" Gunnar suggested archly, "You're hooked, and you know it! The car is ready to drive away now, and at only two years old, you could give me *your* car for nothing, still pay the full asking price, and you would *still* have gotten a bargain!" "You've got no bloody chance!" Andreas retorted, "In fact *you* should pay me for taking this foreign shit off your hands!" Walking away, Andreas knew that Gunnar badly wanted his people carrier for some reason or other, and if *that* were the case, he would almost certainly call him back. And having walked only a few yards, his conjecture bore fruit, "Andreas I'll come clean, I need your car for a special customer, who is willing to pay top-dollar for a classic car. We can do a straight swap, and nobody will lose out. What do you say?" "I'm *not* entirely convinced that I shouldn't receive a little extra for doing you a good turn!" Andreas whinged. Gunnar shook his head, and conceded defeat, "How about if give you half the profit I make on the sale. Would that stop you moaning? Andreas smiled and thought exultantly, *just what I bloody wanted*, but determined to screw as much as he could out of his brother, he stroked his chin thoughtfully, "Well okay, but being concerned about fuel consumption, I'll do the deal, if there's a full tank of petrol thrown in!" "Okay you cheapskate bastard, you'll have your tank of petrol!" Gunnar railed, "You've done me again, you bastard?" Following Gunnar into the office, a smiling Andreas signed the transfers, then sped off, heading for the gym in his shining new car, wearing a broad smile, and reflecting on the great day he was having.

Pulling into the gym car park at speed, he jammed on the brakes, showering gravel everywhere and climbing out of the car he was greeted by an astonished Jimmy, "When did you get that huge thing?" "Twenty minutes ago!" Andreas answered, "What do you think of it?" Jimmy answered moodily, "The car's okay, but the driver's a bloody lunatic. Anyway forget about that, when is Reuben starting here, I could do with a hand just now, what with Christmas and New Year coming up?" "Well he won't be starting college until January, so I'll get him to come in and lend a hand. It'll give him something better to do than driving around the place like a bloody maniac!" And, leaving an open-mouthed Jimmy spluttering in his wake, Andrea headed for the gymnasium, to apply himself to a much needed spot of weight training, and an hour on the punch-bag. At the completion of the punishing session, he showered and headed home, to show Lu the lovely new car that he had acquired from Gunnar. Treating the family to a test drive, the general consensus of opinion, was that he had purchased the most wonderful piece of machinery on the planet, and even Lu showed her approbation while he was driving, by sliding her hand between his legs. And any guilt that he may or may not have had, over securing such a ridiculously favourable bargain, disappeared in that very second, appreciating that later, it could have even more unseen benefits, in the marital bed.

6

Tearing himself away from the warmth of his beautiful young wife's body, Andreas made breakfast for himself and the kids, telling them that the promised day of Christmas shopping in Bristol had arrived. "The big day's not too far away now boys, and no gifts have yet been bought for your grandparents or for that matter your mother!" And spreading themselves out in the spacious rear seating of the new car, they made short work of the crisps and pop he had purchased at the garage, when he had gone there to gloat, while leaving the empties for their doting father to clear up later. It was a beautiful day, and he was looking forward the day out with his boys, but as soon as they arrived at their destination, he realized that Christmas shopping should really been completed much sooner. Everywhere was thronged, and Andreas became more intent on keeping the boys and himself together, than actually purchasing anything himself. It was a relief to their father, when all the boys' presents had been chosen and paid for, by their indulgent, doting *daddi*. Returning to the car park, Andreas found that he had forgotten the registration, make and even the colour of the new car. "I know!" He suggested to the boys, "We'll play a game, the first one to find the new car, gets to stay up an extra half hour tonight!" George much to the chagrin of Victor, won the contest, and Andreas thought *I'll have to think of an excuse for Victor to stay up late too.* Placing all of the presents into the boot and unlocking the car, he relaxed for a few moments before moving off, suggesting that Victor should also have an extra half an hour for not snitching to mum. Relieved to be finally clear of the city, and it's incessant traffic lights, he reflected as they neared home, that it had been a very stressful but satisfactory day. Reaching home and with darkness having fallen, the coloured Christmas lights that Lu had placed in the window, shone brightly in the darkness, giving the whole house a warm, cosy glow. As soon as they entered the house, the boys dashed upstairs with their presents to prevent their mother seeing what they had chosen, and before he could seize the chance of sneaking into the kitchen for a *swiftie*, the telephone began ringing. Andreas announced to the rest of the family, before they rushed to answer, *not much chance of that*, he thought, "I've got it!" Viv had rung to tell him that he had managed to purchase a case of Tolley's from a store an Earl's Court emporium in London. Andreas roared, "Oh that's bloody brilliant, I've been shopping in Bristol all day with the boys, so I'm ready for a drink!" Viv laughed, "In that case I'll be round straight away!" In fifteen minutes Andreas was seated in his chair with his feet on a pouffe, relaxing with a glass of Tolley's and coke. Viv had left almost as soon as he had arrived, so after another of the same Andreas remarked, "I think I'll take a couple of bottles over to Bill Scamp's house, one each for him and Reuben. Would you mind me going love, I've got to see Reuben about working at the club over Christmas?" Lu smiled, "Of course not, you pop off now and I'll get the boys ready for bed!" Telling her of the deal with the boys and the reason for the extra half an hour, she escorted him to the door, and kissed his mouth. "I'll be back presently for more of that!" He promised with a grin. Five minutes later he was knocking on Bill's door with a bottle in either hand, and when the door opened, Andreas proclaimed, "I come bearing gifts!" As soon as Reuben caught a glimpse of what he had brought over, he let out a whoop and got out glasses from the Welsh dresser. "One of these bottles is for your father, so don't go too mad!" Bill made coffee for himself and Andreas, which was duly treated to a good helping of Tolley's finest, while Reuben poured a copious amount of the brandy into a glass, adding a modicum of coke, for good luck. Informing Reuben that he would have to help Jimmy over the holiday period, Andreas drained the coffee and returned home post haste, just in time to kiss the boys goodnight. Remarking to Lu, "I should have asked Viv if there had been any progress made in tracing my father!" She replied, "I'm sure he would have mentioned if there had been, but you probably won't hear anything until after the Christmas break, these government offices have quite a long break!" Andreas remarked with a slightly slurred voice, "Lazy bastards, all they do is sit on their fat arses!" "Yes dear!" Came the conciliatory reply.

7

Paying the price for his predilection for Tolley's, or perhaps the enforced absence from it, Andreas was at least now aware of a store actually retailing the elixir, and made a mental note to put in a standing order. A lazy morning was wasted, idly watching children's television with his three children, and Rosie, now an avid fan of the Flower Pot Men, demanded that everyone else had to suffer puppets with visible strings, jerking along to the accompaniment of condescending voice-overs. Lu nearly jumped out of her skin when the telephone rang, and reaching the phone before her ever-loving, she whispered, "It's Viv, shall I tell him you're not in?" Andreas shook his head, and reaching for the phone, he said in an undertone, "No for God's sake, it might be something more important than Bill and sodding Ben!" Taking the phone he remarked, "I hope you realise that you've just wakened the whole household, so I hope it's something important, like more Tolley's perhaps!" Viv laughed, "No you idiot" And after a pause he said, "I think we may have found your father!" Andreas was taken aback but recovering his equilibrium swiftly he said, "That was quick, how the *hell* did you manage that?" "Pure luck really!" Viv replied. Sally rang the Clifton office where the birth was registered, and asked them to get in touch with the local registrar's office. By pure luck, the woman who had been assigned to the task, remembered your mother's name from somewhere, and racking her brain, she suddenly recalled that your mother had been involved with the relative of a friend of hers. Apparently there was quite a to do about it, as he was a married man, which of course was frowned upon at that time. She could only remember his surname, but managed to get in touch with her friend who supplied the Christian name too. It's not *absolutely* certain, but we believe that this man *is* your father. What an extraordinary set of events!" Impatiently Andreas interrupted Viv's flow of words, "Stop burbling and tell me his name!" On learning the man's identity however, Andreas was suddenly struck dumb, and gently replacing the receiver, he walked into the kitchen where Lu was half-way through making dinner. She looked at him expectantly, and he told her, "They've managed to trace my father!" Shaking his head he mumbled, "And guess what, I'm a bloody Scamp!" Lu began laughing, and looking at her, he shook his head once more, and began laughing in unison, "I wonder if we'll have to change the kids' names?" Failing to stifle her amusement, she spluttered, "God only knows, perhaps Viv can help with that too, and I think Ma and Pa should be told, before you do anything else!" "Yeah you're right!" He agreed. "I suppose I'll have to let Bill Scamp know as well, and Christ only knows what *he'll* make of it!" Wrapping her arms around her husband's neck, she asserted, "Have your dinner first darling, we were always taught not to do anything important on an empty stomach!" So after dinner, and now completely recovered from the previous evenings excesses, he walked over to see the people who had always been his parents in his mind *and* heart, even though he had mannaged to trace his biological father.

"Ma, I have some shock news for you, and I'm not entirely sure whether it's good or bad!" Explaining the news of his parentage, Pa being unusually diplomatic, remarked, "It makes not one bit of difference to us, you will always be a son to us, but how do *you* feel about it?" "I'm stunned Pa, but not unduly upset. I just don't know what to think, it's such a shock!" Pa seemed to have taken over control, "Right!" He said, "I'll get my coat on and we'll walk over to Bill's together!" "Thanks Pa!" Andreas said, knowing all along that the pair of them would always be there for him.

Bill answered the door dressed in his red vest and dungarees, kerchief still tied around his vast neck, and a smidgeon of jam at the corner of his mouth, "Well now, what have I done wrong?" "Can we come in Bill?" P asked, "It's bloody freezing out here?". Bill opened the door and his wife shuffled away to the kitchen to make coffee and as soon as it had been served up, Bill added a drop of Tolley's to the brew. Pa took a sip and remarked, "By Christ Bill, that's powerful stuff. Gotta be the best coffee I've ever tasted, where on earth did you get *that* stuff?" Bill looked at Andreas, who was standing behind Pa shaking his head. Bill's wife Jan ventured, "Although it's always a pleasure Billie, what's the reason for this visit?" Bill glared at her for daring to speak, and Andreas realised that it was now only the second time that he had *ever* heard her speak. Pa looked at Bill and asked, "Do you by any chance know of a *John* Scamp?" Bill replied, "Why has he died, and left me money. God knows I could do with a windfall?" Getting no response to his attempt at humour, he remarked, "Yes

I know him, lives over Bristol way somewhere. Now don't be getting involved with him, he's a real bad'un. A few centuries ago, one of his kin was burned at the stake for being a witch, and consorting with the Devil. And believe me devilry is John's middle name. Pleasant enough cove to me, but apparently he's got kids all over the county!" Andreas looked him in the eye and confessed, "Bill, I can't help being involved with him, I've just learned that *he's* my father. I'm one of those kids he's got all over the county!" "Oh *dordi, dordi,* I bloody warned you to let sleeping dogs lie, but you wouldn't sodding listen, would you? Come to think of you *do* have the look of him, and whatever he may or may not have been, I gotta say he was always a good worker, not like some of those bastards from over that way. He just couldn't keep it in his trousers, if my dear wife will forgive me for saying so in front of her, and I'll tell you one thing Mister Bosworth, I know it's too late now, but I wouldn't let no git of his near a daughter of mine!" Andreas said nothing, but thought to himself, *too late now you old bastard* as he recalled nights of violent passion he had shared with *his* daughter Maria. Bill continued, "I gotta 'fess Andreas, you ain't a bad boy, being brought up good and proper by your Pa, and you've done a lot for folk hereabouts, which fact I put fair and square down to you being a Scamp. Welcome to the family son, *dordi dordi,* wait 'til Reuben hears of this, he'll be tickled pink! Come on let's have another drink to celebrate!" So after another hour of coffee *avits,* and Pa gradually developing a taste for the stuff, Andreas resolved to make sure that his store indoors would be kept under lock and key. When he finally reached home, in a much worse state than when he had left, Lu declared, "If *I* had a car, I could have driven you there *and* back, instead of which you got freezing cold, and it just serves you right!" Andreas commented as he turned out the light and climbed the wooden hill, "I suppose you're right babe, you usually are!"

8

Being woken the following morning by a persistent knocking at the door, Andreas donned his stained, once white dressing gown, and hurried downstairs before the whole household was roused. Finding that it was the delivery man with the washing machine and shower, he urged, "Please make as little noise as possible, especially when you install the shower, there's a baby sleeping upstairs, and I don't want her wakened just yet. The two installations were executed in about thirty minutes, with the household *still* sleeping at the completion of both installations, but realizing that having his long awaited return to work that morning, he would not actually get to witness Lu stepping into the power shower, but feeling only slightly disappointed, he grinned archly, and after a cold jet-propelled shower, he left for the office.

Finally wearying of constant references to his ancestry, Andreas arched his eyebrows and suggested, "I think that's enough on that particular subject for now don't you?" Knowing when it was time to call a halt, Viv quickly changed the subject, "What have you got Lu for Christmas?" Alarm bells instantly rang in Andreas's head! "Jesus, I've got everyone's present but hers, and there's only two days to go. Is it okay if I shoot off and get her something?" "Of course!" Viv replied, "There's nothing much doing here anyway, have you anything in mind?" Looking startled Andreas responded, "I haven't got a clue!" Then smiling whimsically he added, "What can you get for the person who has everything?" Andreas walked toward the door and Viv remarked, "I forgot to tell you, Reuben starts college in Bristol in the new year, on the same day coincidentally, that work commences on the wharf in Melbourne.

Heading for Bristol once more, he saw Maria walking along the road, unfortunately in the opposite direction, but suddenly having the bright idea of engaging her help in choosing Lu's gift, Andreas slowed up. She refused point-blank, but he begged her, "Please Maria, I'm so useless at this sort of thing, and I'm bound to get her something she won't like!" Then smiling archly he promised, "If you help me, I'll buy you something *really* nice!" The inducement was sweet music to her ears and smiling, she was in the passenger seat in seconds, chattering away nine to the dozen. Scarcely listening to the non-stop prattling, he thought *oh yes, I know what buttons to press with Maria alright,* and just as they reached the suburbs of Bristol, her chattering ceased abruptly, "I know *exactly* what she would like. A car. She wants a bloody car. I know that absolutely, one hundred per cent for sure!" Having to stop at a red light, Andreas answered, "What's the point, she can't drive!" Maria advised, "You could book lessons with Dinky too, and just to add a bit of mystery, and romance, you could buy a pair of driving gloves. Put them under the tree, then when she unwraps the parcel, and asks why you thought of gloves, you take her to the open front door, and ta-dah!" "Maria you are an absolute angel. I don't suppose you've any idea of what make or colour?" "Well it's got to be black, sporty, and capable of accommodating three children!" Andreas interjected, "Better make that four!" She laughed, commenting, "Christ, when are you two going to stop over-populating the world? Better make it just sporty and black then, she can borrow this one if she's got to take all of them out. Oh and I would like driving lessons as my reward for this invaluable help!" "That's fine and dandy, but don't think I'm splashing out on a car for *you* as well, but I *will* ask Gunnar to look out for something suitable, that your brother can buy cheaply. As soon as you've passed your test that is!" Two hours later they were on the way home, buoyant, and bloated from the meal that they had eaten after the present had been chosen and paid for. Arranging delivery for ten o'clock on Christmas Eve night, Maria also organised, for the keys to be dropped through the letter box at the same time. With everything arranged, all Andreas had to do now was sit back and wait for Santa to appear, and he decided that it had been a stroke of genius getting Maria on board, realising that without her help, he would never have got so much accomplished in the little time available.

"You're looking very smug dear; I don't suppose it has anything to do with that bloody shower!" Lu asked as soon as he walked through the door. Smiling Andreas said facetiously, "I'm sorry love, I forgot to warn you, and it's not smugness you see on my face, it's that sly look all we Scamps have!" Standing together in front of the fire, they watched as the children came downstairs, carrying presents, that had *not* been wrapped well enough to disguise their contents, and even though the boys no longer believed in Santa, their enthusiasm for the event was undiminished. When all of the presents had been placed under the tree, an evening of television was on the menu, and preparing for Utopia, Andreas brought in an unopened bottle of Tolleys, and a bucket of ice from the kitchen, to accompany the sandwiches laid out on the coffee-table. The youngsters tittered as their father put the drink on the table, prompting Andreas to ask with a smile, "What's the matter with you lot, have you never seen me drinking before?" Giggling even more, he was moved to muse, *dear Lord, please make it Christmas Eve every day.* With bed-time soon arriving, Andreas walked up the stairs with the boys, with Lu following on behind, carrying the sleeping Rosie, *that brandy is a real gift from heaven,* Andreas thought *but it's a bloody good job her highness is unaware of the addition to the wee one's night-time bottle.* Once the children were tucked in bed, and on the verge of sleeping, their parents crept back downstairs to spend the remaining few hours of Christmas Eve, snuggled up on the settee, watching television. Hearing a car pull up outside, and noticing that it was on the stroke of ten, Andreas listened intently until he heard the rattle of the letter-box. "Christ!" Lu exclaimed, "Someone's just posted a card at *this* time of night. Maybe I should ask them in for a drink!" "Don't bother love!" Andreas commented, "They'll be halfway down the road by now. I'll get the card and put it with the others!" Going to the door, he put the car-keys into his pocket, and returned to his wife's side. Having just settled down again, the idyllic moment was suddenly disturbed by the living room door being opened. Rosie murmured, "Mummy, nappy!" And when a fresh nappy had been put in place, Rosie snuggled between them on the settee, falling asleep in seconds, and deciding to call it a day, Andreas tip-toed upstairs, and lay his slumbering princess gently into her cot.

9

"He's been!" Upon hearing those words, Andreas was instantly transported back to a moment in time when Lala, his deceased sister, face aglow with excitement and wonder, had uttered those very same words. Andreas and Lulu's own little girl was now wide awake, screeching with that same childlike excitement as she tore the paper from her presents, and being woken by the caterwauling, her brothers entered the living room, rubbing their their half-sleeping eyes. *Mamouse* and *Daddi* sat smiling as the children joyfully opened each gift, casting the wrapping carelessly aside for someone to dispose of later. Suddenly George exclaimed, "Oh look mum, there's one here for you!" He handed her the present that Ma had insisted on wrapping for Andreas, knowing that he was totally inept at all that sort of thing. Lu's face was a picture of puzzled excitement, and Andreas rose to his feet expectantly, waiting for her approbation on the package, *but* she merely leaned over, kissed his cheek, and uttered, "Thank you darling!" He was impatient for her to ask why he had bought her driving gloves, but the truth of the matter, was that she did not know *exactly* what they were, until she tried them on. Looking at her husband, and being totally bewildered by his stupid grin, she allowed herself to be blindfolded, and led to the door. As soon as the portal was opened, an icy blast made her shiver, and noticing her erect nipples, his baser instincts were aroused, but averting his gaze hastily, in case his appreciation of the fact became too evident, he removed the blind from her eyes. Immediately becoming aware of the reason for his subterfuge, her eyes widened, and squealing with delight, she said with tears in her eyes, "Andreas you fool, you know I can't drive!" It was at that point that he gave her a Christmas card containing a voucher for ten lessons with Dinky. "Oh *dordi dordi*, you are one special husband, you've thought of everything. How on earth did you ever dream all of this up?" Smiling archly, that special husband said nothing, and appreciating the plaudits, he thought slyly, *it's probably better that you don't know my love!* They returned to the living room, and crowded as close to the fire as they dare, bodies convulsing rhythmically, as their bodies became inured to the change in temperature. Lu came in from the kitchen, dragging a huge parcel, which clinked as she placed it beside the tree, betraying it's contents to the recipient. Being delighted when he quickly unwrapped the case of Tolley's finest, he thanked her with a kiss, and propounded, "It's a pity it's so early, or I could have started on my present now!" "Oh go on with you!" She retorted, "It's only once a year!" And *that* was all the incentive he needed.

Ma and Pa came for dinner as arranged, with Lu having done them all proud by cooking a huge chicken, with far more vegetables than they would ever require, and being topped off by pudding and custard, they were fit to burst at the end of the repast. Pa accompanied Andreas to the kitchen where they performed their designated task of washing-up, and spotting the half empty bottle of Tolley's

Pa asked, "Where did you get that then?" When he told him that it was Lu's present to him, he remarked with a grin, "Well she can bloody-well get me some next year. I can't have a Bosworth being outdone by a Scamp!" Andreas smiled as he poured him a generous measure of Tolley's and coke, "God this is wicked stuff!" Pa remarked, holding up the bottle for examination, "It's got *Australian produce* on the label, so I suppose that the go-withers will be that Australian koala, you were going to bring me back?" Andreas smiled indulgently, "Yes Pa that's just what it is!" Downing a couple more large ones, they returned to the fray and watched the kids playing dominoes, poignantly reminding him once again of Lala, who could never get enough of the game.

In the evening, the rest of the family came calling, which unfortunately included, Gunnar's other half Pearl, who had tried on several occasions to get Andreas into bed, and would probably have succeeded, if Gunnar had *not* been his brother. Andreas endured the unwanted intrusion, and for Gunnar's sake, he welcomed her, with a perfunctory kiss, but certainly not with open arms. With Ma prudently keeping a beady eye on her, the evening passed without incident, and with the time approaching for Pa to be dragged home, she took time out to have a little chat with Pearl, with whatever she had said, impacting immediately. Lu went to the kitchen to make bubble-and-squeak with leftovers from the dinner which, accompanied by chips and home-made pickled onions, was a repast fit for a king. Vee, Michael and Lily-Ann arrived, only just in time to avail themselves of the delicious fare, and after a few drinks, everyone began reminiscing of past Christmases. A Tolleys inspired Gunnar, alluded to the time that Pa blotted his copybook by drunkenly passing out, with his head dropping into his Christmas dinner Andreas added, "I think that it was one of the many times that Lu wasn't talking to me for some reason or another, with the incident succeeding in breaking the ice between us!" Vee remarked, "How we didn't all burst out laughing when Ma yanked his head out of the dinner, God only knows and do you remember that bloody sprout lodged in the corner of his mouth!" That particular memory almost caused the roof to cave in with the laughter, and even though they could not have understood why such a thing would have caused such merriment, the kids joined in the laughter too. Gunnar, who was extremely tipsy by this time, slurred, "What about the time, when old Smythe stopped us on the way to the market to tell us that you had inherited a load of money from your mother and aunt, Christ what a day that was!" The room went silent, and Andreas gently led Gunnar gently upstairs, and laying him on Victor's the bed, Andreas ordered his old friend and brother, "Stay there until you've sobered up!" Returning to the party, it was obvious that the air of jollity had been shattered, and standing in the centre of the room, Andreas apprised them of the situation, "It all had to come out sometime, and Gunnar only spoke the truth, so he's done nothing wrong!" Pouring himself a large measure of brandy, he continued, "The Smythes had been searching for me since I left my old home to join this family, and I think the time's arrived when you should learn the whole story. The Smythes introduced me to Viv, who informed me that I had inherited a huge sum of money from my mother, *and* that the relatives I lived with, had perished in a car crash in Spain, also leaving me a tidy sum. Forgive me for not telling you before, but initially it was imperative that nobody knew, and after that, it just didn't seem to be relevant. I'm sorry if I've offended anybody by not mentioning anything before, but I'd rather just forget about all of this, and carry on as we always have!" The room remained silent for a few minutes, until Michael burst into song, *For He's A Jolly Good Fellow*, with the whole assemblage soon joining in, but finding the whole experience embarrassing, Andreas left the room to replenish his glass, being closely followed by Lu and Vee. Lu remarked, "I think it's a damn shame that people were not aware that it was *you* that was responsible for all the wonderful changes around these parts, and I'm *glad* that it's now out in the open, so everyone can appreciate just how generous and kind you are. The song they were singing was their way of showing their appreciation for all you have accomplished for every single one of us!" Vee added, "We're all so proud of you! Now do as you are told, get back in there and *enjoy* yourself!" Noting the same steeliness in her eyes that he had often seen in those of her mother and sister, he did as he was told.

With the party breaking up in the early hours of the morning, Lu organised sleeping arrangements, deciding instantly that Gunnar would stay where he was in Victor's bed. The boys were to top and tail in George's bed, with Lily-Ann sharing with Rosie. Michael and Vee would spend the night in their hosts' bed, leaving *them* to share the settee. With Vee and Michael volunteering to take Ma, Pa, and Pearl home in Andreas's car before retiring, everything had been organized in minutes, and once Vee and Michael had returned, Lu and Andreas were left to make themselves comfortable on the settee. Finding the arrangement rather cramped, both in length *and* breadth, they were reduced to sleeping on the floor, using seat cushions as pillows. With the flickering light from the fire lending a cosy warm glow to the room, they were soon wrapped in each other's arms, and after the loving, she lay on the floor with her jet-black hair spread out behind her on a cushion. Raising himself on one elbow, he looked down at his comatose, wonderful wife sleeping, and noting an unconscious smile playing across her countenance, he kissed her cheek. Rising, he poked life into the fire, and using the old scuttle that he had purchased over a year ago from the charity shop in town, he replenished the sparsely scattered embers. With his chores being almost acquitted, he covered Lu with the blanket that they kept in the airing cupboard for such emergencies, and turned off all the electrical appliances. Satisfied now that everything was just as it should be, he snuggled into her warmth, and just before he fell asleep he murmured sweet nothings in her ear, knowing full well that she was well past hearing him, "This has been a very strange and a very wonderful Christmas!"

10

Being woken by the bitter cold, he decided to put some warmth back in the room, and with the embers still possessing a slight glow, he placed kindling-sticks, under a few lumps of coal, and clearing the ash from the grate, he put the tray outside to cool off. He complained loudly, "Jesus, it's bloody perishing out here!" Darting back quickly into the warmth, he noticed that the fire had already burst into flame, and putting the fireguard back in place, he heard Lu complain grumpily, "Can you keep that bloody noise down, it's enough to waken the devil!" "Huh!" He mumbled, "Is that all the appreciation I get for having my bollocks frozen off, and getting a fire going for an unappreciative mare?" He continued apace, "Thanks a bloody bundle!" Getting back under the covers, he put his freezing hands on her back, and suddenly shooting up into a sitting position, she exclaimed, "You rotten bastard, look what you've done to my nipples!" He did look, and never being able to resist the temptation, he pushed her onto her back, climbed on top of her and began to nibble her ear. She squealed as his cold body touched hers, but not for too long, there was a part of his anatomy that was *not* quite so cold as the rest, and as soon as it touched her, the cold was ignored. Making love with more passion than before, the fire suddenly took on a life of it's own, burning his back, *but* not letting that deter him one iota from his libidinous intent, he remained steadfastly at his post, and once mutual satisfaction had been attained, she pushed him away, instantly relieving her of his weight, and him from the delicious pain of the fire. She murmured semi-consciously, "I've done with your body for the time-being, so you can bloody get off me now!" It was now light enough to see the red marks on his elbows and knees, "Look what you've done to me, I do all the work, and all I get is abuse!" Laughing she remarked, "There *are* some advantages in being a woman, and *that* is one of them!" He got up, poked the fire, and replenishing it's still glowing embers, he went for a refreshing shower.

Returning to the scene, he found that Lu had predictably fallen asleep, and turning on the light, he donned the clothes that he had discarded so carelessly the previous night before, slapped her partially covered rump, and said, "Come on then, rise and shine, or are you going to lay there stinking like a bloody polecat all day long?" Throwing back the curtains wide, he excitedly declared, "Bloody hell, it's been snowing. It certainly wasn't snowing earlier, when I put the ashes outside, and look how deep it is already!" She rose and ran over to the window, "Doesn't it look wonderful!" "Yes my dear, so do you and if you don't hurry up and get some clothes on, all our neighbours and family will see *just* how wonderful you really *are!*" Playfully smacking her backside again, he wrapped her in the blanket and propelled her toward the door. Repairing to the kitchen to make coffee, he sat at the table gently slurping the scalding liquid, but before he had the chance to add anything to it, Rosie appeared at the door carrying her new Teddy, nappy hanging down to her knees, "That bitch knows when to disappear!" He muttered to himself, "I'll bet she's under that spray laughing her bloody self silly, and that wouldn't take too long!" Smiling at his own caustic wit, he soon sobered up, when he removed the sodden, stinking mess. Wiping Rosie's bottom half with a warm soapy flannel, he patted her dry, and applied cream to her bits. Deciding to put on another nappy, he concluded at the successful completion of the task, that he was pretty good at all this changing nappies lark, *I bet there aren't too many blokes, put them on like I do!*

Entering the room suddenly, Lu began berating him instantly, "Look at the hash you've made of putting that bloody nappy on, you can't even be trusted to do a simple job like that? You're bloody useless!" Andreas merely stood and shook his head, while the harangue continued, "You haven't even started breakfast yet. Do I have to organize *every* sodding thing!" Forgetting there was no cushions on the settee, he thrust himself down angrily to finish off his cold coffee, and in jarring his back, he managed to spill coffee onto the carpet. He exclaimed loud enough for Lu to hear, "Bollocks to it all!" Replacing the cushions and turning on the television, he sat down on the settee, until the whirlwind re-entered the room, "Don't think you're going to sit there all day doing bugger all. You can get your arse out here, and help me do the breakfast, there's a dozen people up there who will want feeding when they get up!" Having delivered that particular sermon, she flounced back into the kitchen, and muttering under his breath, Andreas followed her. Noticing that she had the frying pan in one hand and a saucepan in the other, he took full advantage of the fact that she was *hors de combat,* and creeping up behind her, he put his hand up her skirt and grabbing hold of her knickers, he yanked them into the crack of her backside. "There, you mouthy little bitch, have some of that!" She tried to swipe him with the frying pan, and having missed, she put both vessels on the table, and began to laugh loudly, "What am I going to do with you? You're an incorrigible bastard, but you're *my* incorrigible bastard, and I love you!" She put her arms around his waist and kissed his mouth, causing a familiar stirring in his trousers, which she could hardly fail to have noticed, "You've got no bloody chance you horny bastard!" He put his hand up her skirt once more, she asserted, "I told you no and I mean *no*!" Andreas replied with feigned innocence and a grin, "I'm *only* taking the knickers out of your crack!" She shook her head and returning to her pots and pans, she engaged Andreas's help by allowing him to open cans, and get food out of the fridge. The actual cooking was done by his beautiful ever-loving wife, who once more he had succeeded in charming to let him off chores. *God I'm such a devious bastard,* He mused, *it must be the Scamp in me!* "What the hell are you grinning about?" She demanded. "Nothing my babe!" He lied, "Just thinking of you trying to hit me with that frying pan!" She smiled at him and returning to the kitchen, she set about the next phase of preparing breakfast, while Andreas did his bit once more, by rousing the house, which they all thanked him heartily for, and smiling archly, he thought, *I can be a real bastard at times.*

11

With the snow having ceased it's hitherto relentless downpour, the two sisters took advantage by taking their offspring to the hill over by Honeysuckle Wood, and trailing the sledges, fashioned by Walthaar a couple of years prior, behind them. The menfolk meanwhile, still hung over from the previous evening's imbibition of Andreas's Christmas present, staggered to that section of the stream, that had been earmarked for commercialisation some months before by Andreas. Michael commented, "It's so wonderful here, it's almost a shame to spoil it, but I *can* see the potential, and if Viv's given it the go-ahead, it's guaranteed to be a successful venture. How on earth do you think of all these schemes? Every time *I* think of something, it's doomed to failure!" "Don't belittle yourself Michael, what about your shop?" Andreas ventured, "That's been an outstanding success!" "Yes, but what about the cattle that I wanted to purchase just before the disease took hold. If it hadn't been for your intervention, the farm would have gone under, along with all the others?" Andreas did his best to placate him, "That was *not* your fault, I don't think *anybody* could have foreseen it?" "Well *you* certainly did and thank God for that!" Michael averred, "Not really!" Andreas replied, "It was just an inkling, a feeling that all was not as it should be. Put it down to intuition!" "Whatever it was, the farm was saved from disaster!" Not wishing however, to discuss the matter further Andreas suggested, "Come on lads, let's get back. It's getting chilly!"

Considering the depth of snow, they managed a fair pace, and arrived back at the house, to find that the Romany Olympic sledging team had not yet returned. Andreas proposed that a coffee and Tolley's would soon warm the cockles of their heart, and sitting as close to the fire as they could, without being burned, they began to talk business. Andreas brought up the huge problem of storing cider, asking Michael if the cider could be kept fresh, if it were stored in wooden barrels. Michael replied, "That's the way that it was stored for hundreds of years, and if it were stored somewhere cool, it would probably keep fresh longer than the fizzy stuff. The only problem is that it would only be saleable in small amounts to pubs and clubs, and we would completely lose out on the lucrative supermarket trade. We would not be able to turn out the volume of cider needed to satisfy the demand, *and* keep it fresh long enough to make it viable. So we have *real* problems!" Gunnar, who had been listening intently, suddenly entered the conversation, with a suggestion, "Could the problem be solved by hermetically sealing the cider?" They all looked at each other askance, and all of a sudden, Michael's face lit up, "Now that *is* an idea worth considering. They do that with wine in France, so why couldn't we do the same here with cider.!" Has anyone any idea how it's done?" Being now caught up in the excitement, Gunnar replied, "I haven't a clue, but if it *were* possible to seal the cider, it could be churned out in different sized boxes, along with a photo or a painting of the farmhouse!" Michael's face became animated, "Gunnar,

I think you're onto something!" Andreas asked Michael, "How soon could you go to France. We need to find out, just how the process works, and you can bet that Viv will want to ascertain the cost of machinery and boxes?" Michael answered, "I'm busy at the moment, but I suppose that if I twist Pa's arm to put it in a few more shifts, and with Victor now working at the farm, Vee could easily manage the shop on her own!" Andreas suggested, "*I* could always come over and help out at the weekend too. Would your trees, yield enough apples to cope with such a high demand?" Michael exclaimed excitedly, "We can always buy in pretty cheaply. I do that sometimes anyway to vary the blends, and as long as there are enough Delicious and Roman Beauty, I'd be able to fiddle about and get a decent brew!" Andreas remarked, "I didn't realize there was so much involved in the process, I'll appreciate the stuff even more, when I'm supping my freebies!" Gunnar interrupted, "Give him sod all Michael, he's *always* after something for nothing!" With the rest of the family returning at that point, the matter was shelved temporarily, and with the problem of storage apparently solved, the men were in the mood for celebration, but with Andreas's culinary expertise being ordered by the lady of the house, that too had to be deferred.

Dinner consisted of left over cold chicken, accompanied by chips, and a few cans of baked beans thrown in for good measure. All thoughts of *cordon bleu* cuisine were soon forgotten in the wake of good old-fashioned Roma fare, and after the banquet, the children went noisily into the back garden to make a snowman. Sitting back with his hands supporting his midriff, Michael informed the girls of Gunnar's suggestion for storing cider, and with their future in the venture apparently assured, the project was toasted with more Tolley's. By the time the children came in from the garden, excitedly imploring them to come and see the snowman, the assemblage were well on the way to stupefaction, apart from Gunnar, who had decided that his hang-over, now needed Pearl's capable ministrations. The snowman was duly inspected, and found to be another excuse for celebration, and with the passing of time, the copious amounts of alcohol consumed by Rosie's parents affected their ability to function to such a degree, that Victor was designated the task of getting her ready for bed. Andreas, proudly watching his son acquitting the odious task of changing a filled nappy with a skill belying his years, was moved to say smugly to Lu, "He must have been watching me!" Lu shook her head in undisguised astonishment.

Andreas could hardly wait to see Viv to tell him about the idea for storing cider, and rising surprisingly early the following day, considering the amount of alcohol consumed, he rang Viv, inviting him over for a chat. Viv demurred, "That has to be a definite no. Kate and I are both off work together for the first time in ages, and we have plans. So coming round your place, knocking back Tolley's is decidedly *verbotten!*" Andreas insisted that he had something important to explain that could definitely not wait, nor be dealt with on the phone, and promising that it would positively *not* include drinking, Viv replied sternly, "Okay I'll come round but only for an hour, and absolutely *no* alcohol!" Ten minutes later, with Andreas watching from the window, Viv pulled up outside the house, and getting out of the car, he put his leading foot into a puddle of ice-cold slush. Jumping up and down in an effort to shake the freezing liquid from his feet, he succeeded in soaking the other foot too. And being barely unable to contain his amusement, Andreas went to the door to greet his friend, "Come in and dry your feet!" And as Viv was removing his socks, Andreas suggested slyly, "A Tolleys would warm the cockles of your heart?" Viv replied impatiently, "I've already told you *no* alcohol! What *is* this thing that cannot wait?" "Okay Viv!" Andreas explained, "I've got Michael in the living room, and there's something that we'd like to discuss with you!" Putting his socks on the pouffe in front of the fire to dry off, Viv padded through to the lounge, "Okay Michael, perhaps *you* can explain just *what* is so important that I'm dragged away from a nice warm house, to get my feet frozen to the marrow, and have that jackass Andreas, laughing at my discomfort!" Michael briefly outlined the scheme, and listening to the scheme, Viv's eyes widened, "Well, you *do* appear to have solved the problem, and subject to costs, it all sounds fine!" He turned to Michael, "I will require all the figures, the minute you get back from France. The sooner we get this thing off the ground the better, and *if* the project proves successful, we'll get samples out as fast as we can, enabling me to tout them round the supermarkets and breweries!" Becoming more excited by the minute, he added, "We could make bigger boxes for the pubs and clubs, even gallon ones, and incidentally, the idea of a facsimile of the farm on the label is an excellent one. Now if my socks are dry, I'll get back to a woman who desperately needs my servicing!" Attempting the almost impossible task of putting still damp socks onto dry feet, and with Andreas scarcely able to contain his amusement, Viv somehow did achieve the monumental feat, leaving before the rest of the gang deigned to quit their beds to witness his discomposure. Lu wandered down, minutes after the door had closed, remarking, "I thought I heard Viv's voice!" Andreas replied slyly "You did my lovely, but he had urgent business at home!" Michael spluttered his coffee back into his mug.

12

The fact that Michael had never needed a passport before, proved to be merely a minor hitch for the indomitable Viv to arrange, and in little over a week after the scheme had initially been discussed, Vee was driving her husband and brother to the ferry port of Dover. On reaching the outskirts of the port however, Michael took over the wheel who, after sleeping for most of the journey, contrived to take a wrong turning, ending up in a maze of narrow roads and *cul de sacs*, with the remaining two miles being accomplished, thanks solely to the aid of a dog-walking local. Discreetly leaving the pair to say their goodbyes, Andreas made his way to the terminal cafeteria for a welcome cup of coffee, and sitting at a table by the plate-glass window, he spotted Michael's car crawling up the ramp, in a nose to tail queue, heading for the passport check-in boxes. With Vee soon joining her brother, they watched until the car was out of sight three coffees later, then left the docks in a taxi, heading for a bed and breakfast, near the train station, that had been pre-booked by Viv the day before.

After being shown to their rooms, they decided to scour the town for an eatery, and arriving at the town centre, they came across a brightly lit hostelry. Being tempted by the delicious aroma of food being prepared, they entered the warm interior, and when their meal arrived, Andreas asked the waiter if he knew of a place where gypsy folk gathered. Being told that such a pub, could be found located at the other end of town called The Three Cups, Andreas rang for a taxi, when the scarcely adequate meal had been consumed. Happily finding themselves instantly at ease in the almost exclusively Romany clientele, a large brute of a man approached Andreas as he was being served. "Ho friend, what parts are you from?" Andreas replied that they were from the west, near the border with Wales. "Would you accept a drink from a stranger?" The big man asked, and thrusting his hand forward, Andreas replied, "No, but I'll willingly accept one from a friend!" The man responded with a smile, "Well said friend!" His kinsmen also welcomed the pair into their company, with Vee unsurprisingly, receiving special attention once more. Andreas was immediately grateful that Lu had not accompanied him, knowing that if *she* had received the same attention as Vee, there would have been a fight, before the end of the night. One of the younger members of the assemblage asked, "Didn't I see you fighting in Stow a couple of years ago?" "Yes, I've been there a couple of times!" Andreas replied. The youth said to Andreas's new friend, "Hey Luke this is the *chav* I told you about, who finished the week unbeaten!" All of a sudden Vee was no longer the centre of attention, with the boys crowding round Andreas, wanting to know who else he had beaten. Vee suddenly piped up proudly, "He won the British Empire championship Australia!" "Good God!" Luke remarked, "Now that takes some doing. Have you been to America yet, they've got some shit-hot fighters over there?" Andreas replied, "Not yet, but I wouldn't mind going one day, and before I'm not very much older!" Luke asked, "What's your line Andreas, scrap-merchant or roofing? There's plenty of that kinda line round here if you're looking for work!" "I'm a solicitor!" Andreas declared almost shamefacedly. "Get away!" Luke said, "What sort of line is that for an upstanding man like yourself?" Andreas replied, "Forget the past. Our people should be legally represented, and who better than someone they can trust!" Luke responded, "That's true. I wish I'd had you in my corner last year, when I ended up with a two hundred pound fine, and I'll *certainly* come looking for you, if I need a lawyer in the future!" Andreas nodded, and suggested, "You'd also want someone you trust to *dikker* a good deal, if you were buying a house!" Luke suggested with a smile, "That's a fact I'll keep in mind, *if* I ever have enough *gelt* to buy a house. Unfortunately my money all ends up in this bastard's pocket!" He remarked, pointing a thumb towards the landlord's portly torso. A few drinks later, Andreas decided to order a taxi back to the hotel, but his good intentions were delayed some twenty minutes by the boys trying to persuade Vee to stay. He was still grousing about the extra cost, which he put down entirely to Vee and her admirers, when they arrived back at their lodging, he left his sister standing in the hallway, and retired for the night, without a word, *nor* the courtesy of a goodnight kiss.

They were informed at the station the following morning, that due to re-pointing being executed in the tunnel leading out of the station, they would be required to take a bus to Folkestone, where they could then pick up the London-bound train. Noting Andreas's scowl, Vee tried to engineer a conversation, to avert an impending apoplexy, "I wouldn't mind coming here again Andreas, they're lovely folk!" Andreas smiled at her condescendingly, "I don't think Michael would appreciate all the attention that you appear to welcome!" Unabashed, she smiled, melting his cold reserve, causing him to return the gesture, and become aware that his sister possessed the same provocative beauty, with which all the females of the clan had been blessed. With the journey to London being acquitted in just over an hour, they found however, that everything around them was being conducted at break-neck speed, with Andreas losing count of the times he was buffeted by people in a tearing rush to be somewhere two minutes earlier. Deciding to catch the tube train to save money, he realised straight away that he had made a mistake, as descending the moving staircase, proved a major hazard for Vee in her high-heeled shoes. It was also a matter of pure luck that they both boarded *and* alighted at the correct stations, but deciding that although it had proved an interesting experience, it was one to be avoided in the future, particularly when witnessing their homeward bound train pulling out of the station, seconds after their arrival at the platform, and Andreas's ill-humour was exacerbated on discovering that they would have to wait another hour for the next one. The train finally arrived ten minutes later than scheduled, and being so tightly packed that they had to stand for most of the journey, they were forced to endure fellow standees, smoking in the clearly marked no-smoking carriage. The one shining light in an otherwise miserable day was discovering that Viv came to meet them at the station, and with sheer relief, Andreas climbed into the passenger seat beside him, while Vee stretched out in the back, almost immediately falling asleep. Recounting the catastrophic journey, Andreas retorted that the next time he had to undertake such a journey he would take two cars. Viv smiled annoyingly indulgent, "Why didn't you think to have a hire-car waiting at Dover for Michael?" Andreas looked stunned, "I did not know such things existed, would I have been able to drive over the other side?" Viv answered, "With a little difficulty perhaps, but of course, they have specially adapted left-hand drive cars for European travel. It's a bit awkward at first with the steering-wheel being on the opposite side, but you soon get used to it!" Andreas paused then to suggest, "Maybe that's a business we could look into when we get home!"

Being a creature of habit, Andreas went straight upstairs to unpack, and taking his dirty washing downstairs at it's completion, he placed the bundle on top of the washing machine. Collapsing onto the settee, he smiled as Lu placed a steaming mug of coffee *avits* by his side, and declining the opportunity to enlighten his wife on the disastrous journey, he shook his head, "You don't wanna know!" Gunnar arrived soon after, coincidentally just in time for grub once more, the eager beaver that was Andreas Bosworth, broached his notion for a car-hire firm. Gunnar remarked sarcastically, "Is that before or after the self-service store?" "As well as!" Andreas asserted, "It will only take the purchase of appropriate vehicles, and organising a place to store them, which I assume I could leave in your capable hands?" Gunnar replied sardonically "And will you be parking the cars on the grass?" Andreas answered with a grin, "Oh yeah, I never thought about that. I'll get Walthaar to extend the forecourt!" Lu entered the room, "Right you two stop yapping, there's food in the living room, so go and tuck in!" The two friends tucked into chips and leftovers, with Andreas declaring, "You can keep all your fancy restaurants, there is nothing better than left-overs!" Lu beamed from ear to ear, and hoping that the smile portended a carnal end to the evening, Andreas made a mental note to check that there was a bottle of Tolley's open, *just in case*. Gunnar remarked, "It *is* nice Lu but have you fallen so far from grace, that you have to resort to left-overs?" Glaring at him, she flounced out of the room saying, "Look after the pennies, the pounds will look after themselves!"

13

The following day the boys went back to school, and with Andreas returning to the office, Lu was left, with her not so able assistant Rosie, to clean the house, ready for the men's return, but deciding to have a coffee first, she went to the kitchen, with Rosie trailing behind. Having drunk half of the brew, her daughter climbed onto her lap, and in minutes the two of them had surrendered to a deliciously wicked, but totally merited siesta. Meanwhile, her husband, who was industrially contemplating the passing traffic, was about to meet the *new girl in town* at the office. She had been dispatched to summon him to Viv's inner sanctum, and carrying a mug of insipid looking liquid, she delivered the message, that his presence would be required as soon as he had finished his first coffee of the day. Looking at the dishwatery brew, he declared, "I can see that I will have to teach you how to make a *decent* cup of coffee, but thank you for the thought anyway!" She blushed and muttered, "Mister Bailey instructed me to say that he would like to see you within the hour!" "Did he now!" Andreas responded, "Well Mister bloody Bailey, can damned well wait til I'm good and ready!" Having now vented his early morning spleen, he thought, *it can't be anything urgent, or he would have told me on the way home yesterday!* Picking up the "Times" from the desk, he began to lock horns with the crossword compiler, and after what seemed like ten minutes, but was actually in excess of an hour, the door burst open, with Viv standing in the doorway looking like the angel of doom, "I wanted to see you an hour ago! Do you do these things just to annoy me?" "Sorry!" Andreas replied, "I lost track of time!" Viv grunted, "I've got a little job that I want you to do Andreas!" Andreas got up from the desk, and snapped, "No! I don't care what it is, I am not doing it, the last time I did a *little* job for you, it almost cost me my life!" Viv smirked, knowing that the dart of provocation had hit the target, "I may have been a tad economical with the truth, it's not exactly a little job, it's a big one, and before you burst a blood vessel, let me explain. The elder Mister Mowll died two days ago, a fact which you would not have been aware of, because you are never here, and I've been instructed to offer you his position on the board. You start as soon as the funeral is over, and because of his recent illness, there's a fair back-log of work that would require your immediate attention, *should* you accept of course!" Andreas was stunned, "I'm sorry Viv, you've taken me completely by surprise. What is it exactly that you're saying?" Viv explained with a broad grin, "You are being offered a partnership in the firm you idiot!" Andreas sat back down, dumbfounded, but elated too. Taking several minutes to recover from the shock, he smiled and proffered his hand, "You've just got yourself a partner!"

As soon as Viv had left the office he phoned Lu, but receiving no answer, he apprised Ma of his promotion, being aware that it would not be long before the whole family would be acquainted with his elevation to the lofty echelons of power. "I phoned Lu, but got no reply, she's probably on her way down to you!" Sitting back in his chair, with his hands clasped at the back of his head, a habit he'd picked up from his mentor, he intended to hit the ground running, but firstly he had another task nearer his heart, to educate the new girl in the art of making *real* coffee. Calling her into his office, he explained the rudiments of the relatively simple task, and told her that he would expect nothing less than perfection every time. He had the notion that if she manage to acquit the task to his liking, he would ask Viv if she could become his personal secretary, and *if* the plan bore fruit, Lu would have to be kept in ignorance. This girl was *far* too pretty, and Lu would certainly not be happy about *that*. Having little to do in the office, he finished off the crossword, and when lunch-time arrived, he treated his new partner to lunch at the Green Lady, having been a notable absentee from the hostelry for several months. Over lunch he told Viv, that he had seen Gunnar about the prospect of a car-hire business, and that he would have to see Walthaar about developing a larger forecourt to house the cars. Viv remarked, "That won't take long. So you'll have the business up and running as soon as Gunnar purchases the cars!" "We haven't got a name for the business as yet but it's got to be something catchy, and we may have to think about locating the business elsewhere, in all honesty I cannot see it taking off in *this* area, there wouldn't be enough call in such a small area, but we'll give it a go anyway!"

Returning to the office, Andreas found that several files had been placed on his desk for inspection and opening the top file, he stared aghast at it's contents, realising suddenly that he now had sole responsibility for the entire conveyancing department of the firm, with his tenure apparently up and running, *before* the funeral had even been arranged, let alone dispatched. He was just about to make a start when coffee arrived, and gingerly sipping the brew, knowing that she awaited his approbation, he smiled and declared, "Thank you, it's *exactly* how I like it!" Deciding there and then that she would definitely be his *girl Friday*, he went directly to Viv's office, obtaining consent for his new acquisition. Calling her into his office Andreas said, "Mr Bailey has asked me to be a partner in the firm, and as such, I will need a PA!" Then pausing for a second, he continued with a smile, "Having passed the coffee-making test, I'd like to offer the post to you. Mister Bailey has already okayed your exchange, so if the prospect is to your liking, you'll have a six-month probational period, after which we both have the option to continue or call it a day. What do you say?" She smiled, "I'd like that very much Mister Bosworth!" Andreas grinned, "I think I'd like another coffee to celebrate!" Hurrying away to attend to her new boss's needs, she returned in minutes, with a *real* mug of gypsy caffeine, and *that* was how he annexed the soon to become indispensable Rebecca Watkins, who would prove to be his right-hand, confidante *and* friend for the foreseeable future.

Leaving the office early, he picked up Walthaar and took him to the garage to prepare an estimate for the new forecourt area, and taking coffee with Gunnar in the warm office, he left Walthaar to measure the designated area, in the wintery conditions outside. Quickly acquitting the task, Walthaar entered the office, and dropping the clipboard with the measurements onto the desk, he remarked, "The concrete will be no problem, but the grassland will need clearing and levelling before *anything* can be done, which thankfully is only a minor hitch. I can do the whole thing in about three days!" Andreas commented, "There you are Gunnar, the site will be ready in three days, have you any cars picked out yet?" Gunnar answered saying, "Not yet, but I'm going to the auctions in North Wales at the weekend, so hopefully the site will not be empty long!" Andreas turned to Walthaar, "I don't expect you to do this for peanuts just because you're my brother, but a decent discount would not go amiss!" Gunnar cast his eyes to the sky remarking, "Do you ever stop, you cheap-skate bastard?" Andreas laughed, and drove off with the renowned taciturn Walthaar observing, "Do you know, that Gunnar gets more miserable the older he gets!" Pot and kettle immediately sprung to mind, and for the first time he realised just how alike the brothers actually were. Returning to Mowll and Mowll with the estimate, and pointing out the decent discount, he commented, "I think that's a really fair price!" Viv agreed, "Yes that seems reasonable enough, but you will *have* to get out of the habit of reporting in, every time you have completed something. *You* are in charge of your finances now, and I think that you can be trusted to make decisions concerning your own money. On the other hand if you *do* need advice about anything, I am always here, but basically you are free to do whatever you believe to be the correct thing!" Andreas knew that Viv was right, but old habits die hard, and at least he now had Rebecca to try out his ideas on. Reading through her curriculum vitae, he had found that she was a really bright young woman, that he was fortunate enough to have acquired, also realizing that the new concept of having all of a person's education and previous employment all in one folder, was an excellent idea. Looking through Mr Mowll's files and finding that some of the files were in the wrong folder, Rebecca advised him to invest in a computer, pointing out the many advantages, one of which was the ability to store items in an orderly fashion. Andreas was not *totally* convinced, but not closing his mind completely to the idea, he decided to have a word with Viv on the subject. If he was up for the idea, and it proved successful, he could have one installed at the club, and possibly even at the garage. Suddenly the concept of Gunnar sitting at a computer keyboard, brought a smile to his face.

Meanwhile, with Ma having guessed the reason for not answering the phone, she had donned her hat and coat, to go and waken the slumbering duo. When Lu was fully alert, Ma told her of Andreas's fabulous news, "You'll have to pretend that you must have been on the way down to see me, if he asks why you didn't answer the phone. I'll give you a hand to tidy up now, in case he comes home early!" And thus, it was thanks to Ma when Andreas *did* come early to apprise Lu of his good news, which she received with suitably surprised jubilation.

14

Being the wife of a newly-appointed executive sat well on Lu's classically structured shoulders, and as she began to take more interest in the firm's machinations, Andreas became aware of the fact that he would *have* to inform her of the acquisition of a personal secretary. So after dinner one evening, he told Lu that he had been *coerced* into hiring a personal secretary, omitting to inform her of just how young and pretty she was. Receiving the required indifferent response, he relaxed, enough to ask, over a drink or three in the evening, her opinion on the possible acquisition of computers, and found her wholeheartedly behind such a scheme, "Just think of the time and space that could be saved, and if all your case records were in one place, you wouldn't have to go searching for files that you'd forgotten you had!" All of a sudden, he was beginning to see things in a new light, "Hmm, that's true, and as the council offices are now using them, perhaps Viv and I could go along to see how it all works!" With the matter now set firmly in his mind, he changed the subject by asking how the driving lessons were coming along, "Oh great!" she replied, "Dinky is so patient with me, and he's confident that I'll pass my test first time!" Andreas laughed remarking, "Flash the examiner a bit of leg, and you'll pass with flying colours!"

She retorted with, "Do you know *just* how disrespectful that is?" Then added with a pert grin, "But hey-ho, I might give it a go anyway!" The boys were sitting at the table, sharing their attention between watching the television *and* eating supper, while Rosie, sitting at the table for only the second time, had spilled a great deal of her food on the table. "Good job it's a plastic tablecloth!" Lu remarked as she wiped up the mess. Nodding in acquiescence, Andreas picked up the phone to ask Viv's opinion on having computers installed, regurgitating Lu's take on the matter. Viv was doubtful, "It sounds okay in theory, but I would have to find out more about it!" Andreas, now being almost sold on the idea concurred, "Exactly my sentiments, and knowing that the council have just had them installed, I thought I'd give them a ring to see if they'd let us have a look at how it all works. Any day in particular suit you?" Still not being entirely *convinced* Viv replied, "Well Friday afternoon would be the best time for me, and seeing that you never seem to be doing *anything*, presumably *any* day would suit you!" Ignoring the slight, Andreas remarked, "Okay, Friday afternoon it is then!" Returning to the living room, he ushered the boys upstairs for their bath and even though they no longer needed his help, it had become the norm on bath nights, for him to join in playing games with their floating toys. Having the thought that Victor was getting too big to share a bath with the others, he mentioned it later to Lu who averred impatiently, "Oh, let them be children for as long as they have a care to!" And annoyingly he had to concede that she was probably right as usual, just like her mother.

Deciding to contact the council as soon as he arrived at the office, he found them only too glad to accommodate, and when he explained the reason for the coming visit to the council offices to Miss Watkins, she was pleased to have nudged the old fossils, in a new direction. Andreas remarked, "I know that Mister Bailey is out this morning, but will you inform his secretary that the computer demonstration is fixed for one thirty on Friday afternoon!" "Yes Mister Bosworth, and I have a person waiting to see you. He would not tell me his business, wishing only to speak to you!" "Right, I'll see him in ten minutes, just as soon as I've had another of your delicious coffees, and by the way, my name in this office is Andreas, but Mr Bosworth anywhere else!" Smiling, she said, "Coming up right away Andreas, and it's Becky *not* Miss Watkins!"

Ten minutes later, and with his coffee only half consumed, Becky ushered in a down-at-heel, emaciated gypsy, "Ho Gadjo, I've been told you might be able to help me with a problem!" Andreas smiled, "Give me the details, and I'll certainly see what I can do!" "Well sir it's like this!" The man began, "Me and my family have been living in the car park behind the old church for a few years now, and the council have just given us notice to quit with immediate effect. I've been workin' on the scrap metal, and if we've got nowhere to live, I can't get a permit to trade. We always keep the park spotless, you can come and see it anytime you want!" "Right I'll tell you what I'll do!" Andreas declared, "We'll go back to your caravan right now to have a look, but first I'll need your name, and exactly how long you've been living at the park?" "Everyone told me you was a kind man, and I knew that to be a fact, the minute I clapped eyes on you!" Andreas answered firmly, "I *am* a kind man but I'm no fool, and we both know that not all of our people are upfront honest, but if all you say is true, I will do everything I can to help you!" Andreas jotted down his details, and told him, "I'm afraid that I will have to put you down as being *of no fixed abode* for the time-being!" The man replied, "Anything you say sir, anything you say!" Andreas drowned the dregs of his cold coffee, and drove the man to the car park, immediately perceiving a typical, old style, brightly painted, wooden caravan standing in the corner of the park, and with flower pots all around, it was very plain to see that the site *was* indeed neat and tidy. The man's wife came out to shake Andreas hand, while the children stood silently watching from the step, and grasping Andreas's hand tightly, she pleaded, "Please help us sir, we only want to work, and have somewhere to live!" Andreas was not sure of what he *could* actually do, but he was determined to at least try, and returning to the office, he discussed the subject with Becky, who suggested, "The main problem seems to be having somewhere for them to live. If another site could be found, the problem may be solved, but then there is always the possibility of them being moved on again, and that's no life for those poor souls!" "Unfortunately!" Andreas replied, "That is how my people have lived for centuries, and I thought it had been all but eradicated!" Noting her quizzical look he informed her, "Yes, I am Romany too, and proud of that fact!" Becky asserted, "Rightly so Andreas, and we must leave no stone unturned in trying to help these poor people!" Andreas sharply pushed his chair back, and declared, "I'm going home for a while, I might be able to think more clearly there, ring me if anything urgent crops up!"

Knowing that something was troubling him as soon as he walked in, Lu made coffee and sat beside him, gazing intently into his eyes, waiting for an explanation for the sombre demeanour. When he explained the dilemma, she cupped his chin and smiled, "The problem could be half-way to being solved then, the old widow Mary Williams passed away a fortnight ago, and although it's only one bedroom, they could make do, until something more suitable comes along, but at least they would have a fixed abode!" He grinned, "Lu, you're an absolute angel, I don't know what I'd do without you!" He wasted no time in returning to the car park with the good news, and loading the whole family into his spacious new car, he drove them to the old widow's place, and explaining that it was only a one bedroom house, he pointed out however, that at least they would have an address, enabling him to apply for a permit. The couple were thrilled with the house, and the man's wife tried to kiss his hand, but Andreas averred, "Please don't do that, I'm really nobody that special!" "You are special sir, you are *Krallis*, the *king* among men!" Being disconcerted and humbled by the woman's words, he left for home without a word, and returning home, he related the woman's reaction, and Lu commented, kissing his cheek, "Andreas you *are* a good man, and you will just have to get used to the fact that people trust, and look up to you!" Shaking his head, he responded, "I only try to do the best for folk, no more than that!"

Believing the problem to have been resolved, Andreas was surprised the following day, when Becky told him that the same young man was outside waiting to see him. He asked her, "Could you make two of your special coffees, and show him in please!" Will entered the office, seconds after Becky had put the coffees on the desk, and Andreas greeted him, "Good afternoon Will, and what can I do for you today?" "Well sir, I applied for the permit and it was turned down!" "Did they give a reason?" "No sir, a man just came, and said that my application had been turned down, no reason, no nothing sir!" "Okay Will, drink your coffee, and leave it with me. I'll see what I can do!" Having an idea of the cause, *and* how to resolve that particular problem, he was also aware that if what he had in mind failed, *all* hope of a satisfactory conclusion would be lost. He spent the rest of the afternoon contacting people that he knew for certain had knowledge of the locale, and added to family lore, he became increasingly more optimistic of achieving a result.

The day of the visit to the council offices arrived, and Andreas chose *not* to mention the affair to Viv, but thought it wise to have him present, knowing that if he managed to address the problem with a council representative, he would need a reputable witness to anything that transpired. Arriving at the council offices, a few minutes later than the designated time, they were immediately introduced to Simon, their instructor for the day, and after having had everything explained to them twice over, they were allowed to try out the keyboard for themselves. With Viv proving to be more adept than his junior partner, and Simon pointed out just how advantageous computers would be in their line of business, "You will never have to rummage for files again. Everything is there at the touch of a button!" Andreas thought, *that's exactly what that bitch indoors pointed out, clever little sod,* and Andreas could tell that Viv was impressed with the system, when he asked if Simon could recommend a particular company's products. "Tiny are pretty good!" Simon suggested, whereupon Viv said seriously, "I think that if we are going to splash out a serious amount of cash, we'd be as well getting a large one!" It was only later that Viv understood the reason for having caused so much laughter, and when the mirth had subsided, Andreas asked Simon if it would be possible to speak to the person in charge of issuing permits. Simon replied, "I'll see if he's available!" And within five minutes he had returned, accompanied by a large, red-faced man, who testily ushered them into a side office. With Viv looking completely mystified, Andreas got down to brass tacks straight away, "I understand that you have turned down Will Jones's application for a scrap-dealer's permit, may I ask the reason for the refusal?" The man puffed out his chest and replied, "We have had complaints about scruffy tinkers going around the town collecting scrap, and I for one want to see it all stopped. Now is there anything else I can do for you!" Andreas commented, without a hint of the anger that he was feeling inside, "I think that I should point out that this man is neither scruffy nor a tinker, he is an honest man, with no criminal record, eking out a living, by disposing of materials that people have no further use for!" The man's face began to redden, and Viv was tempted to intervene, but sensing that Andreas had the bit between his teeth, *and* that there was an underlying purpose to his suit, he allowed the conversation to continue, "Allow me to acquaint you with the history of the car park where Mr Jones has been living. It was originally called Broome Park, and was part of a vast estate owned by Sir James Broome, a local man who made his fortune in the paper-making industry. When he married, Sir James had a house built in the middle of the park, that had designed by Christopher Bird, the famous architect. On Sir James's death, both Broome House as it was called then, *and* the park were left to the people of the town, and because of the unique design, and the house's connection to a celebrated architect, it was awarded the status of a listed building!" Viv leaned forward in expectation as Andreas paused, "A few years ago, the council had the building demolished overnight, to make way for the car-park, that is now *in situ*. There was a huge fuss, because it was a listed building, and had been left to the people of the town, but due to delays, supposedly contrived by the council, the *brouhaha* was suppressed and swept under the carpet. Now I'm not suggesting for one moment, that the council *were* culpable, but I'm sure that the people concerned in this matter, would *not* want old coals to be raked over. I have several members of the *national* press in my circle of friends, who are *always* looking for something to get their teeth into, and I am led to believe that it could mean hefty fines for an individual or corporation, responsible for the demolition of a listed building for financial gain, and a possible jail sentence, if it were proved that a payment had been made to the person or persons, responsible for the disassembly of Broome House!" The councillor's rotund face turned an even brighter shade of red as Andreas continued, "I have in my possession an affidavit, citing that, four weeks after the demolition, you purchased land, on which you built a large, mansion type dwelling. It would be imprudent for me to suggest that there *is* a connection between that and the demolition, but I'm sure that my friends in London, could dig up *something* of interest!" Smith's face turned from red to purple, and the councillor spluttered, "There is no need for that Mister Bosworth, everything will be sorted out to your satisfaction!" Andreas smiled, "Thank you Mister Smith, and I trust that any future applications will be met with the same consideration!" Returning to the office, they made a detour to the car park, where Andreas told Will,

"I've seen the person responsible for permits, and if you re-apply on Monday, your permit will be granted. "Thank you Krallis!" Will responded, "Thank you so much for all you have done, God bless you sir!" As they left the park Viv commented, "I'm proud of you too Andreas, you have done really well, but how and from whom did you get an affidavit?" Andreas grinned archly, "Actually I do not have one, I was bluffing, but I do have a lot of local knowledge from my kin, and the rest I just made up!" Viv shook his head in disbelief, "You were taking one hell of a risk, and fortunately it paid off, but I do *not* want to hear of you resorting to such nefarious methods again, *ever*. And what the hell is this Krallis business all about?" Andreas was too embarrassed to answer, but when Viv insisted, Andreas told him exactly what the word meant, and Viv repeated the word, "Hmm, Krallis, King of the Gypsies. It's a grand title, but one that I have to say is richly merited!" Andreas had the thought that the real King of the Gypsies might wish to contest that last statement. But Lu *had* hit the nail fair and square on the head, her husband *was* trusted and revered.

15

Receiving an early call on Monday morning from Simon, he learned of a beginners computer course at the old church hall, that would be held every Monday for the following six weeks. Andreas immediately rang to enrol his family, adding Reuben *and* Viv to the list for good measure, whose recruitment in his absence, was a sure way for Andreas to get back at his mentor for all the sly digs thrown his way in the not so distant past. Deciding to involve the new senior partner in his subterfuge, he knocked Mr Mowll's door, to plead his case, "Having already enrolled Mister Bailey and myself, I hope that you won't think me presumptuous, in asking if you'd care to join us on the course Mister Mowll?" Andreas received exactly the reply that he had expected, "It's something that I would love to be involved in, but regretfully, I'm far too busy just at present to take on *anything*!" Andreas replied, "I trust you do not think me too forward in setting up the scheme?" "Certainly not Mr Bosworth, it shows initiative, and I will inform Mr Bailey myself of his inclusion!" Minutes later, sitting at his desk with his hands clasped behind his head, Andreas smiled and thought, *I feel really satisfied with my day's work.* Viv entered the office stating, "I've had a good day today one way or another!" "Have you?" Andreas asked, "That's great. Oh, er Mister Mowll wants a word with you!" "Shit, I wonder what *he* wants!" Viv mused, as he dashed from the room. Andreas put his papers into his latest briefcase, acquired for a song from a charity shop, and smirking, he discreetly left the building. Heading for home he could not help smiling once more at his ingenuity, and as soon as he arrived home he told Lu, "If the phone goes, don't answer it!" Addressing the boys, he told them, "If you kids *do* answer it, and it's Uncle Viv, tell him I'm not in!" George commented, "But that would be a lie *daddi*!" "I know George, but it's what is known as a little white lie, and as such, does not count!" He shouted upstairs to his beautiful wife, "Hey Lu, will you make up the spare bed in the boy's room!" She demanded, "What are you up to, you devious bastard?" When he told her what he had set up, she laughed saying, "You're *both* worse than a couple of kids!" She went through to the kitchen, an after an hiatus of five minutes Andreas shouted, "Better make another dinner too!" She called back, "It's already on!" He added, "Spare razor and towels?" She poked her head round the door, "Done!" He smiled remarking, "*Now* I know why I married you!"

Ten minutes later, the phone rang, instantly becoming a source of much laughter, and no-one answered the phone, nor the succeeding three calls occurring at regular intervals. The fifth and final time that the phone rang, Andreas nodded to George, who ran faster than his brother, to answer the call, "He's not in Uncle Viv!" He heard his son say. Everyone laughed and nobody was surprised when the doorbell rang ten minutes later, with Victor being delegated to answer the door. Viv stormed into the room, "It's a damned good job the kids are here or I'd give you a piece of my mind!" "Sit down. and I'll make us a couple of Tolley's and coke!" With his face as dark as thunder Viv declared, "If I had a drink, I'd lose my licence, then wouldn't be able to drive to this bloody computer course!" Andreas laughed, remarking as Lu came in with his dinner, "We know that Katie is working, so everything has been arranged, you have a meal, a bed, and a disposable razor that has been put in the bathroom, so sit your arse down and relax!" Snatching the drink from Andreas's hand, he downed it quickly and asked with a grin, "Any more of that stuff?" "Steady!" Andreas warned, "We've got work in the morning!" Andreas had to admit that in spite of all of Viv's strange, and at times wicked idiosyncrasies, he did enjoy his company, knowing that *he* in turn loved coming over to see Lu and the kids. The domestic bliss that Andreas had with Lu and the kids was something that Viv coveted, and after dinner and another couple of Tolley's, he admitted as much. "I wish Kate wasn't such a career woman, I could absolutely lose myself in what you have here!" Andreas remarked, "I know that, but Katie is one beautiful woman, and *you* are a lucky man!" Viv replied, "I know, but I *would* like children, to carry on the business after I'm gone. You have three children with another on the way, and I'm jealous!" Andreas averred, "My children adore you Viv. Come on I've had enough maudlin, let's play dominoes with Lu and the kids!" Andreas dropped out after one game in order to apply himself more diligently to Tolley's, a habit to which he was becoming more and more accustomed, leaving George and Lu playing playing against Viv and Victor, ably assisted all round by Rosie, who had been allowed the dubious honour of slapping down tiles for the quartet. The sublime evening was rounded off by Andreas cooking supper for the gang, *and* doing the washing-up, even though he was tempted to leave that abhorrent task for his *ever-loving* to exact in the morning, but having the notion that it could lead to a carnal reward later, he stoically bore the cross, adding a small Tolleys to Rosie's bottle, *just in case*. Becoming tired of running round slapping down dominoes, Rosie sat beside her father on the settee and promptly fell asleep, *without* the soporific mixture being applied, until the sound of tiles been slapped down, an age old family custom, continually disturbed her slumber. At last, during one of her wakeful moments, Andreas managed to feed the bottle to her, then carrying her upstairs, he lay her in the wee bed, that he had purchased the previous week, securing a decent discount for cash. He returned to the living room and asserted, "Right you boys, bed for you too!" "George pleaded, "Oh please dad, can't we stay up a little longer. Uncle Viv doesn't come round often, and I did tell a little white lie for you!" Andreas looked at Viv, and grinning he acceded to his son's demands, "Well okay then, but only for half an hour. Don't forget you've got school in the morning!" "I've had enough now Andreas!" Lu said, "You can take my place!" So for the promised half an hour, Andreas partnered George, where to Viv's patent chagrin, they won every game, and taking the boys up the wooden hill to bed, he popped in to see Lu, finding that she was sound asleep. Andreas and Viv sat downstairs talking and drinking for an hour or so, the way that friends do. "You bastard!" Viv said, "Imagine making that little boy tell lies for you, you're getting more and more devious!" Andreas responded with a grin, "Well I had a bloody good tutor didn't I?" With that they called it a day and retiring for the night, Andreas rounded off a fine evening by waking his dear wife to have his wicked way.

After a morning shower, Andreas roused the children, into which category Viv indubitably fell, and while the boys were in the kitchen eating, Viv remarked, "Jesus, you make a lot of noise when you're having sex, I could hear everything you were up to!" Andreas grinned, "You shouldn't have been listening you bloody pervert, but if you want lessons, I'll give you a good discount, because of our friendship!" Rosie toddled downstairs, and being thankful that she now seemed to be past the stage of having a soaking nappy hanging round her ankles, he sighed deeply, and groused, "It's all bloody go here in the mornings, no wonder I'm buggered by the time I get to the office!" "Yeah, you do too much!" Viv remarked sardonically, adding, "I'll be in late myself this morning, Kate applied for promotion and they're telling her today whether she's got it or not!" Andreas asked, "Will it mean re-locating?" Viv replied, "I wouldn't think so, but I'll let you know later. I'm off now, give my love to Lu!" Five minutes after all the work was done, the crafty bitch deigned to honour the scene with her presence, and Andreas thought, *Now I suppose she'll sit on her arse all day watching television. When you think about it, she's got a good life and bloody lucky she's got me!*

The weather forecast was not favourable, and it had already begun to drizzle, so after bestowing his wife with a perfunctory kiss, and suggesting that she take an operational immediate shower, he drove the boys to school, promising to pick them up at the end of their day. They kissed him on the cheek, then ran off to join their pals, and watching them run across the quadrangle, he thought of how different it had all been when he had been at the school. Looking in the wing-mirror waiting to move off, he noticed Mr Elliott, his old physical training teacher, walking along the path, and though his broad back was now slightly bowed, he still walked with a strong confident stride. Deciding to have a chat with him, Andreas rolled down the window and wished him good morning, whereupon his first ever boxing trainer, looked in awe at the large car, remarking, "You seem to have done well for yourself, but I always suspected that you might!" Andreas told him the good news that he just been made a partner in Mowll and Mowll as a conveyancing solicitor. "The school is proud of what you've achieved, and I have to say that both of your boys show the same drive for life, *and* of course your aptitude for sport. Victor would like to box but apparently his mother will not hear of it, and George shows promise as an all-round athlete!" Andreas replied, "See if you can get Victor interested in football instead, he's a natural!" Relating the tale of how, when he was a toddler, he had embarrassingly run rings round him with a football, in front of the whole family. His former tutor laughed, "I hadn't heard about his prowess on the football field but I'd appreciate you having a word with his mother about the boxing, he shows the same promise that you did at that age, and it would be a shame to waste it!" Andreas shrugged his shoulders, "If *I* say anything to his mother, it will only make matters worse, she didn't like it when *I* was fighting!" As he was about to leave Mr Elliott asked, "Could you see your connections at the club, to see if we can get a boxing evening organised?" "Of course, although ultimately it's the domain of Jimmy Kelly and Reuben Scamp, but I *will* have a word!" Andreas was delighted to have spoken to Mr Elliott and to hear about George, who as far *he* had been aware, had shown no interest in sport of any kind. Entering the office, he looked at his desk, perceiving a mug of steaming coffee sitting on a brand new coaster, beside another two further additions, IN and OUT trays, with the in-tray predictably piled high and the out-tray unsurprisingly empty. As soon as Becky entered the office he praised her solicitation, "Thank you for the thought, it will certainly keep my desk a lot tidier!" Explaining how he had used a little local knowledge to get the permit, and temporary accommodation for Will Jones, she smiled and declared, "Oh that's wonderful news, I'm so happy for them. I think I'm going to love working here!"

Picking up the boys from school, he only just managed to beat the rain, but before they had even gotten halfway home, the rain changed firstly to sleet, then to snow, and on arrival at the house, they had to make a mad dash for the door. Being welcomed instantly by warmth and the smell of food being cooked, Rosie ran up to her father, "Viv! Viv!" Andreas asserted, "No darling, Uncle Viv's not coming tonight, maybe he'll come tomorrow!" "No Daddy, Viv, Viv!" Ignoring her entreaty to listen, he answered the phone, as much to put a stop to it's strident ringing as anything else. It was Viv, and with tidings that could be both good *and* bad, "Katie got the promotion, and she's over the moon!" "That's wonderful news!" Andreas replied, and putting his hand over the mouth-piece, he relayed the good news to Lu, "Yeah we're going to the Green Man for a celebration lunch!" Adding, "We haven't booked yet, but if you want to come along, you're more than welcome, *if* you can get a sitter that is!" "No!" Andreas answered, "It's too late for that now, but why don't you come over here, Lu's made a lovely stew, which would save you having to book *or* hang about in the cold!" "Okay you've twisted my arm!" Viv responded, but with his reaction being a little *too* hasty, Andreas smelled a rat, and he realized that going to the Green Lady had *never* been Viv's intention, *the bastard's getting his own back for last night!* He thought. Planning the sleeping arrangements, he told Lu, "They can sleep in our bed and we'll sleep on the settee!" Then all of a sudden he thought of a better idea, "Forget that, they can sleep in the boys' single beds, and the *boys* can sleep in the living room on the settee!" He grinned wickedly, *he'll have to get up early if he wants to get the better of me!* Swearing Lu to secrecy he declared, "I can't wait to see their faces when I show them to their room for the night!" She laughed, "Do you two ever stop, you really *are* like a couple of kids!" She was right of course but even *she* had to admit that it *was* funny, "It'll do them good to sleep in separate beds for a change!" Andreas remarked with a grin.

The kids had their dinner early, while the hosts awaited the arrival of their guests, and arriving at the appointed time, Viv and Katie were immediately greeted with a Tolley's aperitif. Dinner was served soon after with Andreas more than ready for his all-time favourite meal, rabbit stew and dumplings. "This stew is delicious!" Katie declared and Andreas, hyper from the euphoric expectation of his prank commented, "The meat is courtesy of Riley, who trapped the beast at four o'clock this morning, and the dumplings are courtesy of the rabbits who shit themselves when they saw his ugly face!" Being the only one not killing themselves laughing, Lu delivered *the stare*, leaving Andreas in no doubt that he had overstepped the line, but being reassured of no fall from grace, when he detected the semblance of a grin at the corner of her mouth, and being emboldened by the ghost of things to come, he remarked with a saucy grin, "I was only joking dear, your dumplings are legendary!" Lu's pregnancy had just begun to show, giving her skin an even more beautiful glow, and being determined to make her pay dearly later on for her feigned disapproval of his little joke, he thought, *oh boy am I on form and I've only had one drink!* With dinner over, the kids would not let Katie settle, being all over her like a rash, with Rosie being the worst offender, and as he watched his daughter playing with Katie, Andreas suddenly realized that she had known all along that Viv *would* be calling.

Going to the kitchen, he brought through four glasses, and a bottle of chilled champagne, that he'd purchased cheaply, as it was out of date, but with the Jeroboam soon disappearing, a little *too* quickly for Andreas's liking, he discovered the reason for it's rapid evaporation, when he looked under the table, and saw Rosie, hidden by the table cloth, quaffing her mother's half full glass of *champers*. He thought, *oh well, it'll save me having to add Tolleys to her night-time bottle,* and once the *bubbly* had been finished off, albeit with some extra assistance, a bottle of Tolleys was produced, and within a very short space of time, Katie had developed a taste for the elixir of life. After two or three more hours of serious libation, Viv yawned and declared that he was ready for bed, and realizing that the moment that he had been waiting for all night had arrived, Andreas escorted them upstairs. Opening the boys' bedroom door he said, "I've put extra quilts on the beds, in case you get cold!" The fear of being overcome by laughter, prevented him from looking at their faces, thus spoiling his complete enjoyment of the moment, that *would* have been the icing on the cake. Closing the door slowly and quietly behind him, he descended the stairs, laughing as noiselessly as he was able, all the way down. Lu commented, "That was cruel, *but* I have to say, *extremely* funny!" Later in the night, and after he had received his conjugal rights *without* his daughter's intervention, he thought of the trick he had played, and once more had real difficulty in stifling his laughter, but somehow managing the task, he lay in the dark in his warm double bed, and smirked himself to sleep

16

Immediately calling to mind his prank of the previous evening, Andreas smiled and walked to the shower-room whistling a merry tune, until Lu banged on the door asking him, in an expletive strewn vernacular, to desist. With difficulty in curtailing his merriment, and at the completion of his ablutions, he went downstairs to make his first coffee of the day. Hearing footsteps, he turned round and joy of all joys, it was Viv, "Have a good night?" Andreas enquired. "Yes thank you!" Viv answered coldly, and struggling once more to contain his amusement, Andreas turned the screw, "Comfy?" "You bastard!" Viv retorted angrily, and being unable to contain himself no longer, Andreas screeched with laughter, until the lady of the house, roused from her slumber once more, screamed, "Can you two down there keep that bloody noise down, I'm trying to make up for the sleep I was denied last night!" Viv got ready for work in silence, and said icily as he left for the office, "I do not want to see you today *at all*, so if you need advice on something, don't bother coming to me!" Storming from the house, Andreas was convinced that Viv had to have heard the laughter as he walked down the path towards his car.

Entering the kitchen, Katie looked at him and began to laugh, "You are a sod Andreas. *I* managed to hide my amusement, but Viv certainly did *not* see the funny side at all!" Andreas grinned, "I've got to be honest Kate, I didn't think of it until practically the last moment!" She smiled, "You were always a good laugh, it's one of the things I liked about you when we first met!" He looked at her seriously and assured his friend's loved one, "It's okay, I've *never* uttered a word to anyone about our one-night-stand. After all it *was* before I got with Lu, *and* before you and Viv got together. Actually you could have knocked me down with a feather the night you walked into the Green Man on his arm!" Tittering, she added, "I almost choked when he introduced us, and you told him that you'd already had the pleasure!" Looking at her seriously, he said, "I cannot ever remember a time when I wasn't in love with Lu!" And Katie remarked, "You two are so wonderful together, and the kids are adorable!" Andreas kissed her cheek, and rounded up the boys just in time to see Rosie coming down the stairs rubbing her eyes. Katie assured him, "Don't worry *I'll* see to her!" Blowing them both a kiss, he left with the boys.

As soon as Andreas entered the office Becky said, "Mister Bailey said that he wants to see you, *before* you pick up the *Times*!" Andreas said, "Hmm, must be important, he told me this morning over breakfast, that he did not want to see or speak to me today. I'm afraid he's not too happy with me at the moment!" Recounting the events of the previous evening, and noting her amusement, he remarked, "For God's sake don't laugh when you see him. He'll know that I've told you, and we'll *both* be in trouble!" Walking into Viv's office, he demanded stiffly, "You sent for me?" "Yes!" Viv responded, "I've heard from Michael, and he's coming back on Wednesday. Having now learned how everything works, he's got the quotes for the lot, so it looks as if the project is a goer. I've been on the phone to the breweries and supermarkets, while you were playing happy families, and they *are* interested. It's never been done before with cider, but I'm unsure of whether we can legally protect the concept in law or not, particularly as the supermarkets will attempt to make their own versions, and undercut our prices, which would halve *our* sales and profits. Pubs should not be a problem, with our product being less expensive than bottles, and of course a far superior product, but we really need that supermarket trade to hit the jackpot. I've contacted the Patents Office, and have an interview today. I've already put everything I will need into a folder, but I'm convinced that cider has *never* been marketed in this manner before. The likelihood is that I will be gone all day, and seeing that Mr Mowll is indisposed, you will be in sole charge, so don't go gallivanting off shopping or something equally as mundane, you *could* conceivably be required to sort out a concern of mine, or indeed of Mr Mowll!" "That's great news!" Andreas exclaimed, "Summer is only a couple of months away, so we have just enough time to get everything up and running!" Walking to the door grinning, he assured his friend, "Rest assured Mr Bailey, if I require fresh air, I will open the window!" Viv shook his head and walked out of the building, heading for his interview at the Patents Office.

"Well Becky, it looks as if we are will be making even more money, in the very near future!" Andreas declared, and went on to explain how they had all collaborated in the formulation of an idea to produce cider in disposable hermetically sealed containers. Now it was down to Michael to produce the goods, being the one with the know-how of blending *and* where to get hold of the various types of apples, in large enough quantities needed to mass-produce his special variety of cider. It was an exciting experience being in at the grass roots of the creation of a brand new product and he rang Lu to tell her the good news, immediately getting the impression that she was more impressed with the fact that he was in sole charge at the office, than being on the threshold of a bold attempt to break into the drinks market. Becky placed another mug of coffee in front of him and once he had ploughed his way through the extra work, he picked up the Times and with the help of his new ball-point, his mind went into automatic mode. Viv had still not returned or phoned by the time the working day had finished, so he picked up the boys, and headed home, being thankful that at least, the weather was a whole lot better than it had been the previous day. After dinner, there was still no word from Viv, and guessing that he was exacting revenge for his practical joke the previous night, he phoned Vee to ask if she had heard from Michael. She replied, "Yes and isn't that great news about the patent?" "Yes Vee it's bloody marvellous, and so are you!" Sounding distinctly suspicious, she ventured to ask, "What are you talking about Andreas. What *are* you up to?" "Never mind my darling sister, you're just simply a very wonderful person, and I rang to tell you how much I love you!" Putting the phone gently into the cradle, he smiled, and another plan was beginning to formulate in his arch mind. Going directly to the garage, he related the good news, and purchasing Gunnar's entire stock of congratulatory cards, he asked him to write in one of the cards, then leaving *poste haste* to give everybody else in the family the good news, he coerced every one of *them* to write in a card.

The next morning he went in early to the office, long before Viv arrived, and placing all of the cards onto Viv's desk, he returned to his office. Sitting at his desk with a self-satisfied smile on his face, Becky was moved to remark, "You're looking very smug, what have you been up to?" After he had told her the whole story, she laughed saying, "I don't know which one of you is the worst! "That's exactly what my wife said just before I left this morning, and I want to know the moment he comes in!" Ten minutes later she dashed into the office, "He's just come through the door!" Andreas waited for five minutes, knowing that the scheme had to be timed just right, then going to Viv's office, he knocked the door and walked in, where he found Viv halfway through the pile. Viv observed, "I've never seen so many cards in my life!" When he had almost completed the task he said tersely, "I noticed there wasn't one from you!" Then realization dawned, "That's because they're *all* from you aren't they you bastard. How did you find out?" Andreas smirked and lied, "I've got a friend in the Patents Office, so don't ever think that you can ever hide anything from me. Jesus Christ, it must have cost an arm and a leg to get that patent all wrapped up so quickly!" Viv winked, tapped the side of his nose and suggested, "It's not what you know, it's *who* you know! Oh and by the way could you ring round the firms that make this machinery to get the cheapest quote?" Andreas replied with a smug smile, "I did that yesterday afternoon, and the findings are under the last card, *if* you ever get that far!" As Andreas opened the door to leave he asked, "Have you got time for lunch later, I feel that we should celebrate in some way!" "I have, and *you* are bloody well paying!"

17

Michael duly returned from his exploratory trip to Paris, having also purchased four fifty gallon wooden barrels in France, two of which were old sherry barrels from Spain, with the remaining two having once contained French cognac. "Added flavour!" Michael declared, "I've got a few smaller ones at the farm which will do us for now but I'm hoping that I can get more of the larger type when this scheme goes world-wide, and keep the smaller ones for our own use!" "I like the sound of that!" Andreas asserted, admiring Michael's confidence. Michael continued, "We should have enough from the trees in the *outer farm* to cope. Last year was a bumper crop, and according to the long range weather reports, this year will be a good one too, but to safeguard against the lean years, I've ordered more saplings while I was there, so with the fruit we have now, and what I've managed to buy in, we should have enough to last two to three years at the present rate and that's taking into account *your* consumption!" "You cheeky sod!" Andreas suggested playfully, "I *will* however have to taste the brew, purely to test it's worthiness of course!"

Believing that the initial outlay would be minimal, Andreas had however *not* however taken into account the rising costs, blowing his primary estimations out of the window, but with the optimism from those around him being infectious, he was like a child at Christmas when production *finally* began. The machinery churned out the containers for the cider, and the locally made boxes bearing the facsimile of the farm were filled by hand, but Andreas was aware that it would all change, and hopefully for the best, when the orders started pouring in. Viv too had been busy getting orders from the supermarkets and pubs, but sales were merely trickling in, bringing the fear that their optimism may have been premature, or shock horror, entirely misplaced. But their fears proved premature too, for as word of the product spread, sales increased rapidly, bringing fresh concerns, that demand would exceed stock, but with the containers of the required fruit that Michael had ordered while he was in France, fortuitously arriving just in time, the operation was saved. Michael's foresight, and know-how in blending the various types of apples proved to be a life-saver, and once he had tasted the ambrosial brew, Andreas fully appreciated the demand for it's bitter-sweet taste *and* strength. Supermarket demand was principally for larger boxes, while pubs could not get enough of the brew that *had* to be sold in litre boxes, as the machinery was French made. As demand for Golden Valley cider grew, and feeling that the time for expansion had almost arrived, he was not surprised to be summoned to the office one Monday morning to discuss that very subject. "Do you think Michael will be able to cope with the extra work?" Viv asked. "Without Michael we do not have a marketable product!" Andreas answered, "Getting everything just right is an art in itself, and one that only Michael excels in. Any other blend would not give that wonderful taste, and only *he* knows exactly the right amounts of each apple to incorporate into the mix, so without his skill, we are sunk!" Viv leaned back in his chair, put a pencil into his mouth and suggested, "How about if he were to take on an assistant, somebody younger, who could take over should anything happen to him!" Andreas said, "That's sound logical, but you know how these things are closely guarded family secrets? I can ask, but don't hold out *too* much hope of success!" Suddenly judging Viv's demeanour to portend part of a pre-planned scheme, Andreas prepared himself for Viv's *real* reason for the meeting. Viv's wheedling voice continued, "Michael owes you an awful lot doesn't he, what with you saving the farm?" Completely misreading Viv's inference, Andreas retorted, "Absolutely not, I am too busy in the office, *and* attending to all the other businesses we're involved in, to take on more tasks!" Looking at Andreas with a sly grin, Viv remarked, "I'm not talking about *you,* it's someone *young* we need!" Andreas responded angrily, "What the hell are you talking about Viv?" Leaning back with his hands joined behind his neck, Viv's suggestion was a bombshell, "I'm on about Victor and George!" With Andreas being stunned and momentarily speechless, Viv followed up swiftly, "Think of it!" Viv advocated, "They are old enough now to contribute in some way to the business, and it would be an ideal opportunity for them to learn the business, *but* more importantly, they are family!" Thinking about the notion, Andreas conceded that it certainly warranted consideration, and because they *were* family, Michael could very well go for it. And of course with Viv knowing that fact all along, the real purpose for the meeting was now apparent. Smiling at the subterfuge, Andreas recognized however that although Viv was correct in *everything* he had said, it was the devious way he went about things that really got up Andreas's nose. *I'm glad I'm not underhanded like that*, he thought. Deliberating for a moment Andreas suggested, "You'll have to speak to Michael first, I'm not having the boys getting all fired up, only to be let down!" Looking archly over the top of his horn-rimmed spectacles, Viv declared with a half-smile, "Not *me* Andrew, *you*, and before you go off half-cocked again, just think about it for a second. It would be better coming from you, given your history with him at the farm and all that!" Andreas shook his head, asking, "Why do you always call me Andrew when you want a complex task performing!" Pausing for thought however, he finally agreed to the task, "Okay I'll do it but if Michael agrees to the scheme, *you* can get the boys in here to tell them yourself!" Viv held out his hand, "Agreed!" Ringing the farm immediately, Andreas asked Vee to tell Michael that he would be dropping by later in the day to see him, and having her interest markedly aroused, she asked, "Am I permitted to know what this is all about?" "No!" He replied, "You are not, but you *are* permitted to sit in on the meeting!" Ringing Lu, Andreas briefed her on Viv's suggestion. "I think it's a brilliant idea of Viv's!" She declared, "And I promise I won't breathe a word to them!" Andreas agreed, "I know it's an astute move, but I hate the devious way he goes about things!" Lu laughed, remarking, "Bloody hell, hark at the pot calling the kettle black arse!" An indignant Andreas retorted, "Cheeky bitch, I'm not devious at all!" "No dear and who engaged Vee's innocent help in discovering that Viv had secured the patent?"

Pulling into the yard, he found Michael already there waiting for him, a trait he had inherited from his father, along with the blending of cider. Putting a brotherly arm around Andreas's shoulder, he suggested, "Let's go to the parlour,

Vee is making coffee, and I'm sure I can find something to add to it!" Vee and Lily-Ann followed them into the parlour carrying three coffees, and extracting a half bottle of rum from the Welsh dresser, Michael declared waving the bottle, "Just the thing to oil our throats!" "So that's where you keep it!" Vee remarked. Michael smiled, "The less you know about this room, the better!" And turning to Andreas, he asked, "What is this all about then. It must be pretty important for a high-flying legal eagle to come out of his way to see us?" Andreas hardly knew where to begin, and coughing nervously he explained, "I have the figures here for the cider sales, and as you will no doubt be aware, the product is flying off the shelves. I have to say Michael, that it's almost *entirely* due to your unique blending. Everyone concerned with the venture has contributed in some way, but without you the operation would not have even got off the ground!" The smiles Andreas, received for his flattery, boded well for the next part of the plan. "The demand is so great that we are going to have to get new premises to cope with the demand, and Viv expressed the view, that with the increased work-load, and assuming that you could have difficulty coping, Viv would like you to appoint somebody to assist in the blending!" Michael suddenly saw through the flannelling, "Nobody will get the secret from me!" "Please sit down!" Andrew averred, "Look at this thing realistically. There is more work than you would ever hope to handle successfully!" Andreas held up his hand to silence the angry words, forming in Michael's mouth, "Michael, *hear* me out. Realizing that you would not want the secret going out of the family, Viv has proposed that Victor and George become your assistants, with a view to taking over, if and when you decide to call it a day. Think of it Michael, someone you love and trust to take over the reins, whenever you decide that you need a holiday. God knows you've slogged yourself to a stand-still these last few years, coping with the foot and mouth epidemic, *and* the stream diversion. You've worked non-stop for far too long, you *need* a break!" Vee interjected, "I think it's a wonderful idea darling, we *both* need a break, Lily-Ann too. Andreas is spot-on with everything he says, and you know you love those boys!" Michael shook his head and said, "I'm not sure!" And turning to Andreas, he said, "Let me give you an answer in the morning, when Vee and I have had time to talk it over!" Andreas replied, "That's fair enough Michael. We will abide by your decision whatever it is. You are much too valuable to this venture, for us to go against your wishes!" Andreas shook his hand, kissed Vee and Lily-Ann, and driving along the same road that he had walked as a lad, he thought, *they will talk it over but I feel sure that with Vee's input, we may just pull it off*! Almost as soon as he had arrived home, and before he had finished his first Tolley's, the telephone rang. "Well how did did it go?" Viv asked, "Will he play ball?" "Wait til the morning!" Andreas replied, and gently put the receiver into it's berth, with a long satisfying smile playing across his face. Finishing his second drink, he smiled, and commented, "Well my darling, I'm ninety nine percent certain that our two boys will soon be gainfully employed as assistant cider blenders. Michael will let us know tomorrow, but with our sister on the team, everything *should* go to plan!" He was mentally exhausted, and after dinner, sitting back in the armchair with another of his favourite tipple, lovingly mixed by his beautiful wife, he relaxed by watching the television with his family. But in the odd moment, he wondered idly, about the changes that were likely to arise as a result of his young sons' new adventure. Being content with his present state of affairs, he was aware that massive changes such as this, could have an adverse effect on the ambience, *but* there was no stopping the wheels that had now been set in motion, and at the end of the day, his children had to be allowed to grow up. Rising from the chair, he poured himself another of the same, promptly falling asleep in the chair, before he had even managed half a glass. Lu shook him back to consciousness, "Come on little man you've had a busy day, up the wooden hill to bed you go!" *As always Andreas did as he was told*, and it seemed to Andreas that he had only just laid his head on the pillow, when he was awakened by her warm body, and cold searching hands. He murmured sleepily, "Your hands are bloody freezing!" "Well put them somewhere where it's warm then, *and as always he did as he was told.*

18

Being wakened the next morning by rain drumming rhythmically on the window pane, loud enough to waken any-one, apart from his dear wife, and disentangling himself from her warm, unconscious embrace, Andreas went downstairs to prepare breakfast. The phone began ringing before he had completed the task however, and believing it to be Viv, he had half a mind not to answer, but with good sense prevailing however, and the knowledge that if he let it ring on, Lu would give him a mouthful at being prematurely woken, he decided, fortuitously as it turned out, to answer the accursed inconvenience. And hearing Michael's voice, he became instantly alert. "I knew you'd be up, so I thought I'd ring to tell you of our decision!" Pausing for a moment Michael asserted, "We have decided that it would be a good thing all round, for both the project and us, to accept the offer of two young assistants!" Andreas punched the air, but replying soberly, he replied, "Okay Michael that's great, but for now I'd be obliged if you keep it to yourself, until Viv has had the chance to put the offer to the boys!" "Yeah no worries on that score, your bloody gypsy family probably knew the decision before I did anyway!" Andreas laughed, "You're probably right there!" Wakening Lu with the good news, Michael's notion was confirmed, "What the hell did you have to wake me for, I knew that last night!" Shaking his head, he muttered as he closed the door, "I'll drive the boys to school love, it's chucking it down again out there!" He should have saved his breath. She had already returned to the land of nod.

Rain was still coming down in buckets, as he dropped the boys at the gates, but manoeuvring the car into his parking slot at the office, it suddenly ceased it's relentless deluge, allowing him to access the office, without one drop of precipitation having touched his person. Knocking on Viv's office door, he walked in, and perceiving immediately that *his* hair and clothes were soaking, Andreas asked roguishly, "Oh has it been raining?" But before Viv could utter a riposte, Andreas delivered the good news, "Michael has agreed to instruct my sons in the noble art of cider blending!" Viv was over the moon, "Did you pull the emotional blackmail of the farm?" "Well just a little, but the thing that really swung it in our favour was the fact that it was Victor and George, he adores those boys. What day, would you like them to come to the office?" Consulting his leather bound desk diary, he suggested that the most suitable time would be Saturday, "Even allowing for the fact that Victor will be expected at the farm!" "That'll be fine. I'll see Michael about Victor starting a bit later, and I'd better get George involved with the farm too, it would hardly be fair on Victor!" "Right that's everything solved, and next on the agenda, is looking at possible sites for the new cider production plant, if you're not doing much you can come with me?" "Not today I'm afraid, I've got some catching up to do, but if you want to explore by yourself today, I'll accompany you tomorrow. It's not that I don't trust you, but *I* have a better eye for these things than you!"

Viv added sarcastically, "Well don't let me keep you from your work, and seeing that you will likely be at it all day, I won't see you until tomorrow!"

After phoning Lu to tell her the news, he buzzed Becky for coffee, and deciding to phone Vee while he waited, he kept her abreast of the situation. She answered, "Oh, the same day as Lu's driving test then!" Not letting on that he was actually in ignorance of the day of the test, he continued the conversation with Vee, while thinking, *the bitch kept that quiet.* Becky arrived with coffee, and apprising her of the new development, he asked her to get a congratulatory card, and arrange for a bunch of flowers to be delivered on Saturday morning. Becky suggested, "She may not pass?" "I know my wife! "Andreas replied with a grin, "She'll pass okay!" Thinking to himself, *that will be really handy, she can start getting her arse out of bed in the mornings to drive the boys to school, and the farm at weekends.* Lu had still not mentioned the driving test when Friday arrived, even though he had prompted a mention, by asking how she was getting on with the lessons. She had merely replied, "Fine. Dinky is still very patient with me!" Looking as if he were the cat that got the cream, Viv strolled in and asked, "Well are you ready, or have you forgotten that we are site seeing?" Andreas replied, "No of course not, it's just that I've just learned that Lu's driving test is the same day as the boys' interview with you, and I wondered if that would make a difference" "No that'll be fine!" Viv said confidently, and following Andreas's to his new gleaming car, he remarked, "I've got a few sites in mind, but one in particular warrants close consideration!" "Go on then, hit me with it now, so I can shoot you down in flames!" Sighing deeply Viv replied, "At the site where the old church stood, there's a *huge* chunk of land still undeveloped. Size is not a problem, and with the location, being fairly close to the farm *and* adjacent to the main road, cartage would be minimal, plus fruit deliveries would be speedier, and more easily accessed. We could get Ted and your brother to knock up a building in *no* time, and consider this, *if* you rented a building on another site, you would have to spend a good deal of cash converting it anyway!" Andreas shook his head, "You *seem* to have made up your mind already, and looking at other sites would be merely going through the motions!" Viv continued apace, "*If* the plant were built as near to the main road as possible, you would only have to build a small road from the site to the main road, *and* it would be far enough away from houses not to be a noise problem. It would save time and money all round!" Andreas thought for a moment, and said with a grin, "You've really thought this through haven't you, and though it pains me to say it, I think you've come up with the ideal solution to all of our problems!" The only drawback!" Viv postulated, "Would be in getting the owner's consent to build, and negotiating a decent rental agreement!" "Well seeing that I actually own the land, there would be no no problems there, so I see no point in looking anywhere else. Let's go and have a look at the site, to see if I can plan it all out in my mind!" Parking the car on the foundations of where the old church once stood, gave them an ideal vantage point, and studying the site, Andreas was able to imagine it all, pretty much as Viv had envisaged it, and given his propensity for not dwelling on projects for too long, he suggested, "Let's go back to the office, and get in touch with Ted and Mister Smythe!"

Arriving back at Mowll and Mowll, Viv went straight to his office, leaving the execution of their plans to Andreas, being aware that no time would be wasted in getting things moving. That assumption proved to be an accurate assessment of the situation, with Andreas clearing his desk, and buzzing for a rapid burst of caffeine. Ringing Ted he made arrangements to meet at the site *that* afternoon, and as soon as the contents of the mug had been drained, he contacted Mister Smythe inviting him to join the inspection of the soon-to-be building site, while Becky got in touch with the farm, to request Michael's presence at the site. Walking past Viv's office, he popped his head round the open door to inform *him* of the afternoon meeting. "Oh I don't think I'll be there!" Viv asserted, "I'm *far* too busy at the moment!" Andreas replied sarcastically, "Yeah me too, I have a case that is complicated to say the least, with *my* client having taken on an interest only mortgage, without being made aware of the terms, *and* with the loan period now expired, the mortgage company were looking for settlement from my client, who incidentally hasn't a penny to his name. But, realizing the importance of our cider project, I've decided that it will now have to wait until Monday!" And slamming the door on the way out, Andreas stomped out of the room, returning to his office to calm down, before attending a meeting, that could decide, whether the logistics of such a huge undertaking would be the suitable at the site or not. Actually the meeting at the site went completely without a hitch, in spite of or because of, Viv's absence, with Mister Smythe measuring the planned site, and Walthaar, deputising for Ted, marking out the plan on the ground with French chalk. Being excited by the prospect, Michael remarked, "I'm beginning to think that I *will* actually be glad of the extra help from the boys, it seems a monumental task!" Andreas replied, "Yes it's a *biggie* all right, but one that will hopefully pay huge dividends. Come on, let's go back to my office, we're not needed here now!" Michael demurred, "If you don't mind I'll go back to the farm, I've got a mountain of work to do. Vee's been helping, but she's got the shop to run as well as looking after Lily-Ann. Pa is a godsend, but unfortunately he is not the man he was!" Andreas remarked, "It's hard for all of us, but we will all be making more money than we ever dreamed possible, and once you've got the boys trained, you would be able to take a trip somewhere. It would do you all the world of good!"

Returning to the office, Andreas attempted a start on the conveyancing case in hand, but finding it difficult to concentrate on the poor man's plight, he was relieved when Becky entered the office with a mug of coffee, and explaining the case to her, he said, "I just don't know where to begin, it's such a mess!" "Why don't you start at the beginning?" She suggested, "The problem seems to have arisen by the building society's omission, in *not* explaining how such mortgages work. It would seem on the face of it, that all they were interested in was getting his signature on the paper, and perhaps your client would be better advised in passing it to the ombudsman?" Andreas replied with a sigh, "The only problem with that, is that the termination date has already passed, so he has to sell quickly, before the property is repossessed. The only way that I can buy time is to apply to the mortgage providers for an extension of the settlement date, which *could* give the ombudsman time to work a miracle, I'll be in tomorrow, so I'll see what Viv's thoughts are, and thank you for your help Becky!" Picking up his notes, he put them into his briefcase, and picking up the boys from school, he informed them that Uncle Viv wanted to see them at the office the following day. Victor asked instantly, "What about the farm daddi?" "I've seen Uncle Michael!" Andreas answered, "And he's given you the day off, providing you go in, and make up for lost time on Sunday!" Victor replied with a puzzled frown, "What does he want to see us about?" Andreas informed him, "You'll find out soon enough in the morning, but don't worry, you've done nothing wrong!"

In the morning, George could hardly contain himself, while Victor was his usual implacable self, and even Lu was up and about up early, having Rosie washed and dressed before they left for the office. "You're up early sweetheart?" Andreas remarked. "Yeah!" "I thought I'd do a bit of shopping!" So *still* no mention of the driving test, and when he arrived at the office with the boys, slightly later than the appointed time, he found that, true to form, Viv was conspicuous by his absence, meaning that the poor little buggers were going to be kept on tenterhooks for considerably longer, than he would have wished. Seeking to assuage the boys' concerns of the meeting, Andreas took them into his office, straight away noticing flowers, and a card arrayed on his chair. Viv apologised for being late as soon as he came in, but propelling him brutishly into *his* office, Andreas roared angrily, "Viv, I will tolerate you messing *me* about, but don't you *ever* do that to my children again!" "I'm sorry Andreas, but it was a genuine delay. The car wouldn't start, and I had to ring Gunnar to come out and sort the problem. You had already left, so there was no way of letting you know. Ask Gunnar, he'll tell you!" "Well okay, but I'm really not happy about it!" Much chastened Viv asserted, "Right then, you'd better ask them to come in. Will you be sitting in?" Nodding curtly, *Andreas* left to collect the boys.

"Okay boys, you must be wondering what this is all about!" Viv began, "And I won't beat about the bush. I'd like you both to come and work for the firm!" The boys looked at each other in amazement, Viv continued, "You will be aware, I'm sure, of the success of the cider project, and we have decided to build a bigger plant, so your Uncle Michael, who is blender for the company, feels that it may be too much for him to cope alone, and he has expressed a wish that you boys learn the arts of blending, under his tuition. It is a specialised art, and the blend has to be just right, so tutelage will be time-consuming, and you will *both* have to fit it in with working at the farm!" George's eyes almost bulged out of their sockets. Never in his wildest dreams did he ever imagine that he would work at the farm with his brother, let alone be trained for a grown-up's job. Viv continued, "You will be paid for the farm-work as well as the tuition, and if you agree, we will open a savings account for you at the firm's bank, and being employees of this firm, you would no longer be paid by the farm!" Andreas, now somewhat calmer, had the thought that he could *not* have put it any better, and ever the pragmatic, Victor asked, "How *much* will we be paid?" "If you look on the desk!" Viv replied, "You will find a sheet of paper in front of you, with all the details of pay and conditions. It is a fair day's pay for a fair day's work, and is *not* just pocket money. Read the paper, and if you agree to what is on offer, put your signature in the space provided, but if you need time to think it over, please don't be afraid to ask!" Victor solemnly read *every* word before signing, while George, not needing time to read, signed immediately.

Andreas asked the boys to wait in his office, and Viv asked, "I suppose you'll be taking them home now?" "Maybe not, I need advice on the conveyancing case, and don't forget that Lu's taking her test this morning, so hopefully we may have a surprise visitor this morning!" Andreas returned to his office, remarking to his two sons, "Well boys, you are now working for a living. How does that feel?" In unison they shouted, "Great!" Clearing the desk of all the clutter, and replacing the chaos with the cards and flowers. George asked, "Are they for us dad?" "No son!" Andreas answered, "You'll soon see who they're for!" And fortunately, they did not have to wait too long for the intended recipient, as Lu was ushered into the office by Becky, with Lu *not* looking best pleased at her husband's acquisition of such an attractive young woman, and with pursed lips, she watched Becky closely as she left the room. Her mood changed however as soon as she noticed the display on the desk, and smiling she asked, "How did you know?" "Do you think that you're the *only* one who can see the future!" He answered with a grin, but not wishing to tarnish her moment of glory, he confessed, "Actually I cannot lie. It was Vee who inadvertently let it slip!" "Well it's a lovely surprise, do you think that your secretary could make coffee for me?" Adding, "Or is she just for decoration?" Andreas smiled at the sarcasm, "I'm sure she will!" Andreas went straight away to Becky's office, explaining that the coffee was for his wife, and mentioning with a wink, "She takes it extra sweet!" Two minutes later, Becky placed a steaming mug of coffee in front of her boss's wife, and not waiting for approbation, she silently returned to her office. Lu sipped the coffee, being quite prepared to spit the brew straight back into the mug with disgust, but instead her eyebrows lifted in appreciation, and as she drained the mug, Andreas appreciated that Becky had made a friend for life.

19

Andreas asked, "Could *you* take the boys home love. I have a problem here that I'm hoping Viv can help with, but it should *only* take an hour or so?" "Well don't be *too* long babe!" She replied, "I promised Ma we'd call in later!" Picking up the cards and flowers, she kissed him gently on the lips, and herded the boys towards the door. "What's this problem you need to discuss?" Viv asked from the doorway, and being told the details of the case, he replied, "I'm assuming there was no endowment policy in place. Why was that?" "He alleges that he was never actually advised to have a policy, with the *whole* thing not being explained fully to him, and he just assumed that the money he paid monthly, was being deducted from the amount loaned!" "Well I think that applying for a stay of execution *is* the way forward, and you are correct, there *would* be a case for the ombudsman. Whether or not he will get anywhere with it, is another matter, but securing an extension to the settlement date, *would* give him more time to sell, *should* the ombudsman thing be a no-goer, and *hopefully* he'll get a price that would clear off the amount. It would seem, on the face of it, that there's little else you can do, but do not *bank* on the ombudsman, getting a reasonable extension is the way to go, and as the market is quite buoyant at the moment, he does have a chance. Is he living at the property?" "No, he has a tenant!" Andreas answered, to which Viv remarked, "Well at least your client will have somewhere to rest his head, even if the poor bugger he's renting to, will not. So the answer is yes, you would be right to advise this course of action, and realistically your options are limited in what you can do!" Rising from his desk, he suggested, "If that's all, perhaps we could have a spot of lunch before you return to your domestic duties?" "That would be great!" Andreas replied, adding with a grin, "And I do believe it's your turn to pay Mister Bailey, but I'd better ring Lu, or she'll be sat waiting for me to accompany her to Ma's, and I don't want to miss the opportunity of you treating me to a meal!"

There was a new chef at the Green Man, and apparently lasagne was no longer an option, so Andreas made do with a medium rare fillet, that came absolutely nowhere near to being even on a par, with the fare that he and Reuben enjoyed so much in Melbourne. He thought light-heartedly that if he wanted a decent meal, he would have to purchase the place, and import his favourite chef from Oz. Convinced that he would capture not only local trade, but from miles around too. Viv asked, "Penny for your thoughts?" Andreas smiled, and related his whimsical idea. Viv replied, "Well you can certainly afford it, but you would have to make it a condition that Golden Valley Cider is sold there. Is this place up for sale then?" Andreas shrugged, and shook his head, "I don't think so, I was just fantasising really, but maybe if I make them an offer they can't refuse, who knows!" Viv laughed declaring, "Go for it Andreas, you haven't purchased new property in a while!" Andreas commented, "I was only joking really, but if you're serious I *could* explore the possibility, but on the other hand, perhaps I should look for somewhere less expensive to buy, and build up the trade. It would be great to get my teeth into something again, but I've got enough on my plate at the moment with this mortgage thing, and of course the cider business!"

He found however, that as the day progressed, he could not get the idea out of his head, and talking it over with Lu when he arrived home from lunch, he found that she was all for the idea. Even suggesting that he could look around town later for something more suitable, as long as she could accompany him, and even though it had not *seriously* entered his mind, he was certain that Ma and Pa would relish the opportunity to look after the kids for a few hours, giving *them* the opportunity of a night out together. The lump at the front would determine her abstinence, but that would *not* necessarily have to hamper *him,* and believing that it was no use letting the grass grow under his feet, he rang Ma to see if they would baby-sit. Lu was very much up for a night on the town, and booking the Priory for a night's stay, he decided to drive into town himself, and let Lu drive home in the morning, which would enable Lu to imbibe, *I hope she appreciates my altruism,* but somehow doubting that fact, he thought, *she can be an ungrateful little mare at times.* It had been some time since he had seen Eric, and Andreas was looking forward to renewing old acquaintances. Ringing Viv and Gunnar to see if they would be interested in joining them for a *quiet* night in town, he arranged to meet them in the Red Cow, another hostelry which he had neglected to visit of late. Perhaps they could pop in the Friend in Need, and enjoy a game of dominoes with their two elderly friends. He realized all of a sudden that his whimsical notion of buying the Green

Man, was now paying unexpected dividends, with Lu in fact, being over the moon at the prospect of a night out, getting ready, hours before the proposed gathering. Her husband meanwhile, was lounging on the settee, watching television with the kids, and only just about remembering to call his parents to arrange a sleep-over, as *they* would now be staying overnight at the Priory Hotel. Everything was set fair for a great evening, and an hour before they were due to meet at the Red Cow, Andreas *began* his ablutions, roping in Victor to get Rosie ready for bed, while he luxuriated under the spray. And while her lady-ship was putting the finishing touches to her coiffure, he rang the rest of the family, to ask if they would join them too, unfortunately getting no reply from Guaril after three attempts. Slipping on his blue blazer, he looked in the wardrobe mirror, and admiring his still boyish figure, he thought, *by Christ, she's a lucky woman having a handsome bugger like me.* "Look lively Lu, the baby-sitters will be here any minute!" And making her grand entrance into the living room in seconds, she wore a long, diaphanous pale blue evening dress, *indiscreetly* accommodating the bulge, but with her hair piled high in a bouffant style, she looked stunning. "Wow, you look fabulous Lu, but for God's sake don't stand where the light can shine through that dress, the world will see what you had for breakfast!" The baby-sitters arrived on time, and Lu decided that *she* would drive into town, and feeling a little on edge about it, Andreas was *not* looking forward to the experience of her driving to town. He found however, that her prowess was impressive, boding well for future jaunts, particularly when parking the car adroitly, in the scarcely adequate space, in front of Walthaar's flat.

Strolling to the Red Cow, they found most of the gang already in evidence, and as soon as Walthaar and his latest love had joined them, the troupe was complete, then after a couple of *swifties* under their belts, they were soon under way for the Friend in Need, where Andreas immediately asking the whereabouts of his erstwhile, domino playing friends. Being informed by the barman of their demise, "Sadly they both passed away a few months ago. One of the old gents passed away on Friday, and the other the following Tuesday!" Andreas shook his head and murmured sadly, "I'm sorry to hear that, did they have families?" "No sir, they were both single gentlemen, and I believe they were related in some way, cousins I believe!" Having just the one drink, the next port of call was the Priory, and hearing the jukebox, before turning the corner into the street, the girls immediately went into party mode. This state of affairs unfortunately portending, that Gunnar would have to keep a vigilant eye on Pearl, who was wont to be over familiar with men when she had been drinking, and even when she had not. A fair crowd had gathered, even though it was still relatively early, and spotting them at the bar, Eric made his way across, and being genuinely pleased to see them all, he asked if they were up for a *stop-on* drink later. Andreas replied, "Lu and I are booked in here for the night anyway, and with the rest all living local, we *could* be up for it!" "Business must be good Eric!" Andreas commented, "You've a good crowd in?" Eric shrugged and sighed, "I've got a new band playing tonight, so it's not too bad, but with overheads, it barely pays me to open, even Saturdays are not *that* great. If I could find someone stupid enough to buy the place, I'd sell up and cut my losses!" Having glanced briefly at Viv, Andreas remarked to Eric,

"If you're serious, I could be in a position to throw you a life-line. I have a client who *could* be interested in buying, so if Viv and I could come in to see you during the week, we could discuss it!" Eric replied, "Oh I'm serious all right, pop in on Wednesday. It won't do any harm to, at least *listen* to your client's offer!" Andreas averred, "Don't do *anything* until you've seen us. Now let's forget about business for a while and get down to some serious drinking!"

Andreas noticed Guaril and Barbara walking into the bar, carrying the band's equipment, provoking the thought, *Barbara's son must be performing here tonight, so I don't think we'll be going anywhere else, especially with a stop on, at the end of the night!* Guaril walked across as soon as he noticed the family sitting at a table, hugging them all in turn. Den and Barbara smiled and waved, then continued setting up the speakers, until looking at the clock Den called over, "Come on then Gary, let's get the show on the road!" Andreas thought, *Gary eh, that's a new one,* noticing Guaril strapping on a twelve string. Barbara stood ready at the keyboard, and with her son strapping on one of his array of guitars, they began to play after the customary count of three. With the trio taking turns at singing, and playing the various instruments, they covered a wide spectrum of genres, and at the end of the first half, they received a standing ovation. "Bravo, that was marvellous!" Lu declared, when the stars of the show came to sit with them, and Andreas asked, "What's with this Gary business then!" Guaril's face reddened, "Oh that's a kind of stage name, they call me Cider Gary, because that's all I ever drink!" Laughing, Andreas suggested, "You should try our Home Farm cider, that Michael, myself and Viv are churning out. It's a new concept of producing cider in hermetically sealed containers, and even if I do say so myself, the blend is even better than the old farmer's. I'll bring some over when I can find time!" Den rose from the table, and with the band dutifully following him to the stage, they launched into the second half, with a medley of rock legends that brought the house down once more, moving Andreas to muse, *I wonder if they need a manager?* The end of the show came, and with the band going on to another venue on the other side of the county, *Gary* kissed his family goodnight, and left with his retinue. The bar gradually began to empty, and although it was an *invitation* only stop-on, the clientele were loath to leave, but after an hour, everyone, except the *bona fide* had quit the premises, but after one more round of drinks, they too decided that enough was enough, with everyone leaving in high spirits, and with the surviving couple also deciding to call it a day, it left Eric and his band of workers to wash the glasses, and sweep up. Being buoyed by the amount of drink he had quaffed, Andreas put his hand up Lu's dress as she walked up the stairs in front of him, and suddenly laughing, he exclaimed, "You mischievous little minx, you've got no bloody drawers on, and I am gonna make you pay big time for *that*!" He made love to his heavily pregnant, but highly receptive wife into the wee hours, and rising somewhat later, the hot-blooded pair took advantage of the absence of an operable shower, by sharing a bath, *purely* for the sake of water conservation of course. But thrashing about in the throes of passion, a fair amount of the economised water ended up on the floor anyway, thereby *nullifying* their good intentions for the preservation of the world.

Eating a good sized breakfast, albeit it almost lunch time, they returned to the room to make ready for the return journey, and making their way once more down the steep, rickety staircase to the bar, Andreas shook Eric's hand, and telling him that he would ring mid-week to discuss the matter they had touched on the previous evening, he cited the fact that there were figures that needed checking, before tabling an offer on behalf of his client. Waving goodbye as they left, they returned to the car and once they were under way, Lu asked, "Will you make an offer?" "It's likely!" He replied, "What *sort* of offer will depend on the ifs and buts of what our checks show. The building is a few hundred years old, and *if* it's a listed building, we wouldn't be able to make the alterations, that would be mandatory for turning the place into a going concern. If it is *not* listed, I have to consider if the building is in a fit enough state to allow alterations at *all,* plus with the trade being so poor, bar prices would have to be lowered to encourage trade, and *if* I did take over, would it be viable? I'm not so sure. The whole scheme is fraught with hidden dangers, and it would be folly making a hasty decision!" Arriving home, Ma helped Lu prepare dinner, with Andreas and Pa managing a few Tolley's, in between attempting to curb Rosie's, non-stop racing around the house, screaming for all she was worth, in stark contrast to the way that *they* had been raised, with both Ma and Pa being very much down on that sort of riotous behaviour, but with her grandparents now well past the first flush of youth, Rosie had become a law unto herself. Being relieved by the first call for dinner, Andreas filled two pint glasses of the new cider, from a keg that he had stashed in the cellar, and sipping slowly at the pale yellow ambrosia, savouring each drop of the carefully blended liquid, while waiting for dinner to be served. Pa declared, "I reckon this stuff, is even better than the old man's brew, and you tell that our boys are learning the trade from Michael. If they do half as well this stuff, they would be doing well!" "Until Michael explained that it was all in the blending!" Andreas told Pa, "I had no idea, that there was so much involved in brewing, but I'll tell you this much right now, that our boys will surpass, anything that's *ever* been brewed!" Being well aware that it was the Tolley's and cider chasers doing the talking, the boys were grinning from ear to ear nonetheless, at the plaudits, being hurled their way. Andreas, advised his sons, "Mind now boys, not a word to anyone about this. People get jealous, and the last thing we want, is to alienate our future customers!" Pa interrupted, "Here son, any more cider in that barrel?" Andreas was quickly coming to the conclusion that Pa had developed a more than passing fancy for the brew, but as it could prove to be an inducement in securing, regular baby sitting, he said nothing. Thankfully Ma dragged Pa home, before he could completely drain the barrel, and with Rosie still in hyperactive mode, due no doubt to her grandparents' indulgence the previous evening, Andreas decided that a little extra brandy in her milk, was called for. But getting almost caught in the act, by his ever-loving, he was not able to administer the full intended dosage, *oh well*, he thought, crossing the fingers of both hands, *here goes for nothing*. Later in the evening, Lu suggested another bath together, to which he replied, "You horny little mare, and who is gonna mop up the carpet?" "I never thought of that!" Lu replied. Adding coyly with a mischievous pout, "And I've been looking forward to that all day!" Lifting one eyebrow, Andreas responded hastily, "I'll see about getting the bathroom tiled, first thing tomorrow!" Peeping in on Rosie, he found her laying across the bed, with her feet up the wall, fast asleep, and having righted, and covered his princess with her pink blanket, he thought, *there must have been enough tranquillising liquid in her drink after all.* With the boys also succumbing to sleep early, the house was peaceful and quiet enough for an extended session of debauchery, and in the wee hours, just before dawn, he murmured to his comatose, unresponsive wife, "Hey, crossing your fingers *really* works!"

With a mountain of work to get through at the office the next day, he set off early for a change, deciding en route, that the first task to be addressed would be that of the poor fellow whose mortgage situation was giving such grave concerns. And finding the man waiting in reception, as he passed through the doorway, Andreas told him, "Give me five minutes, and I'll be with you!" As usual coffee was waiting on his desk, and after hanging up his coat, he buzzed Becky to bring coffee for his client. *Determined* to do his utmost for the Roma, come hell or high water, he sipped his coffee, and called in his client, with the interview beginning, as soon as the coffee was placed in front of the overwrought man. Putting on his most sympathetic face, Andreas told his client, "I have to tell you in all honestly, that the situation is not good!" Then pausing for a quick slurp, he added, "What I propose, is to apply for an extension as near to the settlement date as possible, and also bring the case to the attention of the ombudsman, which would likely take about three months to resolve. I'm hoping that the two courses of action will coincide with the extension, but the key to it all, is that it is imperative, we get that settlement date extended, as the property will take at *least* three months to sell, if all else fails. The decision is yours of course, but I *have* to inform you, that there is little else that can be done, but *that* is my advice!" "I trust your advice. It has been good so far Krallis. We'll go for the extension and ombudsman!" Andreas responded instantly, "Right then, the extension will be applied for this morning, and you should get a decision in about two weeks time. The ombudsman will send you a form to fill in, so you will *have* to dig out your mortgage agreement and deeds. You will probably need help filling in the form, so as soon as you receive it, bring the form here, and we'll go through it together!" Realizing the man's Roma roots, by his use of the name with which he had recently, and unfortunately acquired, Andreas paused for a moment, then asked, "Would you mind *not* keep calling me Krallis!" "That is what *everyone* calls you, and you've gotta realize that now, you'll always be known as the Krallis, for as long as you live!" Andreas replied with a smile, "It looks as if I'll have to get used to it then, but do *not* forget to bring in that form as soon as you receive it!" As soon as the man had left the building, he delegated Becky to apply for the mortgage extension form to be sent to his home, and deal with minutiae as soon as possible, while he delved into the machinations of his soon to be property

20

Knocking *on* Viv's door, Andreas walked in uninvited, "How would I find out if a building is listed or not?" "I can see it was a waste of time and money enrolling you on a course, *and* purchasing a computer?" Considering himself chastened, but enlightened, he walked off to Becky's office, and having accessed all the relative information in five minutes flat, he absolved his lack of nous, by patting himself on the back, after all it *had* pretty much been his suggestion to purchase the machine, *if* you discounted Becky's input. Discovering that The Priory Hotel was *not* a listed building, a surveyor's visit was hastily arranged at the hotel, for two days hence, realizing that he needed the green light for the intended extension to the kitchen, which was a must-have, for *other* ideas that he had in mind. Ringing Ted, he arranged to meet him at the hotel in the early afternoon, to begin assessing *everything* that needed to be done, and of course, the cost. Andreas suddenly began to have doubts about the viability of the project, and confiding his fears toViv, who instantly reminded him that everything they had ever undertaken, had been a gamble of one kind or another. He pointed out, that his instinct had always paid dividends in the past, and there was no reason to suppose that this project would be any different. With his confidence having now been restored, he related the morning's conveyancing issues, and informing his colleague of his impending visit to the Priory, Viv had a sudden notion, "I've got nothing important on this afternoon, I'll go with you!"

Having been a paying guest, Andreas knew that the rooms would leave much to be desired, and fearing that the costs would be astronomical, he walked into the hotel with a face like a hung dog. Beginning the inspection at the top of the building, they noticed immediately that the ceiling above the passageway had a damp patch, a problem that could be fixed by the acquisition of a new roof, which he had allowed for in his calculations, and being certain that he could get a council grant for *that*, he dismissed the matter as peripheral. With the full examination over, Ted took the paper with the figures from the clip-board, handing them straight over to Andreas, "There is a fair bit that needs doing, but luckily nothing major. The building is in excellent condition considering it's age, but it will take a tidy wedge, to bring it up to anywhere near the five-star standard that you envisaged. Don't be too down-hearted though, we *can* do it, but it won't be overnight, and it won't be cheap. Structural changes are not too much of a problem, but things like new baths and showers will cost you a fair bit. You'll save a few bob by getting *us* to do *everything*, but if I were you, I'd show that list to the guv'nor, and get a few bar off the asking price!" Andreas commented, "Thanks Ted, I'll keep what you say in mind, and let you know about the work as soon as possible!" Leaving the Priory, Andreas and Viv returned to the office, with Andreas speculating, "If we can pinch the weekday trade from the other pub/diners, it would give us a basis for other ideas I have in mind, but the first thing we would have to do is drop the price of beer, in order to draw the trade in, and once we have them coming through the door, the new décor, and excellent cuisine, will ensure a regular clientele. I've got big plans, that I reckon sadly, will signal the end our cafe, and having seen the figures recently, it's only just about holding it's own anyway. If the pub takes off as well as I anticipate, the cafe would never be able compete!" Viv asked, "It sounds as if you have *already* decided to put in an offer, but assuming that you something else in mind for the cafe, you have to be aware, you would never be able to sell it as a business?" Andreas answered, knowing that he *had* indeed decided to take the gamble, "If the price of the hotel is reasonable enough, I could offset a huge chunk of it by converting the cafe building into two maisonettes!" Weighing up the pros and cons once more, and deciding to take a punt on his plans, he suggested, "If it *were* possible to bring over the chef from Melbourne, it would swing *everything* in my favour, he *really* is that good, and *yes* I *have* decided to take a chance!" Viv was all for it, "I think it'll be a great little earner, once it's up and running, and if it *should* fail, the land is ideal for re-development, being right in the middle of town, and as such would bring in a pretty penny by selling!" "Exactly my thoughts!" Andreas remarked, "But as long as we keep bar prices reasonably low, and the food up to a high standard, I'm convinced that we will be onto a winner. It'll be just what this town needs, somewhere in the town centre, where you could eat and drink at reasonable prices!" Viv remarked, "If this Aussie chef is as good as you say, why don't you send for him!" Andreas agreed, "I'll phone him tomorrow!" Viv looked at him in disgust, averring, "If I have to mention that bloody computer again, I'll be in danger of being labelled a nag!" Andreas sent the message, then left to deliver the cafeteria's death sentence to Carol Ellis, and on arrival at the eatery, he was glad of the fact that there was only a handful of customers in the place, and pointedly changed the door-sign to CLOSED. When the last customer had left, he locked the door, and straight away Carol asked, "What's this all about Andreas?" He replied, "I'm not going to beat about the bush Carol, I'm closing the cafe, for good!" Her face dropped, and he continued, "The good news is that I'm opening a new hotel, and will need someone diligent and trustworthy to run the place, and I'm offering the post to you. It will entail more hours, but would prove more satisfying than running a small cafe, and you would only be required to manage the hotel and bar, as I am sending for a chef from Melbourne. There will be two flats at the hotel for both you and the chef, the wages will be top whack with no over-heads. I don't expect an answer immediately, but I *would* like to know before the end of the week!" Still looking somewhat shell-shocked, she asked, "Andreas, just what is all this *I* business?" He smiled and explaining his role in the matter, he told her, "I'm sorry Carol, but I own this cafe, lock, stock and barrel, along with various other properties, and have done for almost as long as you have known me. I should have told you before, but I was a student, still living at home, and it would have been an unnecessary diversion if people knew that *I* was the owner!" She laughed out loud declaring, "So technically, I have slept with my boss. In the past of course!" Andreas rose from the table slightly embarrassed and smiling, he said, "This is an ideal opportunity for us both, it will not be happening, over-night, but it *is* in the very near future!" As he walked back into the street he thought, *I think I will have made a very good choice, if she accepts*!

Viv was in total agreement with the choice, "She is the *ideal* choice. Er have we had a reply from Melbourne yet?" Andreas answered, "I haven't had time to look, but I think Becky would have told me if we had. Let's leave it for now, I'm tired, and I want to go home, so I'll see you in the morning!" He drove home with a fair bit occupying his mind, but as soon as he entered the front door his mind relaxed, knowing now what he was going to do, *and* exactly how he would be conducting the negotiations with Eric. When the kids had all gone to bed, he discussed the matter with Lu, knowing that she would be one hundred percent behind him, whatever he did. He was focussed enough on the matter to ring Viv, and inform him of the decision, omitting to tell him how *much* he would offer. "Good!" He stated, suggesting, "We'll see Eric tomorrow, *if* we're not too busy doing our proper jobs!" Andreas felt as though a load had been taken from his shoulders, and putting Ted's list, the surveyors report and a pile of blank sheets of paper, to make it look as though he had more information than he actually had, into his battered old briefcase, he rang the Priory to arrange a meeting for ten thirty.

As was the norm for them, Andreas and Viv purposely arrived a few minutes later than the appointed time, and being met at the door by Eric, they were ushered into the ground-floor living quarters, and with his wife making herself scarce, they were left in peace to discuss the possible sale of their home. Handing over a facsimile of Ted's list, Andreas waited until Eric had read the bad news then commented, "You can see that the outlay for bringing the old place up to scratch, runs into tens of thousands, and we have been assured that the extension for a new kitchen will be double that figure, so unless a reasonable compromise on the price can be reached, there will be no deal. Being aware that the hotel has been allowed to become, shall we say run down somewhat, and *if* our client does *not* buy, you would be forced to re-mortgage, just to bring everything up to scratch in order to make it more saleable, plunging you even deeper into the mire. I have to tell you that the offer will probably not come up to your expectations, *but* you will be paid fully in cash. What you do with the money would be your concern, but off the record, I would *not* put it into your bank, and handing him another facsimile, "Here is the surveyor's report, which also does not make good reading!" Eric read the report, and shaking his head, he commented, "I thought you were a mate!" Andreas replied stonily, "Not here and not today!" Eric replied wearily, "You seem to have me over a barrel, and I realize now that I should have had my solicitor here, but I did not expect an offer to be made today!" Andreas handed him another slip of paper with the offer written on it, "I suggest that you show this to your solicitor, and we want an answer before the weekend, *or* I can assure you that the offer will be retracted completely. The offer is non-negotiable, and the *only* one that you will receive from our client!" Andreas shook Eric's hand as he left, more as a gesture than anything else, and Viv asserted, as Andreas threw his briefcase into the rear of the car, "I have to say that you handled that pretty well. I'm impressed. What did you offer?" "Fifty!" Andreas replied. Viv laughed, suggesting, "He'll never go for *that*, it's worth more than treble that!" Andreas remarked, "Didn't you notice the suitcases in the corner of the room, it's my guess that they are already packed, ready to do a runner, and as soon as he gets cash in his hand, he'll be long gone. He *will* agree, then in a week's time, we can make a start. The money that I make from the two maisonettes will pay for the hotel, so it won't have cost me a damn thing, plus the fact that most of the alterations will be paid by grants from the council!" "Got it all sewn up pretty quickly haven't you?" Viv observed. Andreas smiled, "I'm a quick learner!"

Spending the rest of the day, and the following morning trying to persuade the bank to let him have fifty thousand pounds cash of his own money, he finally swung things his way, by threatening to withdraw *all* funds, and deposit them with another bank. One hour later, after stashing five large white envelopes into his briefcase, he returned to the office, and having been back for half an hour the phone rang. Answering the call, Viv made arrangements for a meeting with Eric that afternoon, and with work continuing in the usual way, they had an early lunch, courtesy of the chippie, with a fresh, cheeky-faced young woman serving the appetizing repast, and Andreas idly wondered if Walthaar had managed to get *her* between his sheets yet. When the meal had been washed down with unlaced coffee, he prepared himself for the confrontation by dousing his hands and face in cold water.

Entering the hotel with the briefcase full of cash, Andreas and Viv did not receive the same cordial reception afforded the previous day, with Eric snarling disparagingly, "We have decided to accept your *kind* offer!" Unlocking his briefcase, Andreas handed over the envelopes advising, "It would be best to count it, you just never know with banks these days!" "Oh I'll count it all right!" Eric growled, "Just in case you may try to steal even more money from me!" Andreas retorted sarcastically, "That's not a nice way to talk to an old friend!" Turning his back on the former landlord, Andreas left Viv and Eric's solicitors to sort out the paperwork, and walking across the road to the railway station he purchased a carton of milk, not trusting British Rail coffee. Taking a good long swig, he threw the remains of the carton into the litter bin, and returned to the hotel to sign several dotted lines. Eric's face dropped a mile when he realised the connotations of Andreas signing the documents, and he snarled, "You didn't tell me that it was yourself buying the place, you bloody Judas!" Answering the remark with like, Andreas replied, "Think yourself lucky I didn't claim ten percent discount for cash!" Suspecting the outcome of any altercation with Andreas, Eric allowed himself to be restrained, then slumped into a chair, while the two colleagues, partners and friends, returned to the office in silence. Andreas remarked as they sat in Viv's inner sanctum, "Well *that* went without a hitch, and although I *was* confident, I did not think it would go quite so smoothly!"

Eric left the hotel later that night taking all his possessions, and of course the five large, white envelopes, leaving his wife still asleep in their bed. She rang the office in the morning, tearfully apprising Andreas of the position, and believing that it *could* work out to his advantage, he told her that she could stay on at the hotel, until the new manageress took over. After coffee, Andreas rang Mister Smythe to inform him that his team would be required to design a kitchen extension at the hotel, and two maisonettes from the framework of the cafe, then arranging a lunchtime meeting with Ted to discuss all the work, he considered that all was now in place. Immediately beginning to catch up on all the case work that he had neglected in his haste to get the hotel purchase up completed, he discovered that the mortgage company involved with the hapless Romany *had* been in contact, and had agreed to extension of six months. He had not seen the man since applying for the extension, but ten minutes before he was due to leave for the meeting with Ted, the man turned up, looking for help in completing the ombudsman's form. "John!" Andreas declared, "I've got a meeting in the Green Man in ten minutes time, can you come back around two o'clock this afternoon?" John's face dropped, "I've got to pick up a load of scrap this afternoon, I'll call in tomorrow instead!" Perceiving the disappointment on his face Andreas suggested, "Look John, why don't you join us for lunch, *if* you have time?" His face lit up, "Do you mean a proper sit-down meal. *Dordi dordi*, what a proper gent you are Krallis, and no mistake!" Wincing once again at the constant usage of his newly acquired title, he ushered the man into the street. Andreas turned up for the meeting accompanied by the redoubtable John, and with the form being completed before the meal arrived, Ted and John obviously knowing each other of old, began reminiscing of the old times. Andreas interrupted the nostalgia by saying that he wanted to get the matter of the conversion sewn up as soon as possible. Ted replied, "Sorry Andreas we are just relatives, reliving the past. Right then, I hope you realise that it will involve sub-contracting, to have both conversion sites completed in time, and each lasting two or three months, it will cost a pretty penny!" Andreas asked, "Does that include the time needed to *demolish* the cafe?" Ted answered, "That is *everything* included, and there will be no need to worry about the disposal of the scrap and debris. John here is the answer to that particular problem!" John told Andreas, "Krallis, I am your man, you need have no further worries on that score, I will get rid of *everything*!" John looked at the clock and remarked, "I'll have to leave you gents" I've got scrap to pick up, and thank you Krallis for helping me with the form, *and* for the nosh!" Andreas watched as he disappeared through the door and smiled, "I wish they'd all stop this Krallis business!" Ted said, "The people love and trust you Andreas. Don't be offended by it, they mean it in the nicest possible way!" Ted suggested that it would be better to apply for planning permission for both projects at the same time, "Better to get it all done at once, you know where you are then!" He stood up, shook Andreas's hand, and as he was leaving he said, "You'll have no worries about John Scamp disposing of the scrap, he's a good man, it's just a pity he can't keep his dick in his trousers!" Looking down at the form, Andreas read the signature. J.Scamp, and realizing with incredulity that the man he had just been having lunch with, could conceivably be his father, he sat back in his seat stunned.

After the kids had gone to bed Andreas told Lu of the machinations of the purchase of the hotel and, shaking her head in disbelief, she scolded him, "How could you treat Eric like that?" "If the roles had been resolved!" Andreas said, "He would have done exactly the same, and don't waste your sympathy on him, he's buggered off with the money, leaving his wife in the lurch, but fortunately for her, I've allowed her to stay at the hotel, and work the bar, until the new management takes over!" Being silent for a few moments, Andreas wore a worried frown, and Lu asked, "Come on then, out with it, what's eating away at you, whatever it is, it cannot possibly be pangs of guilt!" He smiled at the slight, and slowly revealed, "I might have had lunch with my biological father today!" She sat up bolt upright, and turned to face him, "How on earth did that happen?" He told her the saga of how John Scamp had come to be at the meeting, and she commented, "What a strange and wonderful coincidence, if he *is* your father. Do you think that he knows?" Andreas replied, "I wouldn't think so, he keeps calling me Krallis!" "Will you *tell* him?" She asked. "Actually Lu!" He responded, "I'm not entirely sure of how to play this, and I think that just for now, I *won't* mention it. After all it's not a hundred percent that he is, although my intuition tells me that he *is,* but I *will* have to mention it to Viv, in case it's not ethical to represent your own father. The only problem is that our people have set me up as a sort of king, and would not trust anyone else, so if Viv feels that it is *not* right, I would have to do all the work, and turn it over to him to finalise!" She suggested, "There's little else you can do love. It's a strange situation, but by the sounds of it, one that you don't have to deal with straight away. How do you feel about it?" "I'm not sure, but if his case is *not* resolved favourably, I will help him in some way nonetheless, whether I reveal my identity to him or not!" She laughed, "Come on big boy, let's go to bed, and I'll help you forget all about it, well for a couple of minutes anyway!" *And as always, he did as he was told.*

Deciding the following morning to keep the boys dry by driving them to school, he posted John Scamp's ombudsman application, inexplicably kissing the envelope before pushing it into the box. And desperately needing that particular problem to be resolved as soon as possible, he organised an estate agent to put the property on the market. Coincidentally, the source of his interest dropped by later in the morning to ask when the cafe was being developed, and telling him that he'd had no word of when the conversions would be starting so far, Andreas informed him that he would let him know when there *was* work for him, also informing him that *he* would have to go to the estate agents, to sign papers enabling him to get the property on the market. John left immediately, and Andreas walked to the window, watching a man cross the road, who was in all likelihood his father.

Feeling mentally drained, having had a busy few days one way or another, he went to Viv's office for a chat and explaining everything to him, he asked if there *would* be any ethical problem involved. Viv told him that there would not necessarily be any problem, even *if* the client was indeed his father, "It sounds to me as if you need a weekend away somewhere, Go to the travel agents, and see what they have to offer, but the boys would obviously not be able to go, they're *far* too busy at the moment!" Andreas thought for a moment and agreed, "That *is* a good idea, although the boys will definitely not be pleased!" Viv suggested, "Don't worry, they'll be fine at Ma's, and *I'll* make sure that they're too busy to miss you!" Immediately ringing Lu to see what she thought of the idea, and finding that she was all for it, he asserted, "I'll book it now, and fill up the car on my way home!" Walking to the travel agents in the square, he booked up and paid cash, thereby obtaining the usual reasonable discount, and returning to the office, he found that the IN tray had been filled in his absence, and pushing it aside, he rang Ma, to find if it was okay for her to have the boys, and rung Lu immediately after, to inform her of the destination. Applying himself diligently, he succeeded in filling the out-tray by the end of the working day, and filling the car at the garage, Gunnar strolled over and enquired, "What's afoot, you don't usually fill up on a Thursday?" Andreas told him, "Your sister, myself and Rosie are going to Brean Sands for a long weekend!" Gunnar remarked, not for the first time, nor certainly the last, "You cheapskate bastard, all the money *you've* got, and you're going *there,* and I'll *bet* you got a discount!" Andreas remarked with a smile, "Of course, and we're going there *because* it's not too far away. Lu is all for it, so don't knock it!" "Ah well, enjoy yourselves, and if it's any good, I might count my pennies to see if *I've* got enough for a couple of days!" Andreas hung the nozzle back on the pump, and suggested, "Maybe I'll take Ma and Pa next time, *they* could do with a break!" "They'd love that!" Gunnar conceded, "As far as I can recall, they've never been to the seaside. Come to think of it, none of us have, and just imagine that, all the resorts around us, and we've never seen the sea, how weird is that?"

21

Friday morning arrived and with the boys having already been dropped off at the school gate, with strict instructions that they must *not* be late arriving at Ma and Pa's after school, Andreas began packing his case, the second he arrived back at the house. Lu had already filled a case to excess with her and Rosie's *essentials*, so as soon as breakfast had been finished, the girls boarded the car, leaving the pack-horse, that was Andreas Bosworth, to stow the cases in the boot. Exacting the task with a sarcastic smile, he mused, *she think it's three weeks, not three sodding days.* However, setting off for Brean Sands, Andreas found his daughter's excitement contagious, and having now had the grumps expelled, he sang along to every tune blaring out from the radio, making up the lyrics that he had forgotten, or simply did not know. By the time they drove through the camp gates, they were all in holiday mode, and after enduring a barely adequate lunch, they strolled back through the gates, heading for the beach with towels, and a pre-packed lunch, all crammed into a wicker basket, purchased from the camp's rip-off market. Their first glimpse of the sea, reflecting the sunshine, like a million diamonds, was an awe-inspiring sight, and then they noticed the debris, left behind by couldn't care less fools. The water was surprisingly cold, and Rosie refused point-blank to enter the water any further than reached her ankles, but with Andreas's hardened conditioning to freezing water, tempered by swimming in the glacial, mid-winter conditions in their local stream, *he* struck out for deeper water. And after an hour of frolicking in the strangely buoyant water, he noticed Lu waving frantically to him, and guessing that it would have something to do with Rosie, he swam swiftly back to *terra firma*. With the cause of the frenetic waving, being entirely down to his young daughter's desire for ice-cream, they shook the sand from their discarded clothing, and headed for a kiosk, where he was forced to pay top dollar for a cornet, topped with fragmentary chocolate flake, and a *soupcon* of strawberry juice. When the licked-dry cornet had been completely devoured, Rosie excitedly raced over to an arcade, where a walled off area, containing a host of coloured plastic balls, proved an instant magnet. And with her parents being barely able to keep up with her, she dived head first into a sea of red, yellow, green and blue, with Lu pointing out a notice advertising a rip-off child-minding service, Andreas growled tetchily, *nevertheless* being forced to take advantage of leaving her in the charge of people, who were barely out of short-trousers themselves, they watched Rosie beginning to frolic for all she was worth, and shrugging their shoulders, they meandered back to virtually the same sun-kissed spot on the beach. Spreading out the towel, they lay down in the baking sun once more, whereupon Andreas, always sensitive to propitious conditions, leaned over to kiss his voluptuous wife. With the heat of the sun, predictably awakening his baser instincts further, his kisses became more ardent, *until* being pushed away by the recipient of his overtures, *"Andreas* behave yourself, people can see us, and you, oh my God just look at you, sticking out a mile in front!" Andreas grinned lasciviously, and laying his hand on her naked stomach, he declared, "I really don't care!" Having now slid his hand into her bikini bottom, his irate wife removed the offending limb hastily protesting, "Pack it in you bloody fool, people are watching us!" With propriety however, finally gaining the upper hand, when his antics began attracting too *much* attention, she finally put a stop to his shenanigans, by sitting up sharply, declaring that she wanted to go to the chippie. So, the dishevelled pair, collected Rosie, and made their way to the rip-off chippie, where the food *was* at least flavoursome. Rosie, dispensed with eating utensils altogether, earning a sly grin from her father, and *the stare* from her mother. When the meal had been finished they trudged wearily back to the chalet, where Lu and Rosie began to get ready for the evening, while Andreas leaving them in peace, donned a shirt, and a brand new pair of matching Marks and Sparks trousers, purchased by his ever loving, especially for the trip, and headed for the entertainment hall.

A session of bingo was already under way, and being conducted in almost total silence, he adjourned to a side room, from where he thought he would be able to see the girls when they put in an appearance. Playing the slot machines, he soon tired of the peevish pursuit of throwing good money after bad, and returning to the main hall, he found bingo finished, and the entertainment started. Spotting his family sitting at a table near to the stage, he realized that he had been so intent on losing money, that he had not seen their entry, and making his way across, he received a broadside for not having secured a table. Lu commented huffily, "I was bloody lucky to get this one. If it hadn't been for the old couple that *were* sitting here, leaving as soon as bingo finished, we would *not* have had a table!" Andreas retorted sharply, "Well you can come over early the next time, I'm buggered if I'm sitting here in silence, while those bloody half-wits play housy-housy!" Striding to the bar, he bought crisps and pickled eggs to accompany the drinks, and immediately querying the amount required, but finding the charge to be correct, when it had been itemised, he remarked, "Bloody rip-off!" And returning to the table, Lu commented shirtily, "You've been a while?" Andreas replied tetchily, "*You* can go for the next round of drinks, if you think you can do it any quicker!" The entertainment was not Andreas's cup of tea, being aimed principally at children, and he was convinced that with their caterwauling being at such a high level of decibels, it had to have been audible in the next county. But even so, Andreas's mood lightened somewhat, due in no small way to the brandy and coke, he was quaffing in copious amounts, and after a while, Lu rose from the table to get more drinks, as had been suggested by Andreas in his tantrum. He gestured her to sit down, "Sorry for my huff love. you park your arse, it's too much for you in your condition!" Returning to the table, his improving mood soon dissipated when Lu remarked, "What's that on the back of your trousers?" Looking over his shoulder, he noticed a big dollop of something blue, stuck to the seat of his new trousers, and wiping most of the goo off with Rosie's wipes, he deposited the package into a metal bin, before reporting the incident to a member of staff. He was informed that it had happened the previous evening too, and Andreas commented, "It's probably a child, but surely the parents must be aware of what their kids are doing. I'm telling you now that if I catch the brat, I will beat the shit out of the father, and *that* is a promise!" Storming back to the table, he found that Rosie had fallen asleep, and deciding that she too had suffered enough puerility, Lu suggested they return to the chalet. Arriving back *home,* Andreas removed his trousers, hurling them savagely into the corner of the room, and donning a pair of jeans, he returned to the entertainment hall, where he stood at the bar drinking cider, scanning the crowd for the culprit. Noticing two boys dressed alike, blatantly misbehaving, while their parents looked on laughing, he decided to focus his attention on the quartet, and noticed the elder of the two boys, extract a clear plastic bag from his pocket, that Andreas could plainly see, contained a ball of blue slime. Then dropping a dollop of the stuff onto a vacant chair, he hastily ran back to his parents, whereupon they all began laughing fit to burst, *until* Andreas walked across to the table. Addressing the father politely, he said, "Go to that chair and scrape off that blue shit, now!" The mother replied,"What's the matter, they're only having a bit of fun?" Ignoring the woman's inconsequential justification, Andreas warned the children's father, "I strongly advise you to do *exactly* what I say!" The man stood up pulling himself to his full height, but within a nano-second, Andreas had grabbed the man's throat, and by simultaneously kicking the back of his legs with his heel, he brought the man to his knees. Applying more pressure to his throat, Andreas growled calmly, "Wipe it off!" Unable to speak, the man lifted his arm in capitulation, and Andreas watched closely as he picked himself up, and walking away meekly to the chair, he removed the goo with his hand. Turning up seconds later with a member of staff, his wife remarked,

"This is the bloke!" When Andreas explained the situation, the family were banned from the entertainment room, but *he* was also given the warning that he would also be banned, *if* there was further violence. Andreas shrugged his shoulders, and walking away, he said resignedly, "Fair enough!" Returning to the chalet, he stated calmly, "That bloody cider is crap over there, I wonder if I could interest them in some of ours!" Lu smiled fully aware of where he had been, and why, "Get it all sorted did you?" Considering that an answer was not required, and with Lu being patently aware of exactly what had probably taken place, the warrior was bestowed with a reward, that had been fanned by the flames of passion on the beach much earlier.

The rest of the weekend would have passed without further incident, *but* the morning following the incident in the entertainment hall, they decided, at Andreas's insistence for saving a few bob, to use a small supermarket situated just across from the camp gates. When the time came to pay for the goods, the assistant who was deep in conversation with his co-worker, a young lady with alarmingly huge breasts, nonchalantly threw Andreas's change across the counter. Leaving the money sitting between them, Andreas glared at the youngster, until finally turning to Andreas, he asked, "Was there something else?" Andreas got hold of the young man's tie, and pulling him down until their faces were almost touching, he said, "Pick up the change, and *hand* it to me. I do not like having money thrown at me!" The trembling, youth obeyed, with Andreas remarking, "Thank you, that is so much more civilised!" Lu was not amused by the spat, but when Andreas pointed out that the youth *needed* a lesson in good manners, she surprisingly conceded that he was probably right

The whole idea of the weekend away, was for Andreas to relax and wind down, but he was increasingly getting to the point, where he was actually, even more up-tight than he was before. Seemingly, he was the only person on the camp, *not* enjoying the pseudo-camaraderie of half-wits dressed as Disney characters, which merely served to isolate him from his family, with Lu and Rosie loving the caricatures, who seemed to appear round every corner of the camp at opportune, and inopportune intervals during the day. Evenings were passed in never-ending bingo, and being entertained by artistes, most of whom would never make the big time, while the remainder had already tried and failed. Andreas had seen far better in the Priory, but Lu and Rosie, could not have cared less whether the acts were good or not, they wildly cheered the seemingly never-ending stream of untalented journey-men and women. Andreas spent most of the time at the bar, leaving Lu to her bingo, ably assisted in the noble art of losing a few quid by Rosie, and on the whole, the holiday was judged by Andreas, not to have been *his* cup of tea, but seeing Lu and Rosie enjoying themselves so much, did give him an unselfish, and *alien* for him, sense of gratification. On one of his sojourns to the bar, he spoke to the bar manager, about the possibility of them stocking Home Farm cider, and exchanging phone numbers, Andreas promised to give him free samples, just to see how they fared.

At mid-morning on the last day of the holiday, they quit what had been their home from home, and headed west, with Andreas being aware that he really *should* have filled up with petrol, *before* leaving. But finding the local, and every garage after, that they encountered along the way, too expensive, he passed them all by. Stopping at a roadside cafe, they ate a reasonable meal, and checking the petrol gauge before once more setting for home, he opined that they had *just* enough to get them home. His reckoning proved to be unerringly accurate, as the car was running on empty, when they arrived at Gunnar's garage. "Why the bloody hell didn't you fill up before you left?" "Because they were all too bloody dear!" Andreas protested. Gunnar looked at his old friend in amazement, "I suppose *I shouldn't* be surprised at that, and at the risk of being repetitive, you are one cheapskate bastard. Besides having to worry about the price of petrol, did you enjoy yourselves?" Andreas said with a straight face, "Oh yeah, it was great. Peaceful and stress-free, you should try it some time, but for Christ's sake don't tell them that your name is Bosworth!" Gunnar shook his head in puzzlement as they left the garage, and Andreas wondered that at what point, Gunnar would realize that he had not paid for the petrol again, *just the price he had been seeking all day!*

22

It was back to earth with a bump the following morning, and even before the first coffee of the day had been consumed, Viv sent word that he wanted to see him ASP. Andreas hated being summoned in that manner, after all he *was* now a partner, albeit it a junior one, and as such, he decided to finish his coffee, before going to Viv's office. "Jesus!" Andreas remarked when he finally made it to Viv's office, "What is it that is so important, that I had to cut short my first coffee of the day?" Viv told him, "It's going to be a very busy day for you, a good piece of which, you will find in your IN tray!" Adding sarcastically, "As no doubt you will have already noticed. More importantly, Mr Mowll has collapsed, and has been hospitalized, which will mean both of us having to share *his* work as well as doing our own, not that he does that much anyway, but it just makes our work-load a little heavier. There is a problem at the club, Jimmy's wife is ill, and he has to stay at home to look after her, and with Reuben being not quite ready to take over yet, we have to get somebody in pretty quick to take over the reins temporarily. That will be up to you to sort out, it *is* after all your concern, and *I* have to be in court this morning, so *you* will be in sole charge here, you also have the building work at the cafe *and* the hotel to

"

organise, all having to be acquitted from *your* office. The new cider plant is behind schedule so you'll have to arrange to bring in builders from outside. But it's not *all* gloom and doom, thank Christ, Carol has accepted the post of manageress, and the building plans have been approved for the hotel and cafe. This is a busy time for us just now, and we cannot have you swanning off on holidays at the drop of a hat!" Andreas retorted, "*You* were the one that advised me to go away for a long weekend, and I chose a site, where in an emergency, I was near enough to be summoned back!" Viv remarked, "Hmm, yes well, it's likely that we may have to think about getting in a *locum*. all this *had* to happen sometime I suppose, but why the hell when we are so bloody busy. Have you had a reply from Melbourne yet, and if not, you will have to engage someone else pronto. I've got to dash now, enjoy your day!" Breezing out of the office, he left Andreas totally at a loss to know where to begin.

Sitting behind his desk, Andreas made a list, deciding to split the tasks into four sections, and knowing that Becky would inform him of anything that came through from Melbourne, he deleted that from the list. Opting to begin by sorting out the situation at the gym, which unfortunately would entail a visit that needs must, would have to be acquitted fairly quickly, and driving swiftly to the gym, he found Reuben already in a state of panic. Andreas told him to concentrate on the training of the young boxers, as *he* would be pop in each evening, to clear up anything that needed paying or ordering, "I am extremely busy at the office just now, so if there is anything that you think warrants my immediate attention you can phone me at home. Get off to college now and I'll make sure that the bar staff know exactly what to do!" Gathering the bar and catering staff together, he explained the situation, "Until Jimmy returns or Reuben takes over, I am putting Daniel in sole charge of catering and the bar!" He turned to Daniel, "Can I see you in the office before I leave?" And once they were in private Andreas informed him, "You will be paid a manager's wage, for however long it takes for this situation to be resolved. I will be forever in your debt for this favour, and when all this is sorted, I'll get you in college, on a management course. I urge you to seize this opportunity with both hands, and if you work hard, I will see that you have the chance to join the company as manager, in one of the many outlets that we have. The money will be good, and the future secure!" Daniel thanked Andreas, but just before leaving he asked, "Andreas I hope you don't mind me asking, but are *you* in charge of all this?" Andreas replied, "Daniel, I'm not only in charge, I *own* it!"

Calling in at the spot being prepared for the new cider making plant, he was gratified to find everybody at the site toiling ceaselessly, and approaching Ted he suggested, "We are going to have to employ more men here. There is way too much work, with the cafe plus the hotel on top of it all. Are there any other companies run by our people, that can be relied upon to get a job done fairly quickly? I would rather put money in the pockets of our own, than employ Gadjo cowboys!" "Leave it to me, but it will cost you!" "Listen!" Andreas asserted, "We've known each other since I was a boy, and I've thrown a lot of money your way. If I want something doing quickly, I have *always* been prepared to dig deep into my pockets!" Ted laughed, "Every job you give me, you want quickly, but don't worry, I'll get you the men, and good ones at that. We'll soon have everything sorted!" Leaving him to it, Andreas moved on to the cafe.

"I'm glad you've decided to join us Carol, and I've just about got time to take you to the hotel to explain what I have in mind, *and* show you where your apartment will be situated!" "I'd love that. I'll just tell the girls that I'm popping out for a while!" As they got in the car she remarked, "You've done really well for yourself, and I want to tell you, that I appreciate what your company are doing for me!" He smiled, "I'm only too glad to be of service, and it has advantages for both of us. I will be getting the best manageress on this planet, and you will be getting a damned good boss!" "You appear to be in charge of this project, and if that's so, I must say that you've reached the top pretty quickly?" Believing that there was now no need for secrecy, he confessed, "I told you that I invested in the purchase of your little place, along with a few other properties, and I have to be honest with you, Carol I *own* this whole project, as well as the new cider processing plant! Seeing the need for change and the opportunity for profit, I invested, and fortunately it has all borne fruit. You'll be able to move in as soon as the hotel is ready, and you can install your *old* furniture or *we'll* buy new, whatever you are more comfortable with!" When they reached the hotel he was once more impressed by the diligence, and application of the work-force, recognising a few faces from the old camp. Hearing a shout he turned round, "Ho Krallis, I see you got yourself *a bit on the side*, better watch your old woman don't find out!" Andreas stated, "Don't take any notice of them Carol, they're rough diamonds, but good men at heart!" After he had shown her round amid more wolf-whistles and ribald remarks, he told her, "We'll have to get you on a management course, we can't have our staff running circles round you!"

As soon as he had driven her back to the cafe, he headed straight for the office where he was given a sheet of paper along with the mandatory mug of coffee. Sipping his drink and appreciably smacking his lips, he glanced at the paper, noticing that the chef from Melbourne had agreed to join the company. He smiled broadly, and remarked to his increasingly valuable acquisition, "Becky, it's all coming together at last. Now for that bloody IN tray!" Putting everything in some kind of semblance of order, with the least important being at the bottom, he began his proper job, and soldiering on steadfastly through his lunch break, he managed to complete everything by the end of the afternoon, and addressing his indispensable secretary, he remarked, "I'm going home now, but I've got to call in at the club first to see if there are bills to settle, or more ordering to do. I've put Daniel in charge, but I want to go through the ordering process with him, he's never done it before, and it's a vital part of the business!" At that point he put on his jacket, and while his mind was in over-drive, he had a sudden thought, "Could you get Michael on the phone for me?" When he was put through Andreas told him that he wanted a case of pre-packed cider, along with a small barrel, sending to the holiday camp in Brean, telling him that he would sign for it, as it was a freebie. Being aware that the proceeds of the ambrosial liquid would end up in the bar manager's back pocket, he considered it merely a sprat to catch a mackerel. Musing, *after all, if we can secure an order from this camp, maybe others will follow suit, and the disastrous mini-holiday may prove to have prodigious unforeseen benefits. God knows, I deserve to get something from that shit-hole.*

Arriving at the club, he sent for Daniel, and going through all the ordering procedures with him, he pointed out how low each item could be allowed to reach, before re-ordering, and noticing that the lager was already a little low, he let Daniel order it himself. Now satisfied that all was in hand, he decided to leave for home, and walking through the restaurant, with the aroma of food being prepared, his taste buds were aroused, but not daring to succumb to temptation, he walked from the club, knowing that Lu would have prepared a feast, and there would be the devil to pay if he did not do it justice.

After finishing the mountain of food that had been placed in front of him, he rang Viv who asked immediately, "Did you manage to get some of the work done?" "No, I did not get some of the work done, I got *all* of the work done!" He revealed, "Ted is arranging more men on the ground, and I've put Daniel temporarily in charge of the bar and catering. Reuben will be employed in conducting the training for the young boxers, plus attending college, and *I* will call in at the gym each evening to pay bills, and solve problems. Presuming that you'll be sloping off somewhere again, I'll be free to do Mr Mowll's work tomorrow!" Ignoring the sarcasm Viv remarked, "You've done well, but I didn't really expect anything else!" Andreas told him of the idea for sending samples of the cider to the camp, and he agreed wholeheartedly, "That's a great idea, the steward will obviously push the stuff because it's money in his pocket, and if the punters take to it, they'll demand more of the same. I don't suppose you have any of that Oz brandy left?" Suddenly the real motive for his ringing had risen to the surface, "Oh I understand the reason for the call now, Katie's working, and you want somewhere to park your arse for the night. There *is* some left, and don't forget to bring your work clothes and pyjamas, I don't want my family in hysterics at the sight of your body first thing in the morning!" Andreas heard the click and grinning, he replaced the receiver gently.

Complaining to Lu he asserted, "I can see that I'm going to have to order a regular supply of Tolley's, just to keep my friends and relatives happy, I'll be running out before I've had time to re-order the bloody stuff!" Lu commented, "Well it's one way of ensuring that we have a constant stream of visitors. You surely didn't think that they came to see *you!*" Viv's arrival fortunately prevented a reply, being probably just as well. Viv asked, with the worst impression of an Aussie accent that anyone had ever heard, "How're you doing cobber?" "Not you too!" Andreas averred, "One comedian in the house is too much!" The fire began to die down, and Andreas put another couple of logs into the embers, instantly making the room cooler, but with brandy already hitting the parts responsible for warming the cockles of the heart, it was enough to ensure warmth, albeit only to the inside. After a few minutes the wood burst into flame, and putting a shovelful of coal-dust across the top, he sat back to enjoy the heat. "There's nobody gets a fire going like you love!" Lu attested, obviously trying to get into his good books. Viv nodded his confirmation of that fact, but Andreas had not seen the gesture, being occupied in visualising the many gifts that he would be bestowing on his coquettish wife, *later* in bed. Grinning, he thought, *I'll have to take a handkerchief with me, to shove in her mouth. I can't have our guest's sleep disturbed by our noisy, and passionate sex games.*

Going over everything he had managed to accomplish that day, he was in turn enlightened of the case that Viv had been engaged upon, and trying to listen, Andreas found that the brandy, and the warm glow of the fire had induced a premature soporific effect, making it difficult to concentrate on Viv's words. The kids as usual were all over Viv like a rash, and having the thought that he would make an excellent father, Andreas asked suddenly, "How come you and Kate have no kids, there's no *physical* reason is there?" "No!" Viv replied, "Kate is a *career* woman, who is convinced that she is destined for higher things, and she is probably right, but I *would* like an heir to succeed me in the firm, and I'm certain that given the chance, she would be an excellent mother. We *have* spoken on the subject, but she just doesn't want to know!" Andreas suggested, "Why don't you get her pissed up and hide her pills? I'm sure she wouldn't mind if she *did* fall pregnant, and of course it would be too bloody late by then anyway!" Viv laughed, "Don't think that I haven't thought about it, but I know that she would hold it against me. It has to be *her* decision!" Entering the room, Lu who had heard every word, said to Andreas, "That's just like you to suggest something like that. You two had better stop scheming or I'll tell her everything!" "Bloody whistle-blower!" Andreas smilingly commented, but grinning archly, he thought, *it's too bloody late for that anyway. I've already got a plan in mind, that I'll tell Viv about in the morning, before madam honours us with her presence!* The kids were in bed fast asleep, with Rosie now no longer needing a nip of brandy to enter dreamland, so cuddling up to his wife's warm body, nature took it's sweet course, but having forgotten to bring the hanky to bed, he had to put his hand across her mouth, only just about stifling her throes of ecstasy, when that special moment arrived.

Enlightening Viv the following morning of his plan to engage the *drabardi* in his quest for a child, Andreas explained, "Sarah's potions are not drugs, so there would be no after-taste, and Katie will believe that it has *all* been of her own volition, so there'd be no come-backs on you. Give it a try, what have you got to lose?" Andreas could tell from Viv's face that he'd stimulated a modicum of interest in the scheme, and pressing home the advantage Andreas ventured, "Look Viv, if she gets promotion, it might mean re-location, which *could* result in breaking up your relationship. *I'll* see the *drabardi* later, to get the potion, and you can please yourself whether you use it or not!" At that juncture they were interrupted by Rosie, "Daddy, I've wet the bed!" Andreas suggested with a grin, "See what you're missing!" Turning to Rosie he placated her obvious distress, "That's okay darling, there's nothing for you to worry about!" Taking her upstairs, he washed, and dried her, then dressing her in a clean nightie, he took her back downstairs to watch Floella Benjamin on the television. Throwing a couple of logs on the embers, he cleaned out the grate and returned upstairs to strip the bed, depositing the sopping bed-clothes into the wash-basket on the way. Waking Lu he kissed her forehead, "Come on love you'll have to get up, the fire's glowing, and Rosie's downstairs lying on the settee. She's wet herself, but it's okay, I've washed and changed her!" Lu remarked, "I hope you didn't moan at her?" Looking at his wife in dismay he affirmed, "I'd *never* do that Lu!" Going back downstairs, he told Viv, "I can't leave until Lu gets up, Rosie can't be left on her own, and the boys are not up yet!" Viv answered archly,

"Don't worry, I'll do *your* work as usual!" Beating a hasty retreat before Andreas could exact retribution. With Lu and the boys rising at the same time, Andreas saw it as the green light for him to leave, but having a necessary task to exact first, he announced, "I'll give you boys a lift, so there's no need to bolt your food. I've got to see a man about a dog anyway!" George exclaimed excitedly, "Great dad, what sort of dog are we getting?" Andreas explained, "A dog is the last thing I would want. It's just an expression that means that I've got something to do, that doesn't necessarily concern you. Right, I'll be about ten minutes, so you two had better be ready by the time I get back!" Going to Sarah, *the drabardi*, he explained the situation, and handing him two sachets she explained, "Tell him to slip the green one into her drink half an hour before they go to bed, and do the same with the brown one, first thing in the morning!" Noting her dishabille, Andreas remarked with a grin, "Sarah do you *ever* wear clothes that cannot be seen through?" She laughed, "You never complained before!" Andreas kissed her cheek, whereupon she said pertly, "And *you* didn't always kiss me quite so chastely either!"

Going back to the house, he picked up the boys, drove them to school and walking through the main door of Mowll and Mowll, he patted the pocket containing the potions. Smiling archly, he knocked on Viv's door and entered, having to wait for his secretary to leave, before handing over the sachets. Repeating the instructions twice, then once more for luck as he was about to leave, "Now don't get it wrong, green for the evening, brown for the morning. It's almost poetic really, so don't you forget!" "Thanks for your trouble Andreas, but I'm not altogether sure that this the right way!" Smiling, Andreas told him,

"Let me know how you get on!" He left his colleague's office, knowing full well that Viv's conscience *would* weigh heavily, but being totally confident too, that not wanting to chance losing Kate, he *would* use the potions. Repairing to his office, Andreas found the predictable mug of coffee waiting on his desk, and noting that although there were files to be dealt with, most were actually the senior partner's. When at last he got round to completing the work pending, he left to check on the work being done at the sites. Ted who was busy overseeing work at the cider plant, dropped everything as soon as Andreas arrived, "I've just returned from the hotel, and left Walthaar in charge. Everything is coming along fine, but there are a few hitches at the cafe as you will see when you arrive. I estimate that it will take two to three weeks before *this* site is finished, then I'll set these men, working on the cafe conversion, and the *whole* caboodle should be wrapped up in five to six weeks!" Andreas smiled, "That's great Ted, but I would *really* prefer the two sites to be completed at the same time, allowing both Carol *and* the chef to move in on the same day. Then with the hotel up and running, I can sell the maisonettes, pay everything off, and the venture can then proceed on an even keel!" Changing the subject, Ted suggested, "What are your thoughts on a *new* name for the hotel, the Priory got a bit worn at the edges towards the end, and a new name could be just the thing to kick-start the business!" With that in mind Andreas went to the conversion, and consulting Walthaar on the matter, found that he too was in favour of a new name, "You need something quirky that would attract people from out of town, but still have a ring of familiarity about it for the locals!" "Hmm!" Andreas concurred, "Perhaps you've got something there,

I'll certainly keep that in mind. Ted told me that there was a problem at the flats?" Walthaar replied, "There are serious alterations needed, that principally involve the foundations *and* planning permission, the problem being that we can't assess exactly what is required, with rubble and scrap metal hindering progress!" Andreas confirmed, "That will be sorted out today. I've got to see John Scamp later anyway!" Getting back into his car, he decided to postpone any further visiting, opting instead to see his prospective *father*.

Pulling into the camp, he got out of the car, noticing immediately that the mud, omnipresent at every single site, had splattered his shiny car, necessitating a *freebie* at the garage later, providing that Gunnar would have forgotten that he had not paid for the petrol on his last visit. Perceiving John's old truck parked by the side of what he presumed to be his dwelling place, he immediately vowed to help him get a more suitable property, when the house was sold. Having seen Andreas's arrival, John opened the door, "Ho Krallis, what brings you out here?" "Two things John. The mortgage company have given you a six months extension for the settlement of the sum due, which is good news, and the other thing is that you are needed at the cafe site to shift all the debris and scrap metal. My brother told me this morning that even *more* structural work is needed, so there will be quite a bit more for you to dispose of!" "Thank you Krallis, I'll shift the lot this afternoon, you'd be surprised at just how much I can get in the back of that thing!" He asserted, jerking his thumb in the general direction of the battered vehicle, and casting a weather eye on the van, Andreas saw no cause to doubt his words. Returning to the office just in time to join Viv for lunch at the Green Man, he reported the current situations at the sites over a lunch of almost tasteless fish and chips, "I can't wait for the hotel to open!" He remarked, "This meal is absolute crap, and we've been charged top dollar for it too!" Ted entered five minutes later and noticing that he was not in his dirty work clothes for a change, Andreas asked, "Would you like lunch, we've only just started and it's Viv's turn to pay!" To Viv's blatant chagrin, Ted agreed saying, "Yeah I wouldn't mind. Is that *fish*?" Andreas replied, "Yes, but I have to warn you that it's only just about edible, but then again, it's probably the best thing on offer. I've been telling Viv how well the building work is going and the cafe conversion will proceed a mite faster now that I've got John Scamp going round there this afternoon!" Ted commented, "If he'd come even twice a week, we'd be able to get on a bit better!" Turning to Viv, Andreas said, "Everyone I've spoken to thinks it would be a good idea to re-name the hotel, with Walthaar believing that it should be something quirky, and attractive to both outsiders and locals. Got any suggestions?" Viv thought for a moment, then suggested with a grin, "Well how about calling it *The Krallis,* it's quirky, and I'm sure it would be popular with everyone around here!" Ted agreed, "That's a brilliant idea, I can just see that name up on the sign!" "No, that certainly will *not* be the name!" Andreas remarked, hating the thought, but with his co-diners both persisting, and Viv reminding him that they only had a month to come up with *something*, Andreas began to re-think, and noticing Andreas wavering, Viv pressed home his suit, "It really *is* quite quirky! He commented, "The name alone would create a lot of interest in the place initially, and if this chef is as good as you say they would keep coming back. People who dine out on special occasions are all well and good, but for this project to *really* succeed we need a regular clientele, who enjoy good food and drink at reasonable prices!" "I'll think about it!" Andreas averred dismissively. "Well don't think about it *too* long!" Viv persisted, "The signs have to be in place *before* the opening. Talk it over with Lu, she'll make you see sense!"

23

Returning to the office with Viv, Andreas rang the local college to arrange a course in bar management for Carol, discovering that happily, even though it would be a fairly short course, it would provide her with a certificate *and* give her the grounding she would need to run a bar, then ringing the cafe to tell her of the course, he informed her that she would be able to move into the hotel in about a month's time. Needing to check on how things were going elsewhere, he drove to the club, and finding everything in order with the bookwork, catering and bar stock all up to scratch, he was satisfied that the club was in good hands, being *now* appreciative of how well Jimmy had run *everything* on his own. Knowing that he would not have been expected home so early, he went to the gym below, and had an hour's workout, vowing once more optimistically, to have a workout at least once a week. After the rigorous session, he left to pick up his sons, telling them that a stop would be required at the garage on the way home to get the car washed, and fill up with petrol. Not seeing Gunnar anywhere, he asked the stand-in petrol pump attendant his whereabouts, and being told that Gunnar had gone to a holiday camp for two days, Andreas paid the required amount in full, using the new pay-machine for the car-wash. Over dinner Andreas told Lu about the work at the hotel, being only a month off completion, telling her the name that had been suggested, "What a wonderful idea!" she purred, and with that, Andreas was forced to admit defeat in the matter, "The Krallis it will be then!" Noticing however, that throughout the evening, Lu was continually wincing, and holding her bump, he was moved to ask if everything was okay. She replied with a wan smile, "I'm fine, just a few twinges. I reckon he's gonna be a footballer!" Andreas remarked, "I should have known that you would know the sex of our unborn child!" Putting the incident out of his mind, with his own world of buildings and finance, consuming all else, he finally settled down to a relaxing evening, watching television.

Phoning Andreas the following day at the office, Reuben asked "Are you going to Stow with me this year? I could do with the company!" Going to Stow was the furthest thing from his mind, Andreas replied, "I've got too much on just now, what with Lu being near her time, and all the building work going on. Maybe next year!" He then thought, *Jesus Christ it's going to be really busy in a few weeks time, and if I weren't so pre-occupied, I wouldn't have minded going there, just to get away from this pressure-cooker existence!* Forgetting all about the call until later when Lu asked him the same question, he told her that he had already turned Reuben down. She suggested, "Maybe you *should* go, it would do you good to get away for a few days, you *have* been looking really tired lately!" He thought, *how typical of her, thinking of me, when she is so near her time!* She remarked, "Pa asked me this morning, and not looking forward to Bill Scamp's driving, he asked me to ask you. There's no need to worry, if you *do* wanna go, Ma will look after me, and it's only for a few days after all?" Andreas replied, "I'll give it some thought, but I've got such a lot on here!" Changing the subject he remarked with a grin, "Did you know that Gunnar's gone to Brean Sands?" "Yes, he came here to ask what name he should use, as you had told him not to tell them that his name was Bosworth!" Andreas laughed and confessed, "I'm afraid, I did say that, but I was only pulling his leg!" "Well taking it to heart, he's gone and booked in under the name *Gunari Scamp*, but for God's sake don't tell him I told you!" *How am I ever going to resist that one?* He thought with a wicked grin.

In the morning, he asked Viv if he could be spared for a few days as he had to drive the crowd to Stow, Viv asked incredulously, "With Lu being so near her time?" Andreas smiled, "It was her idea!" he answered, "She said to me, that bastard Viv has been driving you too hard lately!" Viv scowled, "Mr Mowll is now well enough to return to work, so you may as well go!" Adding, "And I can't have a beautiful woman, saying things like that about me, can I?" "You flannelling bastard!" Andreas suggested, but changing the subject he asked, "I don't suppose there's a chance that you used the Sarah's potion last night?" Viv's face turned a deep shade of crimson instantly, "As a matter of fact I did, and I have to be honest, I've never known her so wild before. Perhaps we should have that stuff analysed, we'd make a bloody fortune. I was scared of using it at first, being totally in ignorance of what effect it would have on her, but I've really *never* experienced anything like it in my life. It was almost like being raped, and the good thing was, that she never noticed any difference in the taste of her milk last night, or this morning!" Andreas chuckled, and suggested,

"Oh well it looks as if you'll soon have an heir to carry the name on. Perhaps I should offer my congratulations now!"

After ringing Reuben to tell him that he *would* after all be driving them to Stow, and immediately feeling guilty about leaving Lu, he almost had second thoughts, but the die had now been cast, and strangely his guilt was somewhat allayed by learning that Michael had expressed a wish to accompany the motley crew. After packing his holdall early the next morning, Andreas kissed Lu's pale forehead before leaving for the journey, even though he was not entirely sure that he *should* leave her. But arriving at Ma's to pick up Pa and Michael, he was reassured by the lady of the house that Lu would receive *her* close care and attention. And as usual she had prepared enough food to feed a regiment, with Pa and Andreas, stealing a march over the others, by helping themselves to some of the delicacies *before* picking up Bill and Reuben. Riley as ever, would be the last pick-up, with the habitual tongue-lashing he received from his wife Dolores, becoming an integral part of the Stow trip, and as always, the issue was always further compounded, when Dolores, would be like putty in Andreas's hands, after delivering his customary kiss to her sallow face. He soon found that, this year she had not searched Riley's pockets with the same diligence as usual, for as soon as they were under way, he produced a bottle of scotch from a hidden pocket in his padded waistcoat, occasioning the three oldsters to be roaring drunk by the time they arrived in Stow. With the whole trip being steeped in tradition, it was left as usual, to Andreas and Reuben to clean up the mess from the car, with Michael's presence providing a helping hand. And when their stalwart assistant had disappeared into the hotel, with cases in either hand, Andreas turned to Reuben, "Remind me to introduce him to Molly-no-legs!" The crumbs as usual were thrown into the river, and noticing that this time, that no seagulls were present to contest feeding rights, he thought, *hmm probably having a day out at the sea-side!"* Walking through the hallway of the hotel, Andreas could see all the regulars standing at the bar, and as soon as the luggage had been deposited in the correct rooms, Michael accompanied Andreas and Reuben on their customary walk into town. Taking him to what had turned out to be their usual eating establishment, the last time they had visited Stow, Andreas was conversely, once again both glad *and* disappointed that his ex-lover Jan was conspicuously absent. After they had eaten, they took Michael window-shopping in the numerous alley-ways, each containing a plethora of antique shops, until finally arriving back at the hotel, they entered the bar to find that not surprisingly, Reuben's first fight had already been arranged. Putting his lips to the glass of cider, Michael *instantly* spat the insipid looking brew back into the glass, whereupon Andreas advised him to drink Guinness, a drink that although being totally unlike their usual tipple, *did* actually possess a strong bitter-sweet flavour. Molly was looking all gooey-eyed at Reuben, until being introduced to Michael, and eyeing him from head to toe, her cunning eyes twinkled as she gazed up and down his body, immediately finding him the more attractive or more likely option. Reuben nudged Andreas, and the two of them beat a hasty retreat, leaving the two of them together, and walking across to Pa, he said, "What do you reckon Pa, don't you think they make a lovely couple?" Pa remarked, "That's bloody cruel!" Adding with a grin, "But funny!" Becoming suddenly serious, Andreas asked, "Do we know Reuben's opponent yet?" "It's someone called Docherty!" Pa replied, and with a puzzled look, he asserted, "I recognise the name from *somewhere,* but can't quite put a face to it. I think he's Irish or Scotch. Can *you* remember him Andreas?" "Oh I remember him alright!" Came the response, "He's the bastard that kneed me in the crown jewels, and kicked me in the head, while I was bent over in agony. I'll have to make sure that Reuben knows the score, but he *shouldn't* have any problems anyway, so get your life savings on him!" Pa answered with a grin, "They're already on him. If he loses I'm stony, and so is everybody else!" Andreas laughed, "He won't lose. If he does *I'll* jump in, and kick the shit out of him!"

With his entourage walking slowly up the hill to the *arena,* Reuben jogged on ahead, keeping himself warm in the chill of the early evening. Docherty was already there with his party, with Andreas noticing that *his* retinue had doubled in size, from the time he had fought him, and still harbouring a grudge against Docherty's backers for threatening to do him in, after he had floored their man, he hoped that they had backed *all* their money on this one fight. Noting that he was a good stone heavier than when Andreas had fought him, he made Reuben aware of all of his tricks, advising, "Take him out as fast as you can. He's only ever been beaten once, and *too* bloody dangerous to mess around with!" Docherty was certainly a huge, cunning specimen, who would likely give Reuben a rough ride, but Andreas was confident that with his training and fitness, Reuben would prevail. The fight started and Docherty began kicking at Reuben's legs in an effort to slow him down, but Reuben was too quick for the cumbersome Irishman to fall for tricks like that. Circling each other, they were both trading light, distancing blows, but drawing first blood, the Irishman lumbered forward, following the punch with a vicious kick to Reuben's calf, bringing him to his knees. A follow-up kick to the middle of Reuben's back, drove his face into the dirt, but rolling over quickly, Reuben almost avoided the intended follow up kick, but when the kick landed heavily on his forearm, Reuben let out a yelp of pain, a totally out of character occurrence, and all of a sudden, alarm bells began to ring in Andreas's head. As Reuben rose from the ground, arm hanging loosely by his side, the brutish Irishman rushed forward, sensing the kill, but Reuben called on his fitness and training, by sliding to the ground, with one foot rigid in front of him, and the other hooked behind his opponent's foot. The big man stood for a moment, and being unable to balance, he toppled face down, with his leg still being gripped between Reuben's feet. Rolling across the big man's leg, Reuben bore down with all his weight onto Docherty's right leg, and all of a sudden, there was a collective groan, as the crowd heard the leg being snapped. One of Docherty's handlers ran to the telephone, situated halfway down the hill, to call for an ambulance, and with the crowd stunned into silence, the pitiless brutality of gypsy fighting, was evident, as many had witnessed. Some of the crowd stayed on to watch more battles, but the majority, having been shocked by what they had witnessed, walked down the hill, swearing that they'd had enough for the present, but it's as sure as eggs is eggs, that they *would* be back the following night, for more of the same. The ambulance arrived within minutes, and Reuben, accompanied by his father jumped into the rear of the ambulance, joining his still screaming adversary, with his handlers, attempting to make their man as comfortable as they could. Andreas suggested to Pa, "I think Reuben's arm's broken, so it looks as if there won't be any more fighting for Reuben, not on this trip anyway!" And when the family's winnings had been paid out to their satisfaction, they all walked solemnly back to the hotel, and with Andreas not being in a drinking mood anyway, he awaited Reuben's return in the bar without toasting the victory. Everything changed however, when Reuben and his father made their entrance into the bar, and with raucous cheers ringing out, the bar soon became it's usual riotous self. Reuben was unfortunately not able to shake all the hands being thrust forward, with his plastered arm being supported across his body by a sling, and smiling for his admirers and well-wishers, he was strangely distant. Andreas walked across and asked him if he was okay, and shaking his head, he remarked. "I've had pain-killers, and I feel as if I'm going to vomit at any minute!" Andreas told him, "The pills and the trauma, have likely upset your stomach, so let's go for a walk. The fresh air will do you good!" Leaving the clamour of the bar behind, they walked out into the cold night air, and when Reuben beginning to shiver, Andreas took off his jacket, and draped it around his shoulders saying, "It *is* cold, we'll have a brief walk around town then call it a day!" Reuben remarked, "You were spot on with everything you said, he *was* a hard fighter, and I was fortunate to have beaten him!" "Fortunate nothing!" Andreas remarked, "You saw a way to beat him, and went for it. That's not luck, it's called having the will to win!" Reuben asked, "Will this mean going home now?" Andreas replied, "I haven't given it any thought to be honest, and not being too sure of what the others will want to do, I'll ask them tomorrow. If they want to stay, I'll run you home then come back for them, when they're ready to leave. I'm a bit worried about Lu anyway!" "There will be no need, for you to do that!" Reuben replied, "If they decide to stay, I stay too!"

A meeting was held, and a vote taken, with the majority opting to remain. Andreas would have to abide by the decision, and a visit home, was now out of the equation. Riley suggested loudly, that perhaps *Andreas* could maybe take Reuben's place, and turning on his uncle angrily, Andreas left them *all* in no doubt, that there was absolutely no chance of him antagonizing Lu, particularly in her condition. After the meeting Michael took Andreas aside and said, "I'm sorry Andreas, but that could be my fault. I let it slip that Vee had mentioned you winning the British Empire championship in Australia, but don't worry, I didn't tell them who your opponent was!" Andreas commented, "Well thank God for that, but I don't want to fight any more. Australia was a debt of honour, and at the time I took on the fight, I was not aware of that my opponent would turn out to be Lupe, Reuben's brother. Michael confessed, "I have to be honest, I knew that this kind of fight would be tough, but did *not* realise just *how* brutal it actually was. Is it always like that?" Andreas replied, "I'm afraid that all sorts go on in this style of fighting, biting, head butts, gauging, anything short of using weapons!" Michael stated, "Well in that case I don't blame her for not wanting you to fight!" Andreas shrugged his shoulders, "She's always hated it, even when I was boxing at school! Pa and Riley only want me to fight, so they can make money, and I'm not standing for it any more!" The two friends walked across to where Reuben sat nursing his arm, obviously still in pain, and Michael suggested, "Those painkillers should have kicked in by now!" Reuben admitted that he had only taken the ones that had been spoon-fed at the hospital, "You never know what's in those things. It's a pity the *drabardi* isn't here, *her* cures have natural ingredients, not something brewed up by scientists!" Walking through the town, Michael expressed a wish to visit the antiques shops again, and with Reuben being reluctantly dragged along, they entered the first one encountered. Spotting a Welsh dresser similar to the one at the farmhouse, that had been marked up for three thousand five hundred pounds. Michael commented, "If I'd known it was worth that kind of money, I'd have sold it years ago, it's a bloody eyesore!" Andreas pointed out, "Eyesore it may, but if you hang on it for a few years, more, it could be worth double that!" Adding with a smile, "And *where* would you store all your booze?" Finally tiring of being dragged in and out of junk shops, Reuben suggested lunch at their regular eatery, and once having eaten, Michael went to the bar, and after ordering three halves of bitter, he spent a few minutes chatting to the middle-aged barmaid. When he returned, Reuben commented, "You're a dark one, did you get anywhere with her?" Michael's face reddened, "I've actually been making arrangements to meet with the owner, about supplying them with our cider. It seemed too good an opportunity to miss, and with folk from all over Britain flocking to the Fair, word of our product could spread, and who knows maybe we could eventually collar the whole country's trade. It may need a few samples to swing it, but if it were to prove successful, it could reap rich rewards!" Leaving Michael in the pub, the two comrades-in-arms made their way back to the hotel, where Andreas noticed Pa and Riley involved in a deep conversation with a sharply dressed individual. Andreas guessed that *he* was the subject under discussion, when they all looked in his direction. He walked across, and before they had the time to ask, he said, "The answer is no!" Pa pleaded, "Andreas, the family honour is at stake here, and I'm sure Lu would understand. People are calling you a coward because you will not fight, and to restore the family's good name, I have offered to fight their man tomorrow night instead of you!" Seeing through the attempt to earn money for them, Andreas reiterated, "There will be *no* fighting for me, we came here to support Reuben, and that's all, so please do *not* mention the subject again!" Andreas was angry at Pa's attempted emotional blackmail, and walking upstairs, he spent an hour, luxuriating in the shower. Joining the others on the hill later in the evening, and still being angry with Pa, Andreas barely spoke to any of them, but his demeanour lightened somewhat by making money on every fight. Avoiding Andreas at breakfast, Pa was patently aware that Andreas was still angry with him, and in that assumption he was absolutely spot on, with Andreas remarking to Michael, "I can't get over Pa pretending to be forced into a fight, just to get me involved in his schemes, it would cause one almighty row if Lu got to hear of it!"

Strolling through the town after breakfast, Andreas caught sight of a woman a few hundred yards away, turning into the street opposite the pub, that from a distance, bore a strong resemblance to Jan. Irrationally running towards to where he had seen her disappear, he found that whoever it was, had vanished into thin air. Resolving to be in the area the following morning, *just in case*, he returned to the hotel, and found Riley alone at the bar. Asking Pa's whereabouts, he received a shock response, "He's out training for tonight!" Andreas looked at him aghast, "What do you mean?"

Reuben replied for Riley, "He's going to fight for your family honour. That bloke he was talking to was pouring insults on your family, because of your reluctance to fight, Pa lost his rag, and told him that he would fight instead. If this arm hadn't been hurting so much, I'd have killed the bastard myself, there and then!" "Hell!" Andreas responded, "I thought Pa was just trying to goad me into fighting. I *can't* let him fight, I just hope Lu will forgive me! Where is he training?" He asked. Riley replied sullenly, "He's down by the river, about five minutes upstream!" Taking Reuben aside, Andreas gave him instructions of what he would have to do, then walking along the river path, he came upon Pa, stripped to the waist doing press-ups. "You will need to do better than that!" Andreas remarked, "Would you like me to help?" "Well yeah okay that'll be great, I haven't done any of this for years!" Working Pa hard for an hour, Andreas called a halt, and stripping off, they cooled themselves in the river, laying in the warm sun to dry off. As soon as they were dry enough to dress, Andreas remarked, "I reckon you're ready now, so we may as well make our way back. You wouldn't want to keep your opponent waiting now would you?" Reaching the hotel, they strolled into the bar, Reuben walked across and reported, "It's all arranged Andreas, you will be fighting in an hour's time!" "*You're* fighting too?" Pa said, "What's all this about, you've been refusing to fight? What the hell is going on?" Andreas grinned, "You didn't think I'd *let* you fight did you? *I'm* restoring the family honour!" Angrily turning on his son Pa complained, "You mean you've had me sweating like a pig for an hour, and you'd already arranged to fight instead of me. You are one lousy, rotten bastard!" Andreas ran out of the bar, with Pa in close pursuit.

Smothering himself in grease, Andreas descended the stairs dressed in Reuben's strip and Pa's tattered old gloves. With the hour's work-out with Pa whetting his appetite for battle, and his mind sharp and fully focussed, he felt that he was almost back to full fitness. Making no contingency plans for stringing out the grudge match, Andreas wanted blood and plenty of it! Arriving at the top of the hill, he found that his opponent had already arrived ahead of him, and noting that his foe was the *flash Harry* from the bar, he conceded that he looked an entirely different prospect without the gaudy clothing, being two or three inches taller than *he,* without an ounce of fat. Suspecting immediately that the fight would not be easy, Andreas hoped to have enough experience, and tricks up his sleeve, to exact a fitting retribution for goading Pa into fighting. Reflecting the bad feeling that was now known to exist between the pair, a huge crowd, had placed a fair wedge of money, with the *bookies.* And recognizing one of the man's handlers, Andreas chose not to acknowledge the gesture of familiarity from Luke of Dover, focussing solely on the task in hand. Stripping off his track-suit top, Andreas jogged on the spot, and with no preamble or shake of the hand, they walked toward the centre of the circle, and taking a boxer's stance, they moved warily around each other. Striking the first blow with a straight left, Andreas noticed immediately that Pa's old gloves had done their job, raising blood once more, but being stung into action, the man delivered a left jab of his own, that Andreas swatted away with his forearm, but the sting from that blow, was enough to make Andreas realize, that this man could be *more* than capable of inflicting serious damage. Exchanging a flurry of punches, Andreas suddenly fearing that his fitness would let him down for the first time in his career, he decided to slow his opponent down by punching his biceps, and kicking at the sides and backs of his legs. Becoming conscious of the fact that his plan was working, when his adversary's punches, did not seem to have the same venom as those delivered earlier. Andreas continued the onslaught, until the premature end of the round arrived, but believing that it was merely postponing the inevitable, and being totally relaxed, he watched Luke frantically rubbing the man's limbs with *wintergreen* in an effort to bring life back to his muscles. Pushing his fighter to the centre of the *ring,* Luke closed his eyes in dismay, as Andreas continued the barrage, and being aware that his opponent would make a last-ditch attempt to get back into the fight, Andreas was prepared for the rush when it came. Side-stepping the charge, he delivered a perfect karate kick to the kidney region, and before *Flash Harry* had the time to recover his equilibrium, Andreas landed a *punch* in exactly the same spot, dropping his rival to his knees. Crossing the short distance between them, Andreas pulled back on *Flash Harry's* long mane, completely exposing the throat, and pausing for a second, he posed for the crowd, raising his fist above his helpless combatant, then tiring of the charade, he suddenly struck downward at lightning speed. *Flash Harry* clutched at his throat, his mouth open and his eyes wide in terror, but there was to be no mercy for the man, who had dared to prod Pa into a fight. With face set in stone, and sanity now abandoned, Andreas savagely kicked him head, but before he could administer the coup-de-grace, Luke threw in the towel, and Reuben pulled him away with his good arm, "Leave him be Andreas, he's done!" But *Andreas* was not done, and would not be restrained, but finally with Pa joining Reuben in the constraint, they managed to avert a tragedy. Luke walked across to congratulate him, "Andreas, that chavvi you just hammered *was* the unbeaten champion of England!" Andreas retorted angrily, "He should never have challenged my Pa, and tell him when he comes round, that he's damned lucky to be alive!" Luke shook his head, "I'm afraid that was my fault, it was the only way of getting you to fight, and believe me, I would *never* have let him fight your Pa!" Andreas was stunned, "You stupid bastard Luke, you could have gotten your friend killed. I'll maybe see you later for a drink, I might have calmed down by then!" Walking down the hill towards the hotel Riley reported, "We've made a killing today, that bloke you fought was well fancied to beat you!" "They should have gone with you then shouldn't they?" Andreas suggested sarcastically, "You only bet on certainties!" When they reached the hotel, his blood had still not yet cooled, and excusing himself, he went to his favourite spot by the river, and diving head-first into the cold water, the impetus drove the air from his lungs, and panting for breath, he regurgitated the water that had entered his lungs. The exercise, succeeded in calming his mindless fury, and becoming inured to the water, the rage cooled in congruity with the stream. Surfacing, he fancied that he thought he detected a movement on the far side of the stream, and instantly recalling Jan's penchant for skinny-dipping, he stood stock-still in the water for a few moments to see if he had been mistaken, but seeing no ripples on the surface, he shrugged, and dismissed as a figment of his agitated imagination. Swimming around in the clear water, he wiped away the blood and sweat from his body with his hands, then laying out to dry on the bank, a sudden evening chill induced a shiver, warranting a swift return to the hotel.

Walking back to the hotel, Andreas could not rid himself of the feeling that someone *had* actually been watching him, as he bathed in the stream, and not ever having been wrong in the past with his hunches, he decided that he would seek a new bathing site. Entering the bar, he saw a slightly inebriated Michael, holding a glass of cider up to the light, and pretending to taste the insipid concoction. He pulled a face remarking, "I think I'll have to go home, and bring back a supply of decent cider!" Everyone laughed, but his flippancy, had kindled an idea that Andreas had been considering ever since Michael had mentioned supplying their usual eating house, with Golden Valley samples. Taking Michael aside, he told him, that if he had a mind to fulfil his whimsy, they could drive home straight away, to bring back a couple of barrels, and explaining his concerns for Lu's well-being, it would kill two birds with one stone. Michael was suddenly all for the suggestion, and with Andreas volunteering to drive, after an hiatus of just ten minutes, they were on the road heading for home, leaving their perplexed companions scratching their heads. Unhindered by traffic, he was able to make good time, and as soon as they reached his home, Andreas relinquished the wheel, enabling a now sober Michael, to visit Vee, *and* load up barrels of Home Farm Cider.

Lu was surprised, but delighted when Andreas walked through the door, "What the hell are you doing back here at this time of night?" Andreas replied laughing, "I missed you so much, I just had to come home and see you!" She cocked her head to one side in disbelief, and then he told her the truth, "Michael came up with the idea of coming home, to fetch some cider for the locals up *there* to try out, and I thought it would be an ideal opportunity to come and check that you're okay. And before we go any further, I have to confess that I've been fighting, *before* you notice the bruises on my face!" She shook her head in disapproval, until he told her the full story of Reuben's broken arm, and Pa being goaded into fighting for the honour of the family, after *he* had refused, "I couldn't let Pa take a beating!" She replied, "Okay, you are forgiven *this* one time, but you will end up over my knee, if there's any more of it!" "Hey!" He reminded her, "You're supposed to put me *off* fighting!" Swooping her up into his arms, he carried her up the stairs, making love more gently than ever before, to make everything as comfortable as he could for her, and after the deed was done, he lay on his back staring at the ceiling and asked, "Are you *really* okay Lu? I wanted to come home when Reuben's arm got broke, but I was out-voted. It was only Michael's suggestion of fetching cider to sell in Stow, that provided me with the opportunity to come home!" She replied, "Of course I'm okay. Really I'm fine. Now then, if I know my sister we've got one more hour, so get off your back, and give me some *serious* sex!" *And as always, he did as he was told.*

"I could have done with you helping me to load those barrels!" Michael complained, "I had to roll them into the back of the car, using planks of wood, and with the first barrel breaking the slats, the barrel went flying, almost falling on my foot. I should really have picked them up from the *new* plant, they would have been loaded for me!" Andreas's eyebrows lifted, "Oh the plant's open is it, Lu didn't say?" Michael laughed, "You probably didn't give her the chance! Hey, we could call in at the plant, and get some of those pre-packed ciders to see how *they* go!" So arriving at the plant within minutes of turning onto the main road, Andreas gazed admiringly at the completed building, shouting to Michael, "You may as well load another barrel while you're at it!" The samples were speedily loaded by the night shift, and duly signed for. Getting under way immediately, Andreas reflected ruefully that if it hadn't been for certain members of the troupe, they could have travelled over-night on *every* trip to Stow. With the return journey taking only slightly longer than the outward, Andreas found that he was still far from being tired, when they pulled into the dimly-lit, hotel car-park. Alighting from the car, he informed Michael that he was going for another swim to freshen up, "Leave the room door ajar, so I don't disturb you when I come back!" Walking quickly to the river, he hurriedly stripped off, and disturbing the peaceful flow of rivulets gleaming like diamonds in the moonlight, he dived in without hesitation, but not with his previous rashness. Luxuriating in the tranquil ambience, his body was soon overtaken by fatigue from the fight, and the punishing drive, so deciding to return to warm hotel, he clambered from the water dripping wet, and deciding to save time, he thought he would walk *without* clothes, until his body had been dried by the gentle breeze. However as he reached the edge of town, and not having seen a soul, he decided to take a chance by walking the remaining short distance *au naturel,* and with little chance of being discovered, the only living creature he encountered, was an old dog-fox, scavenging in a dustbin. Stopping to watch the spectacle, he and the canine scrutinised each other, both fascinated by the uniqueness of the occasion, until finally the fox scurried away with his tail between his legs. Quietly unlocking the main door, Andreas crept into the room and was asleep within minutes of pulling the bedclothes over his cold body.

Waking a few hours later, he got himself ready for the day ahead, by walking to the grocer's shop for a newspaper, and noticing a row of plastic bottles of water in a refrigerated cabinet display unit, he decided to give the stuff a try. Lifting the bottle to his lips, he took a swig, not really knowing what to expect, but being instantly surprised by the fresh spring-water, he looked at the label, and noticing that it had been imported from France, he thought, *I wonder why nobody has come up with the idea of bottling British water, it would be cheaper than importing inferior French pond fluid!* And finishing the contents, he threw the empty bottle into a bin, and returned to the hotel, making a mental note to mention the bottled water to Michael. Being served with a large, but mostly greasy breakfast, he was soon joined by his companions, expressing surprise that he had been home and back, in such a short time. Riley wanted to sample the goods straight away, but Michael told him firmly, "You can get that idea out of your head right now. This is strictly for business purposes only!" With Andreas adding sternly, "The car will remain locked until *everything* has been moved to the cellar!" As soon as their fast had been broken, Andreas and Michael went to see the hotelier in his office, and being swayed by the offer of a free sample, he readily agreed to give Home Farm cider a trial run. Unlocking the car Andreas and Michael, wrestled a barrel from the car, and once the keg had been lowered into the cellar, the duo also deposited a box of mixed size cartons into the cellar. Re-locking the car, the pair returned to the bar, where the owner began pumping up the cider, until it ran clear,

"Well that's an improvement for a start!" He declared with a grin, "There's hardly any ullage!" Pouring half pints for the assemblage to test, and getting a favourable reaction, the owner asked, "How much is this stuff going to cost?" Andreas replied, "The barrel on tap now is on the house, but the other two will have to be paid for, and I've thrown in a box of the pre-packed stuff too. How much it will cost in the future will be entirely up to Michael here, so I'll leave you to discuss terms, but I'm sure it will be less than your usual brew!"

Informing Andreas that Riley had been trying to get another fight for him, Pa said that he could not find anyone willing to take him on, and looking aghast Andreas remarked, "What part of *I don't want to fight again*, do you two not understand. You made a few quid yesterday, just be content with that, but if you do want to make more cash, go up and have a few bob on the other fighters because I will definitely *not* be available!" The Romany from Dover sauntered into the bar, "Where did you disappear to last night, we were supposed to be having a drink together?" Explaining where they had been Andreas remarked, "It seems to be going down well with the regulars!" The owner poured a half for Luke to try saying, "This one is on the house!" After sipping the drink cautiously, a surprised look came onto Luke's face, "Jesus Christ *this* is seriously good. Now, if you can get some of that stuff sent down to us, it'll sell like hot cakes!" Introducing Michael, Andreas asserted with a wry smirk, "This is Vee's husband, and you will have to organise charges and delivery with him, he is in charge of all that!" Leaving them to it, Andreas and Reuben decided to re-acquaint themselves with the town, and passing the spot where he had seen the fox, Andreas recounted the tale of his naked nocturnal sojourn. "How on earth did you manage that without getting yourself arrested?" Andreas shrugged his shoulders nonchalantly saying, "I didn't think about that to be honest, but I did feel uncomfortable while I was in the water, I was sure some bastard was watching me, but if somebody wants to get off, on seeing me naked, I would suggest that they have a serious problem!" Reuben suggested, "You should be more careful, it could have been someone out to rob you, while you were *hors de combat* in the water!" Andreas answered, "I don't think so, I don't swim out *that* far, *and* I don't carry money either!" Reuben averred shaking his head, "Yeah but *they* don't know that, and if was some-one out to pinch your clothes, you'd have had to walk home with no clothes on!" Their laughter attracted stares from passing shoppers, and they were still chuckling when they entered their favourite eating place. "Now this is more like it!" Andreas said, between mouthfuls of lasagne, and when they had eaten every morsel, he went to the bar and asked to see the owner. "She's off somewhere with her son. She always goes away at this time of year, but if you leave a business-card, I'll make sure she gets it!" Andreas said that he had not brought cards with him, but his brother-in-law had spoken to the bar-maid the previous day, about selling Home Farm cider, "I'll return later with samples of the pre-packed cider, if she'd like to try it out!" "Pre-packed cider eh!" The barman said, "Now there's a novel idea, and as long it tastes okay, I'll certainly make sure that she considers it!" Andreas said, "We've recently had it patented, and so far it has not been supplied to retailers, so she will not be able to get it from anyone else but us. When I drop in the samples later today, you can judge for yourself!" The barman smiled, "I am a bit of a cider buff, as it goes, and if *I* like it, I'm sure I can persuade her to try it out!"

Walking away from the pub, Andreas said to Reuben, "The first thing to do when we get back home, is have business cards printed. Do you know anywhere local that does that sort of thing?" He replied, "Yes there's a sign-writer's shop in town, and I'm sure they do printing as well!" Andreas replied, "Ah yes, I remember now, that's my old boxing captain Cal's brother, so maybe I can get them a bit cheaper!" Reaching the hotel, they found all of the locals, knocking back Farmhouse cider, with the owner declaring, "That stuff is going down bloody well. How many barrels did you say you've got?" "Only another two!" Andreas replied, asking, "Did you come to an agreement over the price with Michael?" "Yes and it's a damned sight cheaper than our usual brew, so if the demand continues, I should do well out of it!" Andreas said with a smile, "You shouldn't have told me that, I might bump up the price!" With Michael making an entrance, Andreas brought up the subject of bottled water, "The shops here are full of the stuff, and it's all been imported from France, is there any way that *we* can produce these things at the cider factory, or would we need to splash out on new premises?" Michael answered, "The plant is big enough, so there's no reason why we can't give it a go. It would be a good little experiment, and if it *did* take off, we may even *have* to think about buying another plant. I'll go into it when we get back!" Andreas replied, "Yes and I'll square it with Viv. Anything the *Frogs* can do, I'm bloody sure that we can do better!"

Rising to his feet Pa suggested, "We're going up the hill to watch the fights!" With Reuben, still under the weather Andreas decided to accompany them as far as the eatery, as he wanted to deposit pre-packed, to whet the locals' appetite. Having acquitted that task, he decided against returning to the hotel, going for a stroll by the river instead, to see if he could find an alternative site for swimming, but arriving at his habitual bathing spot, he sat on the bank for a rest, resisting the temptation to strip off and dive in. And staring almost trance-like at the glistening wavelets, he suddenly noticed the ripples beginning to broaden, instantly returning him to reality. Standing up he looked through cupped hands toward the middle-distance, and perceived the back view of a nude female form, rising and falling dolphin-like in the water. Feeling unsettled by the spectacle, he began to walk slowly back to the hotel, and with the image of the naked form still fresh in his mind, he stopped suddenly, and realizing that it could been Jan in the water, he ran back to the spot, but with the water disappointingly calm once more, he wondered momentarily if he had imagined that too. Returning to the hotel in a more sombre mood, and still being confused about what he had seen, or thought he had seen, he shook his head in bewilderment, and deciding that an early night was needed, he quickened his pace.

Waking the following morning, he thought *thank God this is the last day, I don't think I can come back here again, there are too many ghosts.* Pa was already eating his breakfast when Andreas entered the dining room, "Are you okay son, you look as if you've seen a ghost?" Andreas smiled and answered, "I'm okay Pa I just need a bit of fresh air. I'm going to the shop for a newspaper, do you want anything?" "No thanks son. Give me a minute to finish this breakfast, and I'll walk along with you!" Walking down the road side by side, Andreas put his arm round Pa's shoulder, remarking, "You know Pa, I couldn't love you any more, than if you were my real father!" Pa smiled, "I know you do son, and I know that at times I can be hard work, but you are truly like a son to me!" Andreas purchased his paper and a bar of dark chocolate for Pa. "Good Lord!" Pa declared, "I haven't had one of these in years, not since Lala passed away really!" His face clouded at the thought, and he said sombrely, "It'll be the anniversary of her death when we go back, and it still cuts me to pieces, knowing that it was me who bought that cheap paint!" Andreas remarked, "Don't torture yourself Pa, how on earth were you to know that the paint contained lead, *or* that Lala would acquire the habit of chewing it from the window-frames!"

When they arrived at the hotel the others were busy eating breakfast, and Michael asked, "Aren't you having breakfast Andreas?" Grimacing he replied, "Not in here, I couldn't stomach it two days in a row. I'll walk into town with you, and eat at our usual place. I left samples of the cider there last night, and I'd like to see how they went down!" Leaving Michael and Reuben in the square, he headed for the place that still held memories for him, and thought that perhaps like Pa, he was torturing himself by continually dredging up the past. Entering the bar, he acknowledged a few fellow hotel guests eating breakfast, obviously having also opted to forego the fare dished up in the hotel. The barman greeted him like a long-lost friend, "I'm glad you came in. I have to say that the cider you brought in, was the finest I've *ever* tasted, and a couple of our regular cider drinkers, asked if I could get hold of more. Is there somewhere you can be reached?" Andreas wrote down Michael's name and number saying, "It's the big fellow I came in with yesterday, so you'll know who to look out for, and he is also the person that handles costing and delivery, *if* you wish to place an order!" Having eaten, he joined the others on the hill, and with the bookies busily doing a brisk trade with a large crowd, the first scrap began, but finding the spectacle holding no interest for him, he strolled back down the hill, to the town, where he found locals *and* outsiders, jostling and shouting to be served first in the Friday market. Managing to purchase presents for everyone back home, *and* as usual purchasing Pa's gifts too, he decided to drive to Gloucester for lunch, returning to the hotel to change clothes.

The *guv'nor* of the hotel approached Andreas as he was on the way out, "I've been looking all over for you, can we get the other two barrels in the cellar, I've almost sold out of the first one, and they will have to be chilled before I start serving!" Answering in the affirmative, Andreas replied, "Certainly, but can you get someone to help me lift them out of the car?" So with the assistance of two regulars, the barrels were taken from the back of the car and lowered into the cellar. Andreas called down to the owner, "You can settle up with Michael, he'll be back shortly!" And now having only one carton of pre-packed, he thought he would tout them in Gloucester, to prevent Pa and Riley being comatose when they arrived home. Within an hour of leaving Stow, he was driving down the streets of Gloucester, and searching for a likely place to start, he pulled up outside the New Inn, and taking a bite of the cheese sandwich, that he had purchased, he asked to speak to the manager, who arrived within minutes, wearing a worried frown. Andreas immediately put him at ease, by assuring him that his reason for wishing to see him was purely business, and bringing in the last carton, he handed over a dozen bags, telling the manager, that there was no charge for the samples, "If they fare well, we can be contacted on this number!" He said handing the manager a slip of paper, containing Michael's details. "We are returning home from Stow tomorrow, so we'll pop in for breakfast, and if the cider has pleased your customers, you can get the prices from Michael our master-blender, who is also in charge of sales!" Leaving the New Inn, Andreas walked up the road to The Imperial, a pub specialising in real ales, and ordering coffee, he spoke to the manager about the possibility of *them* also selling Home Farm cider. Leaving more samples, he gave the same promise to return the following morning, and once his coffee had been finished, he set off back to Stow.

Arriving three quarters of an hour later, he headed straight for the bar, guessing correctly where his companions would head as soon as the fighting had ceased. Telling Michael of the potential business openings in Gloucester, he was interrupted by Riley, "Why should we waste time going to Gloucester?" Andreas replied tersely, "Does it really matter to you *where* you drink on the way home? That's where we're going, and that's an end of it!" Knowing that the others would not mind *where* they stopped for breakfast, and deciding that he'd had enough of Riley's shenanigans, he said sternly, "This is definitely the last time that I'll be coming here. It's okay for you lot, you can relax and have a good time, while I do the driving, and see to all your problems!"

Going upstairs, Andreas lay on the bed and falling easily into a deep sleep, he was wakened a while later by the honking of a horn from the car park. Rising wearily from the bed, he looked out of the window, and noticing that his car was causing an obstruction, he splashed cold water onto his face and went downstairs. "I'm sorry mate, if you reverse a few feet I'll shift my car!" Hearing the driver uttering a few foul-mouthed oaths as he opened the car door, Andreas could feel his hackles rising, but in spite of the fact that his sleep had been disturbed, he managed to hold his temper. Sitting in the car, he started the engine, waiting for the other car to begin reversing, and realizing that the driver had no intention of moving, Andreas got out of the car, and walked over to find the driver impatiently drumming his fingers, he asked, "Are you going to *move* your car or what?" The driver turned grinning to his passengers, "Or what!" Andreas went to his car, locked the door, and began walking back toward the hotel, but hearing a car door slam, and footsteps running towards him, Andreas spun round just before the man reached him, and delivered a well aimed punch to the jaw. Hearing the crack of bone, and seeing his would-be assailant crumple to the floor, Andreas walked over to the startled passengers, remarking, "I think he might need the hospital, so if one of you kind gentlemen can sit behind the wheel and reverse, I'll let you out!" Picking up their companion's prostrate body, two of the men placed his unconscious form into the rear of the car, while the other got behind the wheel, and reversed. Smiling broadly, Andreas sarcastically thanked them, and parked the car in another spot. Feeling the need for another shower after the altercation, and ready for a change of clothes, after sleeping in the ones he had been wearing, he went straight to the room.

Believing himself to be almost human again, he entered the bar, finding all the usual suspects in attendance in their usual places at the bar, and with all being special people in different off-beat ways, they were *real* characters. Andreas had the thought that perhaps in a few years time, when the boys were a little older, he would bring them to Stow to meet this disparate crew, and joining his companions, the senior members of whom were already well *oiled,* he was aware that they would be the devil's own job to rouse in the morning. The last night customarily was party time, and the celebrations were already well under way, with Mollie busily plying her trade, finding that nobody was yet that drunk. Laughing Lennie had already given his matinee performance, with his maniacal laughing for no apparent, never failing to bring a smile to everyone's face, and feeling in a much lighter frame of mind, Andreas *almost* changed his mind about not coming back with this lot again.

As usual Andreas was the only member from their band of soldiers to be in attendance in the dining room for breakfast, but looking at the fare dripping with grease, he walked out of the hotel in the hope of finding somewhere else open at that time of the morning. On the way into town he encountered the barman from their regular eating place, and asked, "Is there a chance of you serving food as early as this?" The barman replied, "We don't normally open for business until ten o'clock, but for you, I'll make an exception!" Falling in beside him, Andreas asked when the owner would be back, with the man replying, "Tomorrow, so I reckon your brother-in-law will be getting a call pretty soon!" Within a short time of arriving at the pub, a full English breakfast had been served up, and swiftly despatched, then asking for the bill, Andreas said, "I'll have to get back, the others won't even be out of bed yet. Waving away Andreas's attempt to settle up, the barman averred, "The samples you gave me yesterday will more than pay for the meal, and I've put several pouches aside for the owner to try!" Andreas shook his hand, "Thank you very much for a delicious meal, and I really have to dash, I've got grown up children to organise, and I'll tell Michael to expect a call!"

Returning to the hotel, he found that all except Pa and Riley had risen, and going directly to their room, he banged on the door, then entered, shouting loudly "Right you two, you've got fifteen minutes to wash and pack. If you're not ready, we'll be leaving without you. That is no idle threat, and if you're hungry, you'll have to wait until we get to Gloucester!" Walking towards the door he turned to remind them, "Remember, fifteen minutes, not one second longer!" Going downstairs, Andreas settled his bill, and opening the car for everyone to stow their cases, he enlightened the ensemble of his decision to leave in fifteen minutes. Looking at his watch after ten, he started the engine, and smiling two minutes later, he saw the pair rushing out of the door, carrying half-closed cases in their arms, with Pa's shirt hanging out of his trousers, and Riley almost tripping over his untied laces. The humour of the farce was compounded when Andreas inched the car forward, and in the panic, several items of clothing fell from both cases, and still edging forward Andreas suddenly accelerated toward the park entrance as they drew near. The crowd that had gathered to watch the spectacle roared with laughter, as the pair ran hell for leather to catch up, and finally cramming in their cases, they took their places in the car, and the return home finally got under way. Andreas smiled, noticing that a pair of Pa's underpants had been left on the ground in the park, which all of a sudden determined Pa's Christmas present! Apart from the complaints that he had to endure about there being no cider, the short trip to Gloucester passed peacefully enough, and arriving at the

New Inn, they all ordered breakfast. Andreas introduced Michael to the manager, who informed them that the pre-packed had gone down particularly well, and learning the prices from Michael, he immediately placed an order. With the others still eating, Andreas and Michael walked the short distance to the Imperial, where they received a similar substantial order, and on their return, they found that the usual duo had taken advantage of the unexpected opportunity to have a session. Andreas hated being a wet blanket, but he wanted to get home quickly to Lu, so when they had all returned to the car, he insisted that any further stops would be for toilet purposes only, and that *they* would be made in country lanes. Sure enough after half an hour, he had to accommodate Riley's weak bladder, and when they came to a stop in a country lane, Andreas asked them *all* to take advantage of the stop, "I'm not stopping every five minutes!" Once their toilet needs had been attended to, Andreas did not spare the horses for the rest of the journey, and with no distractions, such good time was made, that Pa and Riley only managed to *half* empty the hip-flask. Pulling up in front of Riley's place, Andreas got out of the car, and raced up the steps to receive his customary kiss from Dolores, an act never failing to produce a scowl from Riley. Finally reaching Pa's after dropping off the rest of the crew, Andreas found a pleasant surprise waiting for him as he carried Pa's case into the house, and embracing his ever increasing family, he remarked, "Are you okay Lu, you look a little pale?" "I'm fine. Did you have a good time looking after everybody?" Smiling Andreas remarked, "Well it's certainly not much of a break for *me,* and I've made up my mind, never to do it again. Reuben can take it on, and you can bet your life that Pa and Riley won't play *him* up the way they do me. I managed to bag another three customers for our cider, while I was there, and they were really impressed by the brew, so I'm hoping it could be the start of something really big. How is the work going with the maisonettes and the Priory?" Lu corrected him, "Have you forgotten that the hotel is now called The Krallis? When the cider plant was finished, half the crew were transferred to the hotel, and half to the maisonettes, so *everything* is coming along fine!" Entering the room with plates of stew Ma said, "If you can all stop talking for a while, you can get some *decent* food down you for a change!" Without a word of protest the two pilgrims sat down, and with tribute having been duly paid to the day-old rabbit stew, Andreas and his family, said their farewells and returned home. Lu and the kids went upstairs, leaving Andreas sitting on the settee, totally relaxed for the first time in days, with a cup of *real* coffee, and as soon as the brandy-laced beverage had been drained, he noticed that Lu had not returned downstairs. Going to the bedroom, he found Lu laying half asleep on top of the covers. He asked, "What's wrong Lu, you are not your usual self?" Getting no reply, he carefully undressed, and covered her with the top layer of bedclothes, but instinctively sensing that something was radically wrong, and with the birth of their fourth child being imminent, he phoned Ma for advice. "Best let her lie, and contact the *drabardi* in the morning!" Putting coal dust on top of the embers of the fire to keep it low, but still glowing, he turned out the lights and went to bed.

24

Sensing that all was not well with Lu, Andreas snapped on the light, and seeing blood all over the covers, he leapt from the bed and phoned for an ambulance, stressing that it was an emergency, "She is unconscious, and haemorrhaging!" Going to the boys' bedroom he gently woke Victor, "I have to take *mamousse* to the hospital, so you will have to see to the others in the morning. Can you do that for me?" "Yes *daddi*, is she having the baby now?" Andreas confessed, "Son, I'm not sure of anything yet, and she's not very well, so I have to get her to the hospital, just to be on the safe side!" Hearing a knocking at the door he told his son, "There's the ambulance now. Don't bother getting up, just make sure that neither you nor the young ones go into that bedroom!" They carried her out on a stretcher, and climbing into the back of the ambulance with her, he held her hand all the way to the hospital, where she was rushed immediately to a side-ward. The doctor drew a curtain round the bed, while a nurse led Andreas away to a waiting room, and in his deeply distressed state, he inexplicably picked up one of the magazines, and began to complete a half-finished crossword puzzle. But throwing the periodical down fiercely after a few minutes, he paced around the room until the doctor returned. With his face full of concern Andreas asked, "Is she okay. Can I see her?" The doctor's face was stern, "She's sedated so I'm afraid you cannot see her at the moment. We've managed to stop the bleeding, so she is relatively comfortable. And my brief examination tells me that sadly, the foetus is no longer alive, and with our primary concerns now being for the mother, she will have a scan, followed by a minor operation to remove the foetus, and we *should* know by then, just what the problem is. She is still pretty poorly, but having stopped the bleeding, we have managed to stabilise her condition, so the best thing all round would be for you to return home, and come back later. The scan is scheduled for nine thirty, so if you come back between ten and eleven o'clock, we will hopefully have good news for you then, and try not to worry, she is in capable hands!" "Thank you doctor!" Andreas murmured, "I'll be back at ten!"

Getting a taxi home, he found Victor sitting on the settee wide awake, "*Mamouse* is really ill isn't she?" "Yes son!" He replied looking at the floor, and believing that telling Victor the truth of the matter, would be the best thing, he imparted the bad news, "She's lost the baby, and has to have a scan, and an operation later this morning. I'd better let your grandma know!" After informing Ma of the night's events, he spent an hour phoning the rest of the family, playing down the seriousness of the situation, as Victor was still downstairs, listening to every word. Going into the living room, he poked the fire until it burst into flame, then added two logs, and a few lumps of coal to the flames. Judging his son *savvy* enough to know the truth, he told Victor the truth, "I'm afraid it's serious son, she was losing blood heavily on the way to hospital, which they have managed to stop. They have sedated her, so she is in no pain, but she is still very weak. I have to return to the hospital at ten o'clock to learn the results of a scan, so why don't you go back to bed now, and try to get a couple of hours shut-eye. I have things to do right now, but don't worry, I'll wake you all in time for school!" Walking his son back to his bedroom, he tucked him in, as he had when he was younger, kissed his forehead and that of his sleeping brother, then peeped in on Rosie, without tarrying too long, as she was such a light sleeper. Entering the bedroom, he stripped the bed, and after putting the bedding into the washing machine, he dragged the blood-stained mattress downstairs to the shed, in case any of them, did happen to wander into the room. When he was satisfied that no more could be done, he sat in front of the fire in his armchair, and stared into the coals until he drifted mercifully into a much-troubled sleep.

Waking with a start, he looked at the clock, and noting that it was eight thirty, he panicked having not yet woken the kids, until he heard their voices in the kitchen, and seeing the children finishing off their breakfast, all ready for school. He told them, "Hang on, I'll drive you to school!" Answering for the others, Victor, "It's okay dad we'll walk, you get yourself ready to go to the hospital!" Putting on their coats ready to leave, Victor paused at the door, "It's all right dad I've told them that mamousse has been taken to hospital, and don't worry, they're okay!" Walking them to the gate, Andreas hugged his children, and silently thanking God for blessing him with such wonderful children, he watched until they were out of sight. Going back into the warmth of the house, he phoned Ma to ask if she and Pa would go with him to the hospital, and putting down the phone, he went upstairs to get ready.

Dressing, his eyes were drawn to the bare bones of the bed, and realized that new bedding, would have to be purchased, *Lu would not want to sleep on a bed that could be considered marame.* Looking at the clock once more, and noting that it was now five minutes past nine, he phoned the shop from where he had last purchased the bedroom furniture, ordering a completely new bed and set of bedding, before leaving to pick up his parents. The journey to the hospital was conducted in almost total silence, with each being afraid of voicing their fears. Arriving at the hospital, Ma began to sob uncontrollably, and with Pa consoling her, Andreas ushered them into the waiting room. Managing to locate the doctor quickly, they walked together to the waiting room, where Ma and Pa were waiting anxiously. Gravely he reported the result of the scan, "I'm afraid that the prognosis is not good. The scan shows that she has choriocarcinoma, something of which I'm sure you will never have heard of. It's an extremely rare, but potentially dangerous form of cancer of the uterus. When the foetus is removed this morning, we'll be able to tell whether the cancer cells will have to be removed then, or at a later date. The latter would be the best scenario all round, as she has lost a fair amount of blood. If the cells have spread, we would *have* to take a chance on removing them, and I have to tell you that she has no more than a fair chance of pulling through such a procedure at his stage. There *is* hope but I'm afraid that you must all be prepared for the worst!" The words were like daggers to Andreas's heart, and with both parents beginning to sob uncontrollably, Andreas put his arms around them both, guiding them to a seat. The doctor added, "We feel that it would not be wise to wait too long, and we will need your signature, allowing us to continue!"

"Of course!" Andreas answered, and following the nurse into the office, he signed the consent form, and was told that they could sit with Lu until she went to the theatre. With Andreas sitting one side of the bed and her parents the other, they held her hands, willing her to pull through the horrific nightmare that had suddenly blighted their lives. A bespectacled nurse, wearing hat and gown, with a mask dangling from one ear, suddenly appeared to tell them that it was time to go down to the theatre, and still holding her hands, the trio accompanied the trolley, as far as they were permitted. Walking back with them to the waiting room, another nurse gently persuaded the distraught family to accompany her to the canteen, "It's almost lunch-time and a cup of tea and a sandwich will do you the world of good!" Sitting in silence, they nibbled on the snack, with the cup of sweet, strong tea being a balm to their frayed senses, giving them a focus, and some semblance of normality. Returning once again to the waiting room, and feeling a little better, the surgeon sent for them after a fifteen minute wait, mercifully giving them little time to dwell on matters. Telling them that the cancerous cells *had* already begun to spread, which left them with no other option, than to operate straight away, "She haemorrhaged badly during the operation, and is now considerably much weaker!" Andreas asked, "Tell us frankly doctor, what are her chances now?" "They're not good I'm afraid! We've done everything we can, but with losing that amount of blood, she may now be too weak to pull through. I'm dreadfully sorry!" He reported sadly, "But it's simply a matter of time either way!" With the kick to his heart strangely having an air of inevitability about it, Andreas asserted, "I'll get the rest of the family!" Gathering the family quickly and collecting Maria too,

Andreas returned to the hospital, finding Michael, Vee and Lily-Ann already in the side-ward. As soon as the hospital padre arrived to deliver the last rites, the children began weeping, and with Andreas encircling his sons, Rosie and Lily-Ann buried their heads into Ma's coat front. Their angel left them, peacefully and thankfully pain-free, fifteen minutes later, and thirty minutes before her body was due to endure more surgery. His wonderful Lulu had gone, and he did not know how he would survive without her, but he knew that for the sake of his children, he would *have* to.

Being stunned and numbed, the family wanted only to go home, and shut out the rest of the world, but with Andreas needing the family's presence to help him console his children, he persuaded them to return to the place that had been Lu's home. Feeling awkward once they were all ensconced in the living room, Andreas, at the risk of his actions being misconstrued, poured everybody a generous measure of Tolley's, to toast the passing of their loved one, and raising their glasses to her memory, the grieving ensemble downed the healing liquid in one *swally,* and with Michael and Victor repairing to the kitchen to make sandwiches, Andreas poured more of the same. To them it was a perfectly natural way of expressing a tribute to one who was adored by everybody, and when the sandwiches had all been eaten, the assembly began drifting away, returning to their homes, to mourn in their own private and personal way. When the last one had left, Andreas and his children were left alone in their shared grief, with the enormity of what had happened hitting them hard. Sitting in his armchair, he wondered how they would all cope, and as a solitary tear trickled down Victor's stoical face, he disturbed his father's mournful reverie, "Come on *daddi,* let's all go for a walk!" Acquiescing immediately, he smiled wistfully saying, "Okay son, we'll do that, but mind and wrap up well, winter seems to have arrived extra early this year!" Walking in almost total silence along the river bank, Rosie slipped her hand into her father's and bitterly regretting that Lu would now never see her children marry or bounce grand-children on her knee, he vowed to do his best to be both a father and a mother. He had not seen Viv, but knowing that he would be aware of what had happened, Andreas made a mental note to ring him later to help arrange things, with the family being too distressed to be of any assistance, being confident that Viv would want to contribute in some way. The soft, chilling breeze blew away the cobwebs from his mind, and he resolved for the good of the family, and his own sanity, to get things running in the home as near as *dammit* to normal, knowing in his heart however, that *nothing* would ever be normal again. Reaching the spot where Michael had re-routed the river, they turned back for home, and being aware that his children's emotional needs were paramount, he resolved to shelve his own feelings, and just be strong for *them.*

Arriving home he warmed up the rabbit stew, that Lu had made the previous day, and after serving the potage in the living room, he poked and re-charged the fire, while his children ate in front of the television, but feeling no need for food himself, he slumped down on the settee, absent-mindedly watching, whatever held his children's attention. Joining him on the settee once they had eaten, with a boy on either side and Rosie on his lap, remarking as she snuggled into his neck, "You haven't shaved *daddi, and* you smell of that brandy!" Smiling, he went to the bathroom, and as the hot spray cascaded over his body, he realized that it would not be good for the children to see him falling into the trap of letting things slide. Returning to his niche between his two sons, Rosie rose from Victor's lap and snuggled into his neck once more, "Do I smell better now?" He asked. "Yes *daddi*, much better now!" She proclaimed. Before too long she grew tired and carrying her to bed, he found on his return that George had also taken himself off to bed. Going to the cabinet, he poured himself a Tolley's on the rocks with Victor remarking, "Do you think that's a good idea dad, you haven't had anything to eat?" Looking at the concern on his son's face, he poured the liquid into the sink, and placing two logs onto the fire, he sat down on the settee. Victor went to the kitchen, returning in minutes with sandwiches, and putting the plate on the table, he ordered his father, "Eat!" Looking up at the boy who had suddenly become a man, Andreas realized in that moment how blessed he was, *and as always, he did as he was told.*

Sitting with his arm around his sleeping son, Andreas heard a knock at the door, and with Victor now fully awake, he went to the door and admitted Viv, then the three men, stood in the middle of the room, arms clasped tightly around one another in silent grief. Andreas made coffee and cream, managing to lace it with a generous measure of brandy, without Victor seeing, then turning off the television, he put a couple of logs on the fire. Asking Viv immediately, if he would organize the funeral, he explained that *he* would have enough on his hands tending to the children, and making sure that they had suitable clothing for the affair. Viv replied, "Of course, it will be an honour, and if there's anything more you need me to do, you only have to ask!" Andreas told Viv that he would be going back to work at the start of the following week, and that the kids would attend school in the usual way, believing that it would be good for them all, *not* to mope around the house. When Viv had left, Andreas asked Victor what he thought about moving house when it was all over, and conceding that it would probably be the best thing for Rosie, Victor commented that he wasn't bothered either way himself. Andreas wanted them disturbed as little as possible from their routine, and at least with Viv taking on the responsibility of the funeral arrangements, Andreas could concentrate on his children's immediate needs. With Victor making more sandwiches, Andreas realized that in the awful aftermath of Lu's sudden passing, Victor had suddenly become his rock. Kissing his son goodnight, Andreas poked the fire, spread coal dust over the embers, and settled down to sleep on the settee. Falling asleep soon after laying down, he woke in the middle of the night, totally disoriented, and automatically reaching out for Lu, he was suddenly struck by the awful reality, of never having her in his arms again. Lying in the dark, with now only the smallest ember from the fire lighting the room, he found a return to sleep hard to come by, and after an hour of tossing and turning, he gave up the attempt. Pouring a stiff one, he turned on the *comfort* of the television set, and with the drink having the desired soporific effect, George found his father in the morning, propped up on cushions, with a blank television throwing out a monotonous humming tone. Wakening when he heard the boys making breakfast, he realized that it was Saturday, and the boys would have work at the farm, so rousing himself, he cleaned out the fire, put on more logs and peat, then put away his bedding. When the boys left an hour or so later, Rosie had still not roused herself, *just like her mother* he thought wistfully, and creeping up the stairs, he watched her sleeping, noting an unconscious smile on her face. His heart overflowed with love, being certain that she would break a few hearts in the future, including his own. She was *so* still, that in a sudden moment of panic, he woke her to see if she was okay, and rubbing her eyes, she looked up into his face with a smile. Lifting her delicate frame from the bed, Andreas hugged her tightly, becoming aware that his children would be a source of comfort to him in the coming days, and *he* wanted so much, to be a support for *them* too. Carrying her downstairs, he sat her in front of the television, and began to prepare breakfast, "Will you be going to school with the boys on Monday?" Andreas asked. "I think so dad, I wouldn't want to miss any lessons!" She answered seriously. Being surprised at her innate pragmatism, he recalled that Lu had once remarked how much like him they all were in their ways, and of course, as usual she had been right. When his sons returned home from the farm at lunchtime, he admitted, "I'm sorry boys, it will have to be chips and something, I forgot all about dinner. Unless you'd like to go for a meal somewhere, maybe the Green Man, but you'll have to tidy yourself up first!" Pulling faces, they trooped off to the bathroom, and despite the overall situation he could not help but smile wryly, and ringing Gunnar, he asked if he would like to join them.

Seeing no appreciable changes in the place when they arrived, Andreas suggested, "Let's sit near the door, so Uncle Gunnar can see us easily when he comes in!" Within minutes of Gunnar entering the old pub, Andreas could immediately see, by his brother's swollen blood-shot eyes that he had been crying, and running across to greet him, Rosie threw her arms around him, while the boys rose solemnly to shake his hand. Andreas was proud of his children, and knew that Lu would be looking down on them feeling that same sense of pride. Andreas gripped Gunnar by the arms saying, "Have you seen Ma and Pa yet?" "Yes!" Gunnar answered, "Like all of us, they're completely devastated!" Andreas murmured solemnly, "I hope you won't mind but I've asked Viv to organise the funeral. I just couldn't face it!" "Of course I don't mind!" He replied, "With him, you can be sure that everything will be tastefully, and respectfully done!" For the sake of the children Andreas changed the subject by asking how things were faring at the garage, and replying that the new self-service was doing well, he added that trade was brisk on *all* fronts. When they had finished eating Andreas announced, "I will be taking the kids to see Ma and Pa when we've finished here. I'm not looking forward to it, but it has to be done!" Gunnar commented, "I won't be in *this* place too much longer anyway, I made arrangements to meet up with Pearl!" Looking at his watch he averred, "In fact I'm already late, so if you'll excuse me leaving so abruptly, I'll make a move. Thanks for the meal Andreas, I'll catch up with you later!" On the way home, Andreas and his family called in on Ma and Pa to see how they were coping, and being as upset as Gunnar had warned, they made an early exit, with Andreas fearing the effect that their grief may have on the kids. Returning home, Andreas made coffee for himself and the boys, while Rosie, having developed a taste for the bottled water, developed at the cider plant, helped herself to a bottle from the fridge. Suggesting another walk, Victor asked, "Can we go to the spot we went to yesterday?" "Tell you what!" Andreas said, "Let's drive instead, then we can visit the new lido!" "That's a great idea daddi!" He answered, and pausing, he looked up at his father, "I'll be driving soon, so I'll be able to drive you anywhere you wanna go!" He realized suddenly, that there was actually, little difference age-wise, between his son, and that of himself and Gunnar, when Dinky had taught them, all those years ago, *doesn't time fly*, he thought, *and oh how I wish those halcyon days were still here.* Walking along the bank of the river, with George tightly gripping his sister's hand, and Victor side by side with his father, discussing the farm, and in particular the blending of apples, Victor suggested, "I reckon there's room to plant more trees in the outer field, *if* Uncle Michael agrees!" Andreas thought, *how like me he's becoming, in nature for sure, but in looks too. George was like him too, but much more of a peacemaker, than I ever was. They will make an excellent partnership if, and when I retire.* Reaching their objective, Andreas looked admiringly at what had been achieved at the spot, and after skimming a few flat stones across the stream, the heavens opened up, with the deluge dampening their already sombre mien. Dashing to the car, he appreciated the wisdom of having driven to the lido, and with the homeward journey being conducted in silence, the horses were not spared, and after poking the fire, the house soon assumed it's mantle of comforting warmth. Tolley's and coke in hand, he rang Dinky to arrange driving lessons for *both* boys, *George will be fine, as long as he doesn't stray onto the road*, he opined. Having exacted that task, he made toast and coffee, with Rosie opting once more for bottled water from the fridge. Eating their snack in front of the television, Viv and Katie came calling, with Victor, having finished his snack, he jumped up immediately, to make sandwiches and coffee for their guests. "I've come to let you know that the funeral is all arranged. It's to take place on Thursday morning, at ten forty five. Andreas nodded,

"Thank you Viv, I really appreciate your help!" When the sandwiches had been eaten, Viv rose from his seat, and looking down at the floor, he coughed nervously, "If we can have a private word, there's something that I'd like to put to you!" Looking askance at his friend, he said, "We'll go into the kitchen!" Realizing straight away, as he walked in the door, that the floor needed cleaning, which was one of Lu's many chores that he had taken for granted, that he would now have to deal with himself, he asked!" "What's the problem Viv?" And speaking almost apologetically, Viv said, "I've an idea for the ceremony, that I'd like you to consider!" After pausing for a moment, he continued, "I know that it's an extremely delicate suggestion, but I had the idea of re-uniting Lu with Lala. Before you say anything, I know that it could be distressing, but in the long run, it could turn out to be less so, with one celebration of their lives, being held each year, and it would be wonderful for both girls, to be together once more. But thinking about it now, perhaps I should have left the idea in my head. I'm dreadfully sorry if I've upset you!" Andreas replied softly, "Please, there is no need to apologize. Personally, I think it's a wonderful idea, but I will have to consult Ma and Pa. If they think it inappropriate, it will definitely not happen. I'll phone them now, while you are here!" Phoning his parents, he could tell instantly that Ma was upset, but after he had explained everything, she agreed on behalf of both of them, and standing in the hall with the phone still in his hand, he was stricken with a sudden sense of loss. All the while that everything was in the future, he did not have to cope with life without Lu, but with arrangements now having been made, he had to face up to reality. With a heavy heart, he bade Viv goodnight, and rang everyone, appraising them of the time and date, a painful but necessary chore. He then relaxed with the kids, in front of the television, until tiring, they trudged the wooden hill, and half an hour after they had left their father, comfortable but solitary, he stoked the fire, scattering the *nest* with a layer of coal dust, then removing the spare bedding from the airing cupboard, he surrendered to the night

25

Shivering from the early morning chill, and with the bedclothes wrapped around his body like a pall, he stumbled to the fire, and poked the embers until small flames burst into life across the blackened stubble. Placing a couple of logs onto the *nest*, he turned on the television, and in next to no time at all, the room was bathed in warmth, and wearily stirring himself, he went to the kitchen to make coffee. Relaxing with his first cuppa of the day, and settling down on the settee to watch the news, he heard of the premature death of a foreign dignitary, and learning of the tragedy, suddenly, and starkly brought it home to him, that in just four days time, his own wonderful Lulu, and mother of his children, would be laid to rest, and feeling suddenly very alone, he indulged himself in grief and sadness, having pre-determined to only show his grief, when no-one was around, and *this,* was one of those private moments. Looking across at the clock, and noting that it was eight o'clock, he began to prepare breakfast from the farm produce, that the boys had brought home with them the previous day, and once the meal had been prepared, he wakened the boys. And with his melancholy now dispelled, he carried Rosie downstairs to join her brothers, who were now sitting in front of the television, eating their meal from a tray. Before going upstairs to get himself ready, he told them that they would all be going into town, to get them rigged out for their mother's funeral, and feeling better after a shower, he entered the bedroom to get changed. And looking across at the still denuded bed, melancholia returned to nibble at his nether regions, compounded when he opened the wardrobe door, and saw Lu's clothes, hanging neatly in a row. Deciding that he would have to dispose of the clothes at some point in the future, he would execute the task as soon as possible, considering it advisable to have *all* the upset more or less at the same time, rather than prolonging the agony. Changing into jeans, he donned a sweater over his tee-shirt, and rang Michael to tell him that the boys would not be in to work, as he was taking them into town to purchase suits for the funeral. Shops in town had been opening on Sundays for a few months, with the stores realizing that market trade, would reward *their* enterprise, in attracting customers, prepared to spend money on items, that could *not* be purchased elsewhere on a Sunday.

The town was crowded as they made their way to the gents' outfitters, and letting the boys choose their own clothes for Thursday's ceremony, he stipulated that the outfits had to be sober and similar, with black ties over white shirts. Choosing wisely they both opted for dark grey suits, with George's differing only slightly by having a broader black vertical stripe, and with their black shoes being purchased from the shop next door, the task was executed quickly. Depositing the bags in the boot of the car, he decided to call in on Guaril and Barbara, in order to make sure that *he* would be suitably clad too, being aware that he had *never* been too fussy about the way he dressed. Barbara commented, "Don't worry about him, I'll make sure he's spic-and-span!" Andreas smiled, "I know you will. I'm going to have to take Rosie back into town in a minute, to get *her* clothes, so would it be okay for me to leave the boys here for an hour?" Barbara declared, "You sit here, and chat to Guaril, *I'll* take Rosie into town, I will know *exactly* what to get!" Andreas thought that being a woman she *would* know of course, and he was truly grateful for her offer of help, having been fretting about the kind of clothes that a girl her age would wear to a funeral, and in particular that of her mother. Donning her coat, Barbara offered her hand to Rosie who smiled up at her, as she grasped the proffered hand. Realizing that in the very near future, he would be needing even more female assistance, being aware that there *was* in existence, things that he had little or no knowledge of, in regard to the raising of young girls, and *he*, like all gypsy males, possessed a traditional aversion to anything that could be considered *marame!* While Guaril was busily making a fuss of the boys, Andreas realized that *all* of his family had been close to his children, with him being absent for much of their early years, and his brothers, possessed a special bond with them, being the only male members of their side of the family, that they would have seen on a regular basis. Andreas silently vowed to re-dress that situation in the future.

Within an hour Rosie and Barbara had returned with bags bulging with clothes, with Rosie parading in her new clothes, and watching her smiling face, Andreas declared to her obvious delight, "*You* will be the prettiest girl there!" Thanking Barbara for her help, they walked to the flat to see Walthaar, who seemingly had another new girl-friend installed at the flat. Andreas recognized her from somewhere, but could not for the life of him quite put a name to the face, and with curiosity finally getting the better of him, he asked, "Where do I know your face from?" "I'm Maria's sister Ruby!" She declared. And standing back to have a better look, he realized, that it now seemed light years ago, that he had seen her at the market selling pegs, along with Maria, and having lost her *puppy-fat*, she had blossomed into a beautiful young woman. "Ah yes, I remember you now. How *is* Maria?" He asked. "She's okay!" Ruby answered, "Crying a lot, but she'll be fine. Can I get you a coffee?" Declining the offer he thought, *she's got her feet well and truly under the table by the looks of things,* and after a further half an hour of chatting, he asked, "If the offer of coffee still stands, I'll take advantage!" Watching as she left for the kitchen, Andreas lifted his eyebrows, while Walthaar, merely shrugged his shoulders, as was his wont. Returning with steaming mugs a couple of minutes later, Andreas found the brew to be, just as he liked it, and appreciably nodding in her direction, he remarked, "Now *that*, is what I call coffee!" With Walthaar noticing that the kids had not spoken since they arrived he asked with a grin, "What's the matter with you lot then. Cat got your tongue? Come on over here, and give your old uncle a big hug!" Dutifully the two boys trooped across to hug him, with Rosie predictably *diving* on top of him. Not being used to their uncle having a woman in the flat, the kids had been understandably subdued, but now that the ice had been broken, the kids were their old selves. Suddenly feeling familiarly comfortable in the surroundings, Andreas noticed however, that the place could do with a lick of paint, with the whole flat beginning to look a little jaded. When he mentioned the fact, Walthaar explained that he and Ruby had been planning on making a start, but due to the tragedy, it had been shelved, and fully understanding the reason, Andreas said no more on the subject. With Ruby's re-entrance with more coffee, breaking the awkward silence, Andreas asked him if he would phone the furniture shop to ensure that *everything* would be delivered the following day, "My back is killing me with having to sleep on the settee!" "Yes of course!" And consulting his watch, Walthaar remarked, "I'd better do it *now*, they close at twelve on Sundays!" Upon discovering that the bedroom items *were* indeed being delivered the following day, Andreas decided that it was time to go, being walked to the door, by the lovebirds.

Calling in at the garage to fill up and get the car washed, he pulled up beside a petrol-pump, and when Gunnar had ambled slowly across, Andreas told him where they had been, "Ruby seems like a nice girl, he could do a lot worse than end up with her!" Gunnar did not answer, and for the first time ever, Andreas fell ill at ease with him, with both being unable to say what was really in their hearts, and it was a relief to both, when Andreas rolled back out onto the road and headed home. Driving home, with the problem of just what to have for dinner being paramount, he wondered what he could make them for a change, but the dilemma had already been resolved however, with Ma having visited, leaving rabbit stew and dumplings in the kitchen. Finding it gratifying to suddenly realize, that he was *not* the only one attempting to return to normality, although sadly he feared that *Pa* would *never* recover from this second body blow. With Viv and Katie arriving, he told them of his fears for both Pa and Gunnar, "I think Gunnar needs less time on his hands!" Viv declared, "We've just had an order for cider from Stow, so I'll get him to deliver it, I'm sure that the garage can manage without him for a day or so. It will keep him busy, and do us a favour at the same time. He can stay over-night if he wants, but in any case, he would be back by Wednesday afternoon at the very latest!" "Good idea!" Andreas conceded, it'll keep his mind from everything here, for a while anyway. I know for sure that he has never been there before!" And making sure the kids did not hear him, he added, "And maybe he'll meet someone decent, instead of that *dog* he's with now!" He hated speaking that way about anybody, and especially in such close proximity to his kids, but she was certainly not the kind of woman, deserving of a man of Gunnar's stature. With bedtime arriving, Katie took Rosie's hand, walked up the stairs with her, and tucking her into bed, she kissed her cheek. And after staying for a few drinks, they made their way home, leaving Andreas to settle down on the settee alone.

Early the next morning, just before Andreas left for work, the new bed and appurtenances arrived inopportunely, but realizing that he had not arranged for Ma to accept the delivery, he thought it *opportune*. Leaving the stuff where the deliverymen had left it, he hastily took the kids to school, having already written notes, to explain the need for their absence on the day of the funeral, reminding Rosie, *not* to forget to hand in *hers* to the teacher. Arriving at work, a little tardy and dishevelled, he strode purposefully into his office, and finding a pile of mail on his desk, most of which were condolence cards, he placed the cards on the window ledge, drunk the mandatory coffee, and asked Becky if there was anything requiring his immediate attention. She informed him that John Scamp had been in, having received a reply from the ombudsman, and wanted to discuss the matter further with him. Mentioning the fact that he had been in most lunchtimes, she suggested that it would probably not require an appointment. Andreas commented, "Lunch-time will be fine if he comes in, as I've nothing on, and I'll be taking a couple of hours off this afternoon, to visit estate agents!" She replied, "There's nothing on, but why don't you *trawl* the internet from the comfort of your own office?" Smiling wryly, he walked over to the computer, and Becky added, "Forgive me for asking, but why are you thinking of moving?" Andreas replied "Well, Lu and I *had* discussed it, when we learned that she was pregnant, because of the need for an extra room, which unfortunately, will not be required now, but I feel that a move might be the best thing in the circumstances, especially for the children. Lu and I had planned to turn our house over to Will Jones anyway, so a fresh start would suit *everyone* all round!" Using the computer diligently, he jotted down the particulars of the likeliest properties, finding that lunch-time came more quickly than he anticipated, when Becky ushered John Scamp into the office. "Good morning Krallis!" John declared breezily, "I've had a reply from the ombudsman, *and* the mortgage lenders want to settle out of court. What do you think?" As no figure had been offered, there seemed little that he could do at that particular moment, saying that when he received a concrete offer, he was to return, and that *he* would do the negotiating for him. John remarked, "I hear you've taking up fighting again, Krallis!" Telling him that he had only fought because Reuben had sustained a broken arm in his first fight, and *he'd* had to fight for the family honour, to prevent Pa from fighting. John commented, "Quite right too with you being a Bosworth, and all that?" Andreas replied, feeling no compulsion to lie, "I was *raised* by Billy

Bosworth, but I'm actually a Scamp!" Andreas was tempted to tell him the truth, but in the circumstances, and having the tragedy to handle, he did not deem it appropriate. "My wife died when I returned from Stow, so I doubt if I'll *ever* fight again. Her funeral is on Thursday at ten forty five at the old church, you'd be most welcome if you would like to come!" "Thank you Krallis, I would consider it an honour to have been asked!" Andreas asked, "Do you know Will Jones at all?" "I've got him working with me on the cafe conversion!" John answered, "There was too much there for one man!" Andreas suggested, "Would you ask him to pop in, and see me, preferably before the funeral?" Looking puzzled John told Andreas that he would be seeing Will that afternoon, "I'll pass on the message Krallis, have no fear of that!" Taking his leave, John left Andreas lolling in his chair with a self-satisfied smile on his face, but before he'd had to chance to rest on his laurels, Viv walked into the office. "Are you busy, I fancy a snack and a beer?" "No can do!" Andreas replied "I've been looking for a new home on line, and I've made a list of the houses, that I intend to visit this afternoon!" "I'll tell you what!" Viv suggested, "I've got nothing else scheduled for today, so why don't I go with you?" Andreas smiled, "Thanks Viv, I'd appreciate that. I've only put down the ones in *this* area as I don't want the kids being too far away from Ma and Pa, or the school!" "You're right about that, the kids need to be near their grandparents at this time, and so do you, if it comes to that!" Viv as ever was unerringly accurate in that assessment, and the two friends and colleagues, walked to the Green Lady for a light lunch, with Andreas remarking sullenly to Viv, "I'll be bloody glad when The Krallis is up and running, I'm fed up with the swill they serve up in here!"

Viv did not reply, having his mouth full at the time, but after he had swallowed the almost inedible pap he suggested, "That won't be too far away. I visited the site on Saturday, and I reckon it'll be ready in less than a week!" Setting off almost immediately for the nearest house on the list, and finding that it ticked most of the boxes, with size and location being ideal, but unfortunately having only a small back-garden. Viv commented, "Why would you need such a large garden now, with the boys almost grown up?" Andreas replied, "I know what you're saying Viv, but Lu and I had envisaged a large garden, with a lawn, cherry tree, and masses of flowers. I want it near to town, but not near enough to smell petrol fumes, with a patio that we could use on warm summer evenings!" Viv remarked cynically, "You're not *too* hard to please then!" Andreas commented, "Lu and I discussed it two or three months ago, so I've got a pretty good idea of what I'm looking for!" Viv remarked, "I know an area, where they have such houses, but I'm not sure whether there would be any for sale. It's a well-sought after location, and houses there, are quickly snapped up, but we could take a look anyway. Do you want to look now, or after we've seen the others?" "We'll go after!" Andreas decided, "I've got to pick the kids up from school, so I don't want to be too far away!" Spending more than an hour searching, and finding nothing suitable Andreas suggested, "Come on let's pick up the kids, I don't think we're going to have any success here!" Picking them up from school, Andreas told them that they were going to look at houses in an area that Uncle Viv knew, so food would have to wait, and arriving at the area, they walked for what seemed like miles. Finally Andreas remarked to Viv, "I think we're wasting our time here!" Rosie suggested, "Don't give up yet *daddi*, I know there's a house here somewhere, and it will be *just* perfect!" Shaking his head indulgently, he had just about given up hope once more, when she let out a piercing yell, having spotted an agent's sign, half hidden by an overgrown hedge. Victor opened the gate of the house, while Rosie merrily skipped up the path, but looking in dismay at the run-down property, Andreas remarked, "There's too much work needing to be done here!" Viv asserted, "I know, but if the back-garden is as large as the front, it could be worth taking on as a project. *I* think it has great potential, and after all there is no need for haste just yet!" Andreas agreed, "You could be right at that. If someone is still living there we could knock the door, and have a *shufti*, or maybe we should just wait, and get the keys from the estate agents?" The kids were in favour of knocking, and Viv suggested as they walked to the door, that if someone *was* in the house, they could steal a march on rivals, by declaring their interest in the property, at the earliest opportunity. Approaching the door, they had to wait while George and Rosie had an altercation over who would be the one to knock the door, but the problem was resolved, by the owner who, having seen them walk up the path, had opened the door, gesturing them to enter. Rosie whispered to her father, "This is the house I was telling you about!" The hallway was lavishly decorated, although a little dark for Andreas's taste, and being disappointed at the sombreness of every room they were shown, Andreas conceded however, that the rooms *were* large enough for all their needs, and re-decorating ought not to be too much of a problem. The kitchen being the last room to be viewed, was disappointingly sombre too, but when Andreas opened the door leading to the rear garden, fully expecting the worst, he was blown away. It was stunning, *and* large enough, reminding him somewhat of the small-holding that they'd had at the camp, albeit laid out differently, and with more symmetry. A small lawn neatly trimmed, was bordered by flowers of varied colour, with rows of fruit bushes, and a three tree orchard at the foot of the garden, one of which he could see was the small cherry tree, that he and Lu had dreamed of. Having made up his mind there and then, that he *must* have the house, no matter the expense, he enquired the cost of the property, and finding the asking price reasonable, the Roma in him *still* managed to pare another couple of thousand from the price. Introducing Viv as his solicitor, he left them to hammer out the details, and returning to the children, he informed them that the house would soon be theirs, which Rosie had known all along anyway. With the next day being the eve of the funeral, there was still a few tasks, needing his attention, before he could focus on the harrowing day ahead, and topping the list was Will Jones's house situation, being aware that if he didn't come into the office soon, it would be left until after the funeral. Dropping the kids at school, he visited Viv on arrival, "What did you think of the house?" Viv replied, "Forget about the house for the time being, and try to relax, you've got enough on your plate, but for what it's worth, you've got a real bargain!" Andreas averred, Concentrating on such matters, keeps me from brooding about tomorrow!" "Of course, you are right!" He said, "I should learn to keep my big mouth shut!" Andreas put an arm around Viv's shoulders, and suggested, "One of Becky's delicious coffees, is what's needed!" And as soon as the coffee break had been finished, Becky re-entered with the news that Will Jones had arrived, and showing him in. Viv said, "Right then, I'll leave you to it!" "John Scamp told me you wanna see me Krallis!" "Ah yes Will, how are you doing at the house?" John answered, "Well it is a little cramped, but a damn sight better than the car park. Why do you ask?" Andreas looked at him, "I don't know if you've heard, but my wife has passed away, and I think in the long run, that it would be better for the family if we move to another house, and when we move, my house will be yours!" A huge grin spread across his face, "Krallis, you've already done so much for me, and I can't thank you for your many kindnesses, It's so kind of you to think of me, in your sorrow, and I'm truly sorry for your wife's passing!" Andreas smiled, "Think nothing of it Will, John will be attending the funeral, and I was wondering if you'd like to come along too?" Will was visibly moved by the gesture, "I would be truly honoured Krallis. You are a fine man, and your great loss is felt by *all* our people!" Shaking hands, Will left on a high, to give his wife the good news, while Andreas, in *low* spirits, mused that Will had hit the nail, squarely on the head, it *was* indeed a great loss, and one that Andreas feared, he would never recover from. Gathering his papers together, he placed them carefully into his briefcase, and left to pick up his children.

They were all unusually quiet on the journey home, and even though they had known for a couple of weeks, that they would be saying good-bye to their mother, the day was now almost upon them, and the enormity of what was about to take place, was hitting them even harder. Entering the house, it seemed emptier somehow, even though Lu had not been in it for the past fortnight, and Andreas was certain that the decision to move house had been a wise one. The kids were hungry, but not being in the mood for cooking Andreas, suggested they eat out, so they ended up in the Green Lady, where the fare was again, no more than insipid, and scarcely adequate. Arriving home from the meal, and being more than a little weary, he was ready for a quiet night in, but first things first, the bedroom had to be arranged. And after that tiresome chore had been accomplished, he walked wearily downstairs, to re-join his children, almost bumping into Ma and Pa as they walked through the doorway. Immediately taking charge of the situation, Victor repaired to the kitchen, and made refreshments for the unexpected visitors. Andreas could see that they were just pale shadows of their former selves, although in truth, they all were, and apart from thanking Victor for the coffee and sandwiches, they hardly spoke at all, but their presence at least took the kids' minds from the funeral. Rosie sat on Ma's lap, promptly falling asleep, and after Andreas had taken her upstairs, he told them about the new house, and not being disposed to question the move, they agreed that their present home, *would* be ideal for Will Jones and his family. The subdued atmosphere was not *overly* low, but with his parents' departure, after an hour, the gloom returned, and Andreas, along with his sons, spent the evening quietly watching the television, until it was time for bed, and kissing their father goodnight, they went without a murmur of protest, leaving *daddi* sitting on the settee, alone with his memories, but at least, he would be sleeping soundly that night, in a bed.

26

Dawn arrived and with it the awful reality of what lay ahead came knocking at the door, and after attending to his ablutions, he put out the breakfast bowls, before ascending the wooden hill, to waken the children. With breakfast being conducted in virtual silence, and feeling the need of a sharp intake of caffeine, he sat down at the table with with his kids, and slurped a strong, but very sweet, mug of coffee. And after the soothing liquid had hit the right spot, he went back upstairs to get ready. Feeling a deep sense of despair, he wondered how he was ever going cope, but finally donning, and brushing the formal attire, *can't have Lu, up there moaning about me*, he stepped out onto the stairway, carrying his black tie. Seeing Rosie at the top of the stairs staring wide-eyed at the ceiling, he carried his small daughter into her bedroom, and laying out her clothes neatly onto the bed he suggested, "Come on sweetheart, you have to get dressed. We've got to go and say bye-bye to mummy. I'll be downstairs waiting for you!" Adding the final touch to his attire, he pulled up the collar of his new, white shirt, tying the black strip in a *Windsor* knot. Drinking more coffee while he waited for his children, he drained the cup, and was busily swilling out the dregs under the tap, when the three of them walked in together, looking vulnerable, but wonderful too. He smiled, knowing that Lu would have been so proud of them. Arriving within minutes Viv took them to the hospital, from where Lu would begin her final journey, and with the drive to the cemetery being conducted in silence, Andreas found it difficult to avert his eyes from the coffin, attempting to make some semblance of sense over what was actually happening. When the long, slow cavalcade had reached it's destination, they found the cemetery already packed with people, noting that Lala's exhumed casket had already been placed at the edge of the prepared grave. Walking with his arms around his children beside the coffin being borne by his three brothers, in symmetry with Reuben, Bill Scamp and Viv, they reached the yawning space that was to be her eternal home. The man who had *joined* Lu and Andreas in marriage, paid his respects to a wonderful and loving mother, then nodding his head to the four gentlemen holding the stout ropes, she was gently lowered into the grave, and when she had reached her final resting place, her sister's remains were also lowered into the tomb. All eyes were cast down in silent homage, but looking toward the heavens for succour, a choked sob escaped Andreas's throat, as he saw a head and shoulders vision of a smiling Lulu and Lala, surrounded by a golden glow, both looking exactly the same as they had, on the day that Lala had passed away. Almost as if they had been frozen in time. With the remainder of the ceremony passing by in a blur, he wondered later if he had been given an insight into another world, or had he merely undergone a traumatic hallucination, but whatever it had been, the experience was as real to him, as if the girls had actually been there, watching over the interment of their remains. Being greatly disturbed by what he had seen, he was in no way alarmed, drawing comfort from the fact that they had both seemed happy and smiling. With the burial now over, they all began making their way to the *Krallis* for the wake, and making no mention of what he had seen, or thought he had seen, he resolved to ask Ma just what he had experienced, at a more opportune time. Being desperate for the wake to end, so that he could return home with his family, he realized that formalities and tradition had to be observed, but when his inner torment had been prolonged to an almost unbearable degree, it *did* mercifully draw to a close. Viv took them home in his car, and being so squashed up, they were able to feel solace from the closeness of the others, and within five minutes of arriving home, they were joined by the rest of the family. With Andreas being too busy attending to his guests, to dwell too much on the morning's events, but finally managing to grab a quiet moment with Ma, he hesitantly mentioned the vision, that he had experienced. And smiling, she assured him, "What you saw was a special moment, one that few people have, or ever will have experienced. You have been truly blessed!" Giving him solace, her words also gave him the fortitude to get through his grief, and be there for his children, knowing that their needs must come first from that moment on. By the time that everyone had left, he felt emotionally, and physically drained, as he and his little brood sat to watch television. Finally wearying, the children took themselves off to bed, and performing his night-time chores, he climbed the wooden hill, thankful that he had sorted out the bed problem, the previous evening.

With the following morning having an air of normality, in spite of the previous day's traumatic events, which was compounded when the kids trooped downstairs, declaring that they were going to school. Shrugging off his desolation, from the harrowing experience of the previous day, he made ready for the office, dropping off his children at school on the way. Not being able to face Gunnar for fear of his disapproval, at returning to work so soon, he filled the car with petrol from the more expensive one in town, and headed for the office. Viv was surprised to see him when he walked in, "I've just been finalising the purchase of your new house, and it will be ready for you to move in, some time next week, but are you sure you're ready to move in so soon. "Yes, the sooner the better really!" "I'll see what I can do to speed it up!" Viv promised, "Do you fancy lunch in your new place?" "Yes that would be nice!" Andreas responded, "I could pop to the school, and fetch the kids, if they're up for it. They could do with a decent meal for a change!" Thus, when lunchtime arrived, everybody trooped into the Krallis, with Kevin the chef, who had arrived two days prior, attending their table, on being informed of their presence. Apologising for not being able to greet him, Andreas asked if he had settled in okay, and receiving an answer in the affirmative, Andreas promised to pop in and see him in the very near future. Looking around the luxurious surroundings, and noting that it was already very busy, he thought that the place had the sweet smell of success. Viv remarked, "You were right, the food *is* delicious, and if you can keep the prices as low as this, it will make a bomb!" Andreas smiled, "Better to make a little often, than to make a lot seldom, and when the word gets round, the other eateries, will be forced to drop their prices, but will *not* have the quality that we do!" When the meal was over Andreas took the children back to school, and returned to the office, but having precious little to do, he decided to go for a walk. And strolling across the square to where the cafe had been, he gazed up at the maisonettes that were now, almost ready to sell on, with their sleek sharply defined contours, blending in well with the surrounding buildings. He reflected on all the projects that he had turned into reality, *all* achieved with Lu at his side. But now, he was on his own, and knowing that Lu would not want him to stop living the dream, he vowed to *still* undertake new schemes, in order to make life better for his people, and arriving back at the office, he noted the work that had suddenly appeared in the IN tray, but with a new vigour, and will to succeed, he applied himself diligently to the task ahead.

THE END